Uncharted Desires

Jillian Sharp

Peace, Love, & Read

Book Cover by Krissy Diggs

First Edition 2024

Contents

Author Note

There are 547 federally recognized tribes across the United States. The representation of my character is based on my and others' lived experiences. We are a diverse people, with a rich culture, and this is just one representation of the Indigenous experience.

For anyone who's ever dreamed, "he's singing this song for me."

One

I f the boat sank with her on it, Katrina Brooks was completely fine with that, her life was over anyway. He had shared the
video on his social media pages. No formal press conferences,
no build up, nothing. The press had scooped it up in an instant, sharing it everywhere. The headline repeated itself as Kat
scrolled through her phone, the words on the screen blurring
together.

"He wouldn't . . . he didn't . . ." she said to no one in partic-
ular, her voice trembling.

NPR, TMZ, ABC; the initialed media of the world all her-
alded the end of her existence as she knew it. Not only would
Kat be out of a job, but she would be out of the industry.

And then it started. The text messages, one after another.

What's going on?

What do you know?

Why would he do this?

None of her supposed friends asked how she was doing. Kat closed her eyes, letting out a steady stream of air as she swiped left on every message, ignoring their demands.

Her phone vibrated again in her hand, and she cursed as she saw the screen.

Mother Dearest.

She wouldn't be answering that one.

Call me back, Katy.

Can't. On the yacht. Poor service. I'll call when we get to Jakarta.

Then how can you text me?

I'm not going to explain Wi-Fi vs cell service to you. I promise I'm fine and will call you in a couple of days.

The telltale three dots appeared and disappeared. Kat didn't wait to see if her mother would respond, stashing the phone in her pocket. She wasn't lying to her mother. Service was spotty on the yacht, and her phone would soon be nothing more than a fancy camera for the last leg of their trip.

"Did you see the news?" Lydia, one of Kat's best friends and fellow backing singer, said, plopping down next to her on the yacht's fluffy couch.

"How could I miss it? It's the only thing anyone has posted," Kat said, exasperated, as she looked out at the ocean.

"Have you watched the video yet?"

Kat turned to her other friend and fellow singer, Cher, an effervescent blonde who had flung herself down on her other side. "No, why would I? I have no urge to give that man more views."

Cher handed her the phone. "Because it's our jobs on the line."

Kat scrunched up her nose, holding the phone at arm's length, glaring at the video in question. She didn't want to see this. The headlines all said he'd retired, but they hadn't said why. Once she watched the video and heard it from his mouth, it would be real; it would be over for her.

After a decade of being the tour pianist and backing singer for Weston Monroe, the king of romantic rock songs, Kat didn't want to see her life falling apart. She barely made ends meet as it was. Now what would she do? A wave of nausea overcame her as she envisioned singing backing vocals for someone else, or worse, playing piano at a dueling piano bar for the rest of her days.

Lydia leaned over and hit play. Kat's stomach did a slight flip at the sight of him. Weston was on the beach not more than a few hundred feet away from where Kat sat on the yacht. A pink and yellow Hawaiian-style shirt hung loose and unbuttoned on his muscled frame—a physique he had toned to perfection over the past year—and after their week-long vacation, his tan skin glowed in the Indonesian sun and his shaggy, dark blond hair glistened as it curled at his nape. A golden Adonis among men, according to *GQ*, and Kat hated to admit they weren't far off.

His swim trunks outlined his toned legs, ending mid-thigh. She found herself drawn to his long, six-four frame, even though she knew she shouldn't be. After spending a decade on stage with him, she'd learned to ignore the attraction that bubbled up inside her whenever he stood too close or bothered to acknowledge her existence. She simply needed to remind herself of his condescending, womanizing personality, and the butterflies disappeared.

The ocean lapped behind him as the sun began its ascent into the sky. The pinks and reds cast an ethereal light around him, only adding to his god-like qualities.

"My friends," he began, giving the camera a deep smolder. The creases at his deep blue eyes only made him appear more handsome, rather than old, as they did her.

"Oh please . . ." Kat snorted.

Cher smiled. "If one thing can be said about West Monroe, it's that he knows how to turn on the charm."

"I don't know how that works on anybody."

"Worked on you once," Lydia quipped.

"Oh my god, Lyd! That was almost a decade ago, and we do not bring it up!" Kat said, turning her attention back to the video.

"There's no easy way to say this, so I'll just get to the point. I am retiring as a musician and performer. The world tour I have completed was my farewell tour, and I want to thank every one of you who was a part of it; you all made it that much more special to me. But there comes a time in our lives when we realize we are ready for something else, something different, and that is where I am. I don't know what the future holds, but for now, I will be taking an indefinite break from music. Thanks, everyone."

"That's it? He's just done?" She looked up at her friends, who both looked as stunned as she felt. "Is he serious with this shit?"

Cher nodded as she chewed on her thumbnail, a nervous habit that drove Kat nuts.

Kat walked across the deck, her long brown hair whipping in the salty sea breeze. She leaned against the bar and smiled at the bartender. "A mai tai, please," she said. Despite the beautiful surroundings of their trip, her mood was soured by the arrogant jerk who happened to be footing the bill for their lavish vacation.

She gritted her teeth and took a sip of her drink, pretending everything was fine. She was too old to start over—thirty-two-year-old women didn't just magically begin music careers out of nowhere—ten years in the industry had taught her that.

Almost a year on the road and Weston hadn't seen fit to mention the tiny detail of his retirement. It hurt more than she cared to admit.

Cher and Lydia joined her, each ordering their own drink.

"We'll find a new project," Cher said, always the optimist.

"Damn straight," Lydia piped in. "We are nothing if not resourceful. We'll ask Declan for our next gig."

Kat stared into her drink. "Declan's a useless prick."

"You always know the best new musicians," Lydia said to Kat. "Whose album should we be on next?"

"Forget that. Let's start our own girl group," Cher joked.

"Yes, because the world is really clamoring for a middle-aged thirty-something girl group," Kat grumbled, downing the rest of her drink and signaling the bartender for another.

"Bitch, please. I think it's just what the world needs," Lydia laughed. "Besides, don't you think society is sick of watching a bunch of skinny children bouncing around singing pop songs?"

"No." Kat dropped her head on the bar. "It reminds them of the good old days. We just remind them of reality, and nobody wants that."

"Damn, Kat, we're trying to lighten the mood," Cher said. "Although thinking about it, I'm not surprised. Didn't you notice how we were in smaller venues this entire tour? I think he wanted out before he became obsolete."

Kat lifted her head. "I know, I'm sorry. I'm just trying to process all this."

"Kat, we will be fine." Cher placed her hand on Kat's shoulder. "West is not going to throw us to the wolves."

Kat wasn't convinced that wasn't exactly what he was going to do.

Lydia nodded, pointing toward the bow of the ship. "There's the man of the hour now."

Weston walked aboard, his chin held high, broad chest pulling his shirt taut, surrounded by his usual group of adoring acolytes. His dark golden hair shimmered in the bright afternoon sunlight. His best friend Luke was laughing like a hyena at something Weston had said—typical of him. Luke's father was some kind of oil baron, and he was wealthier than Weston, but here, fame outranked everything else.

Conspicuously missing this trip had been Weston's on-again, off-again, supermodel girlfriend Gia Patrizia. But unlike all the other times they had broken up, there had been no social media buzz.

The rest of the crew joined them, mingling around the deck, chatting and laughing without a care in the world. Clearly, they weren't worried about Weston's retirement. A light breeze carried the scent of salt in the air while laughter punctuated the surrounding conversations. The guys would be fine. Everything was easier for men in the music world.

Out of the corner of her eye, Kat caught sight of Declan walking down the stairs at the center of the yacht toward the dining room. Maybe, just maybe, he would help her out. He was a manager after all. Lydia and Cher were deep in conversation with the tour guitarist and bassist, so Kat slipped away and followed him.

Finally catching up to Declan in the dining room, she called out his name.

"What, Katy? I'm due on a call," he said, looking at his cell phone.

Kat bit the side of her cheek, annoyed that after ten years he still couldn't get her name right. Declan had always been a domineering presence on tour. Tall and looming, he had big meaty hands that looked like they could snap her neck in two, and being alone with him always made her uneasy, especially when he was high. Forcing herself not to fidget, she pulled her shoulders back, looking him in the eye. "Now that Weston's retiring, would the label be willing to listen if I record some new stuff?"

"New stuff? You? Like what?" he asked, pointing at her, confused she would even have anything to record. She didn't, but that wasn't the point.

"Yeah, that was the whole reason I ended up on Weston's album. You played my demo and said if I sang and played on Weston's record, you'd consider my stuff. Well, it's been ten years." She held up her hands, showing the enormity of ten.

Declan's eyes narrowed to slits and his lips turned upward in an evil grin. He threw his head back and laughed. He kept laughing as Kat stood by awkwardly waiting for him to finish. "It's not that funny," she said to herself.

"I'm sorry," he choked out. "It's just . . ." He took a deep breath, then chuckled.

"Dammit, Dec!" she snapped.

"You're right, sorry," he said, stifling another laugh. "Listen, Katy, fifteen years ago they could have sold your music. People would have been into whatever Vanessa Carlton piano-rock crap you had going on. But, sweetie, unless you update your whole aesthetic, you will be seen as dated: too old, too . . . I don't know . . . Latina? Your vibe doesn't match alternative rock, and it just ain't happening. I mean, shit, even Monroe's a relic at this point."

Ah yes, Latina . . . Racial ambiguity wins again.

Kat stood motionless, tears gathering in the backs of her eyes. The weight of his words hit her like a sledgehammer to her chest—trends were not in her favor, ever. She knew that piano rock was out; her hopes of it making a comeback, like all things early-2000s, squashed. If emo could come back, why couldn't piano rock?

Kat already knew the answer. The world was angsty, it needed angsty music. Kat was a woman, and an Indigenous woman at that. She could pass for White in some spaces, but people looked at her and always wondered just *what* she was. It made record label execs a little iffy about whether she'd sell in the alternative market space.

Her age, gender, and race were all against her, and as much as she wished she could escape it, she was all too aware of her reality. The finality of his words settled deep within her. Her dream of ever being a musical artist in her own right had never seemed so far away or unattainable. It was over before it had even started.

She'd never deceived herself with thoughts of becoming as famous as Weston Monroe; all she wanted was a career where she could use her voice. There were people out there who would have given anything to perform on the stages she did, but it wasn't about that for her. She wanted to write her music to make a difference and to be a voice for others. For those like her who were different and unheard, forgotten, stuck between worlds. That's why she loved music. It gave voice to the voiceless.

While it didn't always bother her, she saw how homogenous alternative rock shows were. Kat and her best friend from high school, who was Black, always stood out in the crowd. The last Indigenous band to make it big had been Red Bone in the seventies. Why couldn't it be her turn to butt into the alternative rock sector? But Declan had put it in no uncertain terms. That would not happen.

"Sorry, Katy, you got a great voice and a talent on the keys. I'm sure we can put you on an old crooner's next album. I think Beckett Moss has a residency in Vegas and needs performers. Don't worry, we'll keep you working," he said as he turned and walked away.

Kat watched Dec lumbering away, trying to ignore the overwhelming sense of frustration and failure that was engulfing her. This was why she never tried. Because every time she did, she was knocked back. It was better to play it safe. Playing for Weston all these years had insulated her from these soul-crushing disappointments, but now she was exposed again. Rejected again.

Swallowing back the tears of self-pity, her anger reignited. She wasn't sure if she was angrier at Weston for not telling her about his retirement, for wasting her youth and talent, or for quitting and uprooting her safe, predictable world.

Looking down at one of the dining room tables she picked up a knife. The metal was cold in her hand. "Ugh. That's such bullshit," she said, throwing the knife at the stairs leading back up to the deck, the metallic sound reverberating through the empty room.

"Whoa, what's bullshit?" A deep male voice floated down the stairs.

Well, she'd thought the room was empty.

Two

West saw the flying projectile just in time. His reflexes were perhaps slower than usual thanks to his day drinking, but thankfully he noticed, or a certain part of his anatomy that he happened to love very much would have been wounded.

As he entered the dining room, he saw the culprit and wasn't surprised by the knife-wielding crotch assassin.

"If you were trying to damage me permanently, sweetheart, you're a bit too early."

"I would have chosen a sharper knife if I'd known you were coming," she said tartly.

He bent down to pick up the knife, catching a hint of her scent. Vanilla, jasmine, and fresh flowers straight from Bali. As he walked closer to her, she retreated until she bumped into the dining room table, trapped with nowhere to go.

Normally she would have averted her gaze, unable to look him in the eyes. He made her nervous, and she always avoided any situation that put the two of them alone together. And yet, West still enjoyed riling her. But today she was staring right at him.

Her dark brown, almost black hair curled slightly around her shoulders and down her back, and West itched to touch it, the silky strands calling to him like a siren's song across the ocean. Her skin was a shade darker than normal, bronzed by the sun to a deep honey color that made her almost glow.

Something was different about her. Maybe it was the sun and sea air? Or maybe it was the way she was looking at him, her eyes brighter than he remembered, with a hint of something that reminded him of the woman she was long ago.

Before he had gone and ruined everything.

"Now," he started, "want to explain why you're throwing knives across the dining room?"

"It's just a butter knife," she murmured.

"You know, all these years, playing such loud music has made me a little hard of hearing." He leaned over, putting his face directly in front of hers. Her breath hitched, and he enjoyed making her nervous. He quirked up an eyebrow in question.

He could feel the magnetic pull of her presence as he reached out to touch her. But as his fingers brushed her arm, her demeanor changed suddenly, and she pushed hard on his chest with both hands. He felt a spark of electricity between them as her fingers swept across his chest, and he stumbled backward, almost losing his balance.

"Do you want to know why I'm throwing knives, you absolute blowhard?" She shifted her stance. "I was practicing for you."

She continued in an exaggerated masculine voice, mocking him. "Mister 'I'm gonna quit singing with no warning, or even telling the people who have been with me for ten whole years because I'm utterly devoid of any kind of fucking loyalty.' But since you've ruined my plan, I will have to generate a new one."

She was breathing heavily, and it surprised West to see his ice queen so affected. Maybe he was wrong not to have given his singers a warning about his decision ahead of time, but ever since *the incident*, as he called it, he'd learned to keep his relationships with his singers platonic or it would hinder their work. His music was important to him, and the whole band knew that, including the girls. He was friendly with Lydia and Cher; it was just Kat who'd always had a layer of ice around her, and West hadn't bothered to chip into it.

His plan had been to tell them with the rest of the band this morning—or so he'd told himself—but they hadn't been there, and time got away from him to find them.

He examined her flushed face, slightly red from the sun, and her beautiful, amber-colored eyes. He saw genuine hurt in them, and he felt bad for being the one who'd put it there.

"The record label said they would take care of you," he said to relieve his guilt.

Her eyes burned with rage and her mouth quivered as she opened and shut it, trying to form the right words. She spun around.

Is she leaving?

To West's surprise, she marched to the dining room bar and poured two glasses of wine, strolling back to him, her gaze never leaving his.

Silently, she offered him a glass, and he reached out with hesitation. She paused for a moment and did something unexpected—she smiled. A beautiful, dazzling smile that took him aback. It was like being struck by lightning, the way it overtook all his senses.

"Well, I guess I should be thanking you," she said, her eyes shining brightly. "Cheers to the mighty Weston Monroe for giving me such a prominent music career, and for all that shall come." Her voice was an octave too high as she lifted her glass as if to toast him and took a drink.

Shifting under her scrutiny, he furrowed his brow. "Er . . . you're welcome."

She lowered the glass from her mouth, her tongue darting out to lick the wine from her lips, and West's eyes tracked the trail it made.

"Dear god, Weston, you have done jack shit for my career. Can you really be that clueless?"

West took a step back; he had severely miscalculated her motives.

Had she just poisoned his drink?

"You never let us work on any of the music with you," she continued, her frustration palpable. "Every time we tried to move on to new projects, you'd have a new album or a new tour. Why? Do you not know what a break is? We have no real music credits, we have no writing credits, we have no actual careers, we have no families, we have no lives, we have nothing, and it's all thanks to you, so yes . . ." She paused, taking a breath. "Thank you very much for my illustrious music career, and especially the heads-up that you were done with us."

With a swift fling of her arm, she threw the remaining contents of her wineglass into his face. The table shook as she slammed it down, then she leaned forward, grabbed the glass he was holding, turned and walked away.

"You don't deserve this," she shot over her shoulder as she disappeared up the stairs, not waiting for his response.

West gaped at her disappearing figure.

What was that?

Dripping with red wine, he made his way to the bar. Other than Gia, who would frequently throw fits, women rarely spoke to him like that. Kat's unexpected fiery attitude was a pleasant surprise. It reminded him of how she used to be before their relationship was shattered by *the incident*.

He could have done without the red wine to the face, though.

Maybe he'd been a little heavy-handed in his approach to making his music, but it was his music, not hers. He had written an overly ambitious album years ago, and when he had gone searching for touring musicians, the label had suggested Kat,

Lydia, and Cher. Women hadn't been his first choice, but he hadn't hated it. Kat playing piano had been a two-for-one, saving them a tour instrumentalist.

Over the years, they'd worked so well together that he figured why break up the band? They never mentioned being unhappy or unfulfilled with him. He had never thought they might have their own projects or careers they would want to pursue. West was starting to wonder if his name belonged next to "asshole" in the dictionary, but that was another thought for another day.

Wiping off more of the wine, he went to his quarters to shower.

Twenty minutes later, he still smelled of booze, but that was probably because of the copious amounts he had been drinking since boarding the vessel.

The hardest part of his journey was over. His retirement was public, and the entire world knew it. Relief should have come. Except he felt only numbness. Sinking onto the bed, he put his head in his hands and took a deep breath, preparing himself to go back out into the fray of his boisterous friends and the party Unwilling to admit his exhaustion, he steeled himself for another night of forced smiles and hollow laughter.

West's phone vibrated on the bed, but he ignored the message. They had all been the same. Friends and acquaintances all wondering what the hell he was doing. West couldn't wait until they pulled away from the port and his phone became useless.

Another buzz sounded. "Christ!" he cursed, reading the message that popped up.

Gia: Call me back, baby.

Hard pass.

For months, he had been wrestling with an inexplicable emptiness. It shadowed him like a dark cloud, and no matter how hard he tried to shake it off, it lingered. Breaking it off with his ex-girlfriend had been the first smart thing he'd done all year.

He clutched his phone, tempted to chuck it against the wall, when it buzzed again, eliciting a low groan from him. With a sinking feeling, he raised the device to his ear.

"What?"

"Really? That's how you greet your dear old dad?"

West's knuckles turned white as he bit back a groan of frustration. Releasing a long sigh, he held the phone back up to his face. "Hello, dear old dad," he said, sarcasm lacing his tone.

"I take it you're proud of yourself," his dad said, never one to mince words.

"I don't know what you're talking about," West lied, punching at the air with his free hand. That's what his dad made him want to do.

Punch things.

"You know very well what I'm talking about. What the hell, retiring from music? You just couldn't handle staying in my shadow. You went and threw away a perfectly good music career, and to do what? Devote more time to your parties and women?"

"Tell me how you really feel, Dad?" West murmured.

"All the lessons, tutors, and connections, and you're just going to throw it all away, give up on your dreams? People would kill to be in your shoes. What are you doing, son?"

A group of his sound engineers walked by his cabin on the way to their own and West pasted on a smile, shutting his door. He was never one to let anyone see him angry or frustrated. To the world, West lived a carefree life of fun and frivolity. Whiskey, women, and his music. That was all Weston Monroe cared about.

"What does it matter? I'm never going to reach the levels of the great Tommy Monroe. You just said so. Might as well quit while I'm ahead, don't you think?"

His dad grunted in frustration. "West, it's your life. When you wanted your softer girly rock instead of manly rock and roll, I didn't stop you."

Like he hadn't heard that one a thousand times. His dad was a typical eighties rock star, with loud guitars, big hair, and tight pants, but West enjoyed sexier guitar riffs and more romantic lyrics. It drove his father crazy, and West relished disappointing him.

"But just quitting? What's your plan?" his father finished.

West had options, but no plan; he would not tell his father that though. Ever the micromanager, he would lose it.

West had never known his mom; she'd left when he was a baby. He assumed it had something to do with his father's strict nature and high expectations. Though his dad loved him, he was also constantly disappointed. He had no tolerance for those who didn't meet his lofty standards.

As a kid, West had learned guitar, drums, music theory, and everything in between at the dictates of his father. He often imagined what his life would have been like with a mother in it—would she have stood up for him against his father's expectations? Years of experience taught him that any attempt to argue with him was fruitless, so he simply listened, deflecting with jokes and sarcasm.

"Can we talk about this when I get home?" West asked, exasperated. His stomach ached from hunger, and he needed another stiff drink. Luke had invited models from France or Spain or some other European country to join them on the yacht, but not even that appealed to him right now. Just a bottle of the boat's best whiskey and some food would do him good.

"This conversation isn't over, Weston . . ."

"Bye, Dad." West hung up before his dad could finish his sentence, dropping his phone on his bed.

He heard the strains of music coming from the deck above his cabin and debated the merits of his next call. To just go upstairs, have a good time, and forget the world existed beyond this boat. He excelled at that.

But he needed to make some decisions, and that required all the facts. Rubbing the back of his neck, he dialed, making the call he had been dreading since they'd arrived in Bali.

"Hey man, how's it lookin'?" he asked.

"Not so good," the other voice said.

Three

After their last day at sea, West was down in one of the yacht's plush lounges with Luke. The final dinner of the trip had gone well, and the entire crew was up on the deck dancing the night away.

The room was dimly lit, with only the soft glow of a few lights casting shadows on the walls. West leaned back in his chair, took a sip of his whiskey, and watched as Luke rolled a joint. The sound of laughter and music drifted down the stairs, a muffled reminder of the party happening above.

"I think that went well," Luke said, the joint now between his teeth.

"You know you'll get arrested if you're caught with that in Jakarta," West reminded his idiot friend.

"It's the last one."

Sighing, West ran his hands through his hair. He was over Luke's antics at this point. "Better be. I'm not bailing you out of an Indonesian prison."

Luke looked unconcerned. "Like you couldn't send them a wire transfer with some zeros and be done with it."

West gave him a scathing glare over his whiskey glass. "Like you couldn't either."

Luke spread his long arms across the sofa, the picture of true indolence. "Since you're done with Gia for good this time, do you care if I hit that?" he asked casually.

West couldn't care less what Luke did with his ex-girlfriend.

"Do whatever you want, man." He tipped back his drink. "But personally, I'd steer clear." He didn't mention that when he broke up with Gia, she'd torn his hotel room in Paris apart in a violent rage. He could certainly never go back to *Le Meurice*.

Luke grinned. "You know I like them crazy, and these models I brought on the yacht are too boring. Gia has something about her."

There was that, West had to agree. She wasn't like many of the other models: she was intelligent, conniving, and manipulative. She used her intelligence and her body to get what she wanted, and it worked for her.

"Yeah, she's also expensive, so I hope you're ready to put that trust fund to work."

Luke took a long inhale of the joint and held his breath for a minute, contemplating West's words, then he released a cloud of white swirling smoke around his head. "You going broke, Monroe? Couldn't afford her tastes?"

West didn't want to discuss his financial problems. His accountant had been his last call before they had sailed away. He had been offered an acting role in a movie, but he wasn't sure it was something he wanted to do. He had to give the movie studio an answer within the week, and he'd needed a clear picture of his finances, especially if he didn't take the job. Turned out he was hurting a lot worse than he'd realized, and something didn't sit right with him about the figures his accountant had read off.

"No, but since I'm retiring I need to watch the bank account a little closer," was all he would say.

At that moment Declan walked into the room, making a beeline straight to the bar and pouring himself a drink.

"Watch your bank account? Why would you do that?" he asked in what West felt was a rather pointed question.

"West is broke," Luke said with the joint back between his teeth.

Declan swallowed his drink in one gulp and slammed the glass on the bar. "No shit? What are you buying, man? I know the numbers are down, but they're not that bad."

West gritted his teeth. Declan dealt with the label and his accountant to make sure they paid him. He knew exactly how much money was coming in, and it wasn't a paltry amount. West had fronted the tour with his own money, and he hoped soon there would be money coming in from all the shows. "I'm not broke," he ground out.

"But you're going to have to take that acting gig?" Declan hedged.

"Don't push it, Dec," West growled. "Something strange is going on with my financials, and when I get home, I intend to have a team go through them. Something's not right."

Declan shrugged, poured himself another drink and looked over at Luke.

"You think your accountant is stealing from you?" Luke asked.

"It's possible. I don't think I've spent that much, not like you." He gave Luke a look over his glass.

Luke laughed and put out his joint in the ashtray. "So, what are you going to do then? You're retired, you're single, you're rich and good looking with no obligations. If you're not going to act, what's it going to be?"

West grimaced. That wasn't entirely true. He was never free, he still had obligations and choices to make.

"I don't know yet, but when I decide you'll be the first to know."

"That's cryptic, buddy, but okay, have it your way, keep your secrets. While you sulk, I'm going to at least have a little fun with the models you don't seem to care about." Luke set his glass on the mahogany table and walked out of the lounge and down the hall to his cabin.

Declan gave a nod. "I'm off to bed," he told West, ambling after Luke.

After they'd gone, West stared down the hall for a time. The silence hung heavy in the air like a thick fog, broken only by the sound of revelry coming from above.

Luke had been his best friend for over thirty years, and yet he felt they were losing their connection, moving in different directions. Luke wanted to keep partying, dating models, and living the same life they always had, but West wanted something different. He just didn't know what that was yet.

He walked over to the bar and ran his fingers along the expensive bottles of whiskey, landing on one he found acceptable. "Widow Jane is the best they got, huh? No Macallan?"

He pulled the cork out and threw it across the room, then headed up to the deck to join the production crew and his band—they were more like family to him than his actual family at this point, and he was ready to lose himself in the music, have a good time, and drink until he couldn't anymore.

The music had ended, and everyone had gone off to bed. Kat sat on the uppermost deck of the yacht, hugging her legs to her chest, staring out into the inky blackness, watching the moonlight glittering off the expanse of water. The yacht cut through the night like a swift arrow, faster than its usual easy pace, and the cool wind brushed against her skin. She closed her eyes and took in a deep breath, attempting to capture this moment forever in her memory.

The sudden sound of voices in the dark made her heart race, and she ducked down into the lounge chair. It was still early in the morning—around three or four o'clock—but like many other nights the crew was rounding out their evening with drunken revelry, on the cusp of passing out.

Kat pulled her hoodie closer to her body and tugged the legs down on her linen pants, trying to keep warm in the cool ocean air. Suddenly, a dark figure appeared sat on the chair beside her.

"Seat taken?" a strong masculine voice asked.

"Jesus." She jumped. "Don't scare people like that, Weston."

"Sorry," he whispered, his lips twitching with a sheepish smile that she could only partially make out in the faint light of the lamps.

"What are you doing awake?" she asked, trying to ignore the bubbling anticipation as her body drew closer to his of its own volition.

"I could ask you the same thing," he said, his voice low and thick like honey.

"Typical deflection of the question," she noted wryly, turning toward him, suddenly aware of how close they were in the dark. The familiar scent of his soap filled her senses, and an electric current seemed to flow between them.

He shrugged. "Couldn't sleep, I guess."

"Me neither," she offered. "It's going to be hard to go back to reality after all this." She gestured around her.

"What is reality going to be for you?" he asked.

"Who knows? It's not like you care," she said, the hurt in her tone obvious. If she hadn't been coming down from her buzz, she probably wouldn't have said anything, but alcohol made her reveal her true feelings.

"That's not true," he said almost inaudibly.

Kat stood and stalked away, her peaceful moment ruined. He couldn't just come around and say things like he cared when he didn't, and never had. Considering her room was currently occupied, she wasn't sure where to go, she just knew she needed to be away from him.

"Kat, wait." West was faltering after her, footsteps unsteady. "What did I say? Why are you walking so fast?"

Kat spun around to face him, their chests bumping against each other before she took a step backward. Her skin tingled at the heat of his body brushing hers. "Oof . . . what are you doing?" She was annoyed and tired, and he was scrambling her brain. She needed to go to bed.

"Me? You're the one who turned around so suddenly," he retorted with a smirk.

Kat glared at him in the dim light. "Well, why are you following me so closely? I thought it was clear that our conversation was over. That's what it generally means when someone walks away. A normal person would get that."

West raised his hands in surrender, taking a few steps back. "I guess I'm not very normal." He winked.

Kat scoffed and turned away, but not before taking note of how his golden blond hair shone in the moonlight against his tanned skin.

"Okay, Kat, I'll leave you alone. I just wanted you to know that I do care about you and the others, and I should have given you a heads-up."

She sniffed as she felt the familiar burn behind her eyes. But she couldn't let go of her anger toward him even after hearing his words. She crossed her arms over her chest and muttered, "That would have been a nice start."

She turned on her heel, leaving him on the deck. She was done with whatever it was her body was trying to do with this man. She knew better than to go down that road.

"Good night, Kat," Weston said. For good measure, she held up her middle finger in his general direction. She wouldn't forgive him simply because he said one nice thing.

He laughed as she walked away, but Kat refused to give him the satisfaction of looking back. She rounded the corner of the deck toward the stairs and stopped to take in deep breaths. Between the alcohol and such a close encounter with Weston, she was struggling to find her equilibrium.

For a moment, she thought she saw a shadow cross the deck and wondered if he had followed her. Turning to investigate, she looked across the dark deck, but seeing nothing, she dismissed it and continued to her cabin.

Kat's annoyance toward him lingered as she made her way back, hoping Lydia was alone. Lydia and the tour guitarist didn't have a relationship per se, but rather a no-strings-at-tached touring friendship that left Kat currently without a room.

A sudden cry for help stopped her in her tracks. She paused and listened. There it was again. Turning, she sprinted up the stairs and ran back on deck, nearly stumbling over the coils of rope on the teak wood. Another cry for help echoing through the night drew her attention to the edge. Trembling, she leaned over the starboard railing's top rung and saw Weston struggling to get back onto the boat. His hands were clenched around one of the railings of the deck below, his feet slipping and sliding against the wet hull as he tried to climb up.

"Oh my god!" she exclaimed.

"Kat," he yelled. "Go get help!"

Her head whipped back and forth, scanning the deck for someone who could help them, but everyone had already gone to bed and the noise of the engine prevented Weston's yells from being heard by anyone not nearby.

"Can't you swing down onto the lowest deck?" she suggested, eyeing his position. It was possible he could make it . . . Maybe.

"No, Katy," he replied, his voice strained with exhaustion. "Not if I don't want to land in the ocean. Can you please just get help?"

With a frustrated whimper, she backed away from the ledge. What the hell was she going to do? Any minute now West would fall into the ocean, and she needed to save him.

Turning, she frantically ran down the upper deck, hoping to find someone or something to help him. How he had flipped off the edge of the yacht was beyond her. She crisscrossed the deck looking for someone to help her, fear and frustration growing inside her at a rapid rate.

He should really give her a large severance package after this. Why was there no one around anymore?

She sprinted down to the deck, catching a glimpse of Weston who was hanging on for his life, waves crashing against the sides of the yacht. She had to do something, and quick. She could tell his arms were getting tired.

Her eyes landed on the bright orange life buoy hanging on the wall.

Why was it hanging so high?

Frantically, Kat looked around for a ladder or something to stand on, catching sight of a large storage bin down the deck. She ran to the bin, unhooking it from the wall and pushing with all her strength. It was heavy, but not immovable. Kat pushed, her muscles screaming at her to stop, but she knew she had to get the buoy. Finally, her energy almost spent, she pushed the box under it.

Without hesitation, she leapt onto a storage bin and snatched the buoy, barely able to reach it. She ran to Weston, urgency pushing her forward, and threw it down to him.

"Here, grab this!"

He observed it swing back and forth, doubt clear in his eyes. "And you're going to do what exactly?" he asked with trepidation. One of his hands started slipping from the rung.

"Jesus, Weston, just grab it." She tied the rope to the railing, pulling on it. "Look, it's tied off; you're not going anywhere."

His other hand slipped off the rung, and he grabbed the buoy. "Now what?" His blue eyes pierced through the dark as he held onto the buoy for dear life. His feet were still perched on the edge of the boat.

"Swing yourself over to the lower deck."

Weston looked at it dubiously, though it didn't look far away from their current vantage point. She watched his hesitation play across his face. "I'm not Tarzan," he grumbled.

"Just do it!" Kat stomped her foot on the deck.

He made a sighing sound and slowly pushed up, his feet walking across the boat, the rope and life buoy protesting under his weight. He was surprisingly calm and sure-footed, while Kat could feel her heart about to beat out of her chest.

"There you go," Kat said as she eased him along. "You're almost there."

One scoot of his foot after the other, Weston had moved as far as the rope would take him. "Now what?" He stared up at her, dangling from the side of the yacht, the deck still too far away to lunge onto.

"Stay put!" Kat yelled, her voice trembling. "I'll find more rope." She scanned the area for another life buoy, desperation seeping in. There was no time to waste, and not a rope or second buoy in sight. Panic welled within her, but she tamped it down. She had to save Weston first, panic later.

"Shit." She heard Weston cry out.

Running back to the edge of the deck, she called out to him, panic rearing its ugly head within her. "What? What's wrong?"

But she didn't need an answer. The rope was coming untied, and Weston was slipping incrementally down the yacht's exterior, past the point of no return. Without thinking, she grabbed the rope before he fell into the sea.

It burned her hands as it raced through them, but she threw her weight into it with every ounce of strength her body had. She grunted in determination as Weston continued to slip down the side of the yacht.

Kat felt herself being pulled over the railing as she pulled against the rope. Her knuckles whitened as they clung tightly to the fraying rope fibers, determined not to let him fall.

"Let go," Weston cried out from below her. "You can't pull me up."

"No! I won't let you fall in!" Kat said through clenched jaws.

"Then you're going to fall in with me. I'm too heavy. You can't pull me up."

"I don't need to pull you up," Kat said with a grunt as she pulled on the rope. "I . . . just need . . . to tie it onto one of these rungs before we both go down!"

She leaned over the edge just slightly; if she could just . . . get . . . some . . . leverage . . .

"Kat, stop, just let me go, and tell—"

But before he could finish, Kat's feet suddenly flipped over her head, and then they were falling together. And loathe as she was to admit it, Weston might have been right. Instinctively, she braced for impact as she plummeted into the void below.

Four

Well, West wasn't drunk anymore. He hadn't been since he had tripped on the deck chair and managed to fall overboard. And then Kat had tried to save him. Now things had gone from bad to much worse.

His body hit the surface with a thud. It hurt like hell. His back was aching from the impact, as saltwater pummeled his face like tiny fists.

In the light of the moon, he watched the yacht race along the water until it vanished out of sight. A slight breeze whipped through his hair, and clouds covered the moonlight, leaving him in complete darkness.

He pulled on the rope to the life buoy, and to his horror, he didn't find Kat attached to it. Somewhere between her falling and hitting the water she had let go of the rope, but West couldn't see anything in the darkness. Terror seized him as he imagined the worst. What if she hit her head while falling? What if a shark ate her? What if she was abducted by modern-day pirates?

His inner imaginings became more and more ridiculous as fear washed over him.

Snap out of it.

He forced himself to focus and stop spiraling. How many times had he pushed panic aside when stepping onto a stage? He didn't have stage fright, but the anxiety of singing a new song live and waiting for the crowd's approval, or lack of interest, always made him nervous. If he could set aside his anxiety then, he could certainly do it now. He had caused this predicament, and he had to find her. The last thing either of them deserved was to be floating alone in the Indian Ocean.

Without wasting another second, West dove into the dark waters, calling out her name as he surfaced, desperately searching for any sign of her. Every stroke through the rough waves felt like an eternity as he tried to conserve his energy, praying that he would find her before it was too late, the waves washing over him as he gasped for air.

His eyes darted across the sea, searching for any sign of life among the dense darkness, but all he saw was an endless expanse of choppy, unforgiving water.

"Kat." He swam, listening for any sounds of her. "Kat, can you hear me? Kat!" He refused to let fear enter his voice, refused to let the frantic thoughts enter his mind. What if she didn't make it? What if she had drowned? It would have been all his fault.

Dammit, Kat. Why had she even been out on that deck? She was supposed to have gone to bed.

"Kat . . . Kat . . . Come on, Kat, where are you?" He yelled until he was hoarse, waiting for her lilting voice to respond across the water, because right now he'd give anything to hear it.

Taking a moment to rest his muscles, he floated on his back, his arms wrapped around the buoy, his ears going under the water. He imagined what it would sound like hearing her voice. She had a beautiful voice; it wasn't too high-pitched and had a nice timbre to it. Surprisingly sultry for a woman who could be quite prickly.

When he had decided to take on backing singers for his tour ten years ago, her voice had immediately stood out to him. It had been smooth and velvety and had wrapped around his soul. It had melded well with his, and, after a test run with various women, he had wanted her.

He imagined hearing her calling his name, always his full name, never West. Only his father and Kat called him Weston. He heard his name again, Kat's perfect voice calling out to him in his imagination. Was he . . . He sat up so fast that he bumped into something, and there she was, looking disheveled, her body shivering.

"Weston!" she said, nudging him. "I thought you were dead for a minute. You were just floating there, and you had this weird smile on your face, and you weren't answering me, and oh my god, why are you smiling at me?"

He grabbed her waist, hauling her into his arms. "You're alive! Christ, I thought you were dead. I was yelling and yelling for you."

She was warm, and he pushed back from her, unwilling to think about the jolt of awareness that had just gone through him. They were floating in the fucking Indian Ocean right now; his body had no business reacting to touching hers.

"Here, hang onto this." He handed her the buoy.

She grabbed it and pushed it toward him. "This isn't *Titanic*." She smiled. "We can both hang on and not freeze to death."

West gave a slight chuckle and grabbed hold of the buoy. For a long moment they just bobbed there in the water, the truth of their situation setting in. He could see the emotion play across her face. They were alive, but now what?

"What now?" she asked him, as if she'd read his mind.

"I don't know, wait to flag down a boat, I guess."

She gave him an annoyed look. "Really? That's your master plan? Wait here like bobbing buoys for a boat? That sounds like the dumbest plan I've ever heard. If you want to float around like shark bait, be my guest, but I'm finding land."

"You asked," he said, anger lacing his tone. "Do you see any land?" He gestured around splashing water everywhere. "Because I sure don't."

"Why are you getting angry at me? This is all your fault."

"My fault?" He thumped his chest for emphasis. "My fault? Why on earth did you think you could pull me up on your own? I told you to get help! If I had fallen in, at least you could have told the captain to turn around. Now nobody knows we're out here."

Kat shivered again, and West was almost tempted to take pity on her, if he hadn't already been so annoyed at her..

Her head turned, mouth agape. "You're mad at *me* for trying to rescue you?" She pointed an accusing finger at him. "You're the one who drunkenly fell overboard."

"You should have run and gotten help—the captain, Luke, one of the guys." He took a deep inhale, forcing his anger down. West never did angry. He spent a lot of time in meditation to harness his emotions, to hold back the anger and frustration he always believed he wasn't allowed to have. But Kat was pushing his last nerve.

"So you're saying because I'm a woman, I couldn't save you?"

"That's not . . . ugh, you know that's not what I meant!" Weston splashed at the water in front of him, and for the first time his façade—cool, unphased rock star—dropped away.

She smiled, which annoyed West even more.

"It's dark, Weston, and by my guess, it's got to be close to sunrise. I bet the sun will come up and we'll see land any moment now."

"Fine," Weston said. "We'll wait for sunrise." He laid his head on the buoy between his arms and closed his eyes. She shivered, and, for reasons completely unknown to him, his hand moved out, grasping for hers. Reluctantly, she gave it to him, and he felt how small her hand was in his. The enormity of their situation hit him like a ton of bricks as he thought about how small they both were floating in such a vast ocean. They were royally screwed, but he couldn't voice that aloud.

"Do you have your cell phone?" he grumbled more to the buoy than her.

She reached into the water, presumably to check her pockets. "No, it's probably at the bottom of the ocean by now."

"I'm not sure where mine is. It didn't work on the yacht anyway, so it's stashed in a bag somewhere."

"You didn't want to use it to take pictures?" Sarcasm laced her tone, but West couldn't fathom why. Did she have something against him not needing photos of the days preceding his unplanned retirement?

He sighed. "Not really."

Dread settled between them, and the air shifted as West realized Kat also knew how screwed they were. He squeezed her hand, and heard her sniffle, holding back tears.

They were floating in the ocean. Their only hope of survival was that someone would realize they were missing and turn the boat around, or another boat would find them. Or maybe a shark would eat them. West's money was on the shark.

They floated in silence for what felt like hours until Kat finally saw the sun crest the horizon. She let out a long breath she hadn't realized she'd been holding. Her salvation was at hand in the east. Her body ached, feeling like she had fallen from a four-story building. She lifted her head from the life buoy, her neck protesting in pain. If a whale could come around and eat her now, that would be great.

Were there even whales in the Indian Ocean?

She sat up in the water, her hair plastered to her face, her whole body shivering. It had only been a few hours by her estimation, but her body couldn't take much more of the water. The Indian Ocean wasn't freezing, in fact it was rather warm from the summer months now that it was fall. She had no idea why she kept shivering, other than it being her body's response to fear.

Off in the distance, she noticed something floating and decided after further scrutiny it was worth a look. Maybe it was food, or a phone?

Keep dreaming.

She started to swim away, but a strong, warm hand wrapped around her ankle.

"Where are you going?" Weston asked, his voice hoarse.

"Something is floating over there." She pointed to the object, then lifted her ankle above the water and peeled his fingers off her. "I'm going to see what it is."

Not to be deterred, he grabbed at her waist instead, and her heart did a flip inside her chest. What a traitorous organ. It wasn't supposed to do that when he touched her. With his well-built arms, he pulled her in tightly. His strength had grown, and his body transformed into an impenetrable fortress.

He'd always been long and lean. God knew as hard as she'd tried not to notice him, he was impossible to miss. The way his long fingers expertly worked his guitar, the way he threw his head back when his shaggy hair would fall in his face, how his tattoos stretched across his back whenever he'd take his shirt off.

He had always been a powerful force on stage. Now he was all tall muscle and sinew, with toned shoulders, defined arms, and abs for days. To Kat, West had become more intimidating than ever. There was water all around her, and yet somehow her mouth had gone dry.

"You can't just swim off. Who knows what that is—we're in the middle of the ocean, it might be some evil deadly fish," West said.

"Doubtful." She tried not to roll her eyes. "For someone who does what they want all the time, you're quite cautious."

Weston released her and gave her an indecipherable look, so she swam away to put some distance between them. "I don't make rash decisions. I have always calculated all the options and angles. It looks like I do what I want when I want, with no care in the world, but that's not me. The media portrays me one way, and I've never changed the image."

Well, that's a lot to unpack..

Almost everything she had ever thought of him wasn't even true, or so he said.

She gave him a dubious glance. "You thought through every last one of those models and actresses you dated?"

He flashed her a lascivious grin. "Of course." Then he swam toward her with heat in his eyes. When he reached her, his finger glided up her arm with maddeningly slow precision, his voice feathery in her ear. "I can promise you, every single one of those women will tell you our relationship was worth their time."

His finger blazed a trail of fire across her skin as it roamed across her shoulder and came to rest at the place where her neck and collarbone met. Kat quivered beneath his touch, utterly entranced by the scorching feel of his skin on her body. She could feel the power he had over her—how just one finger on her body could turn her into a pool of desire.

She caught his gaze. His eyes glowed with amusement, as though he was trying to keep from laughing at some joke only he knew. She quickly lashed out and playfully splashed him in the face. "Stop trying to hypnotize me!" she said.

"What?" he asked, laughing as he wiped the water out of his eyes.

"That's how you do it? You lure all those women in through hypnosis. I knew it!" She pursed her lips, pretending to be deep in thought. "Well, that and writing incredibly sappy love songs that have women falling at your feet," she teased.

Weston laughed this time and splashed water toward her, but she ducked away just in time.

"Whatever you want to believe," he said, before Kat turned to swim away, making her way to the object, which had moved closer to them.

The waves, thankfully, were not rough, but still impeded her progress. The water dunked her under twice, but finally, she reached out and touched something smooth, and definitely not an evil man-eating fish.

"Darn, it's just plastic."

She swam back, disappointed it had been nothing useful, just some random junk thrown into the ocean—a sad reality of how tragically humans treated the planet.

"What a shame," West said, as he wrapped his arms around the buoy, sighing.

She felt instant warmth move through her at the sound. If her body would stop reacting to every little noise he made, that would be great. She certainly wasn't having any effect on him. That trick he had done with his finger was just because he could. She was the nearest female in his vicinity right now, and it was imperative she remember that or she was going to be in a world of hurt.

On the first tour they had ever gone on together, after a night of partying, Kat and West had ended up alone together in a dark hallway at the House of Blues. She couldn't remember how it had happened, but what she did remember was the awkwardness after. She was not his type, and he had made that abundantly clear years ago.

Exhausted, they lapsed into silence. Kat listened to the water as it lapped against her skin. She had always been one to find the music in the world, or at least she used to. It wasn't just through instruments, but in the sounds that were all around her in nature. The spirit had many ways of talking to people, but most never listened.

With every wave that crashed against them, Kat thought of her Indigenous roots, and was filled with apprehension.

Though nature had always been a great source of comfort for her, it seemed almost ironic that she now found herself lost in its waters. Lost in the eerie quiet, waiting for something to speak to her, a message that never came. She wasn't quite that in tune with Mother Earth lately, and being lost in the middle of the ocean terrified her while any other Native would probably have been perfectly ready for the challenge.

The waves occasionally doused them as the sun beat down. Time passed by slowly as Kat hummed to the surrounding sounds, her body sagging in the water, her arms losing strength as she held on. The ocean winds, the lapping water, the birds flying overhead all lulled her into a false sense of peace.

Wait . . . birds overhead?

She shook Weston. "Weston, wake up!"

"Huh, what?" he said, his head rising from the buoy.

"There are birds!" she exclaimed.

"So?"

"So? That's a good thing," she said, excitement lacing her tone. She scanned their surroundings frantically. It had to be around here somewhere, they had to be close. Somewhere on the horizon, it had to be here.

"There!" She pointed excitedly.

"Huh?" Weston squinted in the direction she was pointing. "Is that . . . ?"

"Yes, it is," Kat said, a smile on her face.

"It's fucking land!" he said, releasing the buoy.

Kat wiped the water from her face as Weston splashed on her in his excitement. He grabbed the buoy and whooped loudly.

"Thank god, we're saved," he yelled.

"Might just make me believe there is a god," Kat said.

"You don't believe in a higher power?" he asked her.

Shrugging, she looked around uneasily. It wasn't a topic she especially loved discussing due to her upbringing in a very religious household after her parents had abandoned their true Indigenous teachings.

"I guess I believe there is something out there—a great creator, if you will—but I don't buy into all the pomp and circumstance."

"That's fair," he replied. "Me and my dad aren't religious at all, but I went on that sabbatical with Buddhist monks in Thailand, which changed the way I see the universe and our place in it."

Kat held back a sound of disgust. "Yeah, I remember, you came back all holier than thou with your new age meditation and wheat grass smoothies. Such rich kid shit."

West started kicking toward shore, dragging her along. "What does that mean?"

"It means we can't all just take off on a sabbatical for five months. Most of us have to work, have responsibilities."

"I have plenty of responsibilities," he said, his anger growing.

Kat shook her head, "It's not the same and you know it."

West balked at her statement as he continued to propel them to shore. "I don't think you realize how much work I put in daily to keep everything running. My household, my music, my staff, I have a lot of people I work with."

Kat rolled her eyes, "It's still not the same as us peons going to work every day just to make sure we have a roof over our heads."

"Because your job is so bad," he said sarcastically.

As much as Kat wanted to argue her point, she was exhausted, hungry, and dehydrated. She wasn't sure she could do much of anything, but they were so close to land and she was done poking at him.

"Whatever, Weston, I'm not saying you don't work hard, I just don't think you grasp how easy it is to live your lifestyle. Let's just get to shore please."

He squinted at the expanse of water between them and the land and let out a resigned sigh. "You're right," he said. "We can come back to my *rich kid shit* later." He kicked harder, increasing their speed. Expending all her energy, Kat helped, kicking her legs as much as she could, her body screaming at her to stop.

"I sure hope this island has people on it," he said.

What happened if it didn't?

But she didn't dare voice it aloud for fear she was right.

Five

The sun was unrelenting as it blazed in the sky, and West's shirt felt like a wet rag. His feet dragged through the sand, and he finally collapsed to his knees with a gasp of relief as they stumbled onto the shoreline.

Slowly, he raised his head, squinting against the glare from the sea, and surveyed their surroundings. The beach curved gently around them like an embrace, fringed by rocks on both sides. He looked down at his feet; they were already beginning to sting from the heat of the sand, and he cursed himself for not wearing shoes.

Clusters of shrubs and little trees lined the shore before giving way to tall trees that reached up toward the sky like hands outstretched from a deep green pool. A vast mountain rose in the center of the island, dominating the horizon with its sheer size. Surely someone had to live on an island this big, but there was no sign of life on the beach.

He took his shirt off in hopes it would dry quicker, turning to see Kat behind him struggling to stand, her legs shaky from floating and kicking in the water for so long. She pulled the hoodie she had been wearing over her head, and West glimpsed the swell of her stomach and secretly hoped the shirt underneath would be pulled up farther.

A feeling he didn't want to acknowledge shot through him as he stared at her midriff. She wasn't plain or simple like he had tried to delude himself into believing, she was stronger than he had given her credit for. There was no other woman he could think of who wouldn't be collapsing in fear at their current situation.

Kat plopped down unceremoniously next to him, sighing loudly, her eyes shut tight.

"I think I'll just never open my eyes again," she said, bundling her hoodie and shoving it under her head like a pillow.

He peered down the length of her body, his gaze lingering as her wet linen pants clung to every curve. Since *the incident* he had tried so hard to put her out of his mind, to not see her as a woman, but just as his bandmate. He was an idiot.

Every shade of bronze mingled within her skin. Her hair drenched, and yet still shining in the sun, was the color of melted chocolate, each strand like spun silk. She had an average-sized waist that eased into lush hips.

West's gaze raked up her form. As she lay on the sand, her drenched shirt stuck to the curves of her breasts, revealing the outline of her bra beneath. He could easily imagine his large hands reaching out to cup them. With closed eyes, her facial features had softened, exposing a vulnerable side to her typically harsh expression. Her aquiline nose gave her an aura of sophistication. Her full pink lips glistened under the sunlight, and he wondered what they tasted like, and then instantly admonished himself for such a thought. They had tried that already once, a long time ago, but Kat wasn't his type. She was too good for him and now was definitely not the time.

She popped one eye open and stared at him. "What are you looking at, Weston?"

"Why do you call me Weston?" he asked, deflecting the question. "My friends all call me West; Weston is just my stage name."

She sat up, dusting the sand from her hands. Not that it did anything for the coating of sand along her back. "We're not exactly friends, are we?"

West reached up to swipe the sand out of her hair, smiling as she tried to bat his hands away. "We've worked together for ten years," he pointed out.

"That doesn't make us friends," she whispered.

Her hair felt like silk in his hand, even after hours in the salty ocean. Even once the sand was all gone, he continued to stroke it as he looked into her eyes, tucking a stray piece behind her ear. He remembered now why he had been intrigued by her so many years ago as he felt an unearthly pull emanating between them. She wasn't the type of woman he usually desired, yet something about her made him want to count the myriad shades of brown he saw reflected in her eyes; she was hypnotically alluring.

A bird made a squawking noise in the sky, and he dropped her hair as if it were on fire before he did something they'd both regret.

"West?"

It took him a moment to register she was talking to him, and that she'd used the name he preferred his friends to use.

"Yeah?"

"How the hell did this happen?"

He shook his head and rested it in his palms, the sand scratching at his skin. "I honestly don't know."

Kat made a sound as if she didn't believe him. What did she think? That he'd thrown himself overboard? Things were bleak, but not that bleak.

He stood up, his angry energy making him anxious. "I mean it. One moment I was walking on the deck, and the next I was tripping and falling, and my reflexes were too slow to catch myself until it was too late. But I keep feeling like something happened, like something touched me. I swear I saw a shadow on the deck."

Kat stood up to keep pace with him as he walked away. "You think someone was on the deck with you? Like what? They pushed you?"

He shrugged. "Yes. No. Maybe. I don't remember! It's all such a haze."

She slowed her pace, and he stopped, turning to wait for her. She took in a deep breath before speaking. "You were drunk, that's all it is. You were drunk, and you tripped off the boat, taking me with you."

Fury bubbled up inside him, an emotion he rarely used. "No. You sent us plunging into the ocean. You should have gotten help."

Kat walked up closer to him, her eyes sparking in anger. "No . . ." She dragged the word out. "You were about to fall in. I went to save you, and I would've too if I'd known how to tie better knots."

He snorted and crossed his arms over his chest. "Clearly. But that would also take being able to follow directions, something you obviously don't know how to do."

"What? I've been taking directions from your deluded ass for a decade."

"Pfft . . . when you want to."

"What the hell does that mean?" she said, her voice going up practically an octave.

"I don't think that's the right note, Weston," he said, trying to mimic her voice. "That harmony will sound like shit, Weston; you don't want keys there it will overpower the guitar. Why am I way back here? I can't hear the others."

"Enough," she cut him off. "You're getting off topic here. You're the one who got rip-roaring drunk and fell off the god-damn boat, but you'd rather blame me or the mysterious ghost who pushed you overboard than take responsibility for your actions. Which is rather typical, don't you think?" Her finger pushed into his chest as she craned her neck to look up at him.

"And what the hell does that mean?" he said, purposely copying her.

"URGH! Why are you so infuriating?"

West tried to hide his smile as she breezed past him. "Where are you going?" he called.

"Away from you. There has to be some other human on this godforsaken island that can free me of you once and for all!"

But as she trudged away through the sand, her steps faltered, and suddenly she was falling.

In an instant, he was there to catch her as her legs trembled and gave way underneath her.

"Kat! Kat!"

Slowly, he allowed himself to sink into the sand. His arms supported her weight as her eyelids fluttered open, and she took in their surroundings. He felt the contours of her body against his, surprised by how effortlessly they fit together.

"Wha-what happened?"

West helped her sit back up, but she was still unsteady.

"You fainted," he told her.

She gave him a scathing look. "Fainted sounds so Victorian. Oh, please Mr. Belvedere, go get my smelling salts. I fear I've got a touch of the vapors again," she said in her best English accent.

West tried to smile at her joke but worry for her ate away at him.

"I just need water," she reassured him. "There has to be a stream or waterfall somewhere on this island."

"I'll go search for it. You stay here." He would not have her passing out on him again.

Kat rolled her eyes and squared her jaw with determination. "No," she said, standing up and walking inland, her steps uneven.

West sighed, crossing his arms across his chest. "Kat, you just passed out. You don't need to do this. I'll find water and bring you some."

"I don't need some high and mighty man to bring me water," she said, turning to face him. "One, you have no container to bring it back in; two, who knows how far away it is; and three, you have no navigational skills whatsoever, so you would one hundred percent get lost getting back to me."

West silently cursed under his breath; how did she even know about his lack of direction? She raised an eyebrow in silent challenge and then began trudging into the forest.

"Better get your shirt," she called to him from the trees.

Infuriating woman.

He walked back to where his shirt lay, now covered in a thin layer of sand. He shook out the fabric and ran to catch up with her, wondering how he could be both worried about someone's welfare and want to strangle them at the same time.

Kat walked into the rainforest, following behind West as he moved ahead of her. The awkward silence loomed between them like a knife overhead, and while what she wanted to know was what had happened that night he had left her so long ago, she knew now wasn't the time. Instead, she decided to probe into his personal life to take her mind off their predicament. Or maybe curiosity had just gotten the better of her after Reggie, the tour bassists had gotten drunk and told them all about West and Gia's epic fight in Paris.

"So, why did Gia throw a hair dryer at your head? I heard it was quite the fight."

West moved the brush aside as they made their way inland. A cacophony of bird sounds rustling the trees drew her attention, sending a shiver through her body. She didn't want to think about what lurked behind all the trees and bush.

"I ended things with her."

"You two are always ending things."

"No, she's always ending things," he amended, as he stepped over a large fallen tree. Kat's short legs had a much harder time, and he turned to help her over.

The trees were tall and wide, with thick canopies that blocked out the sun. Monkeys chattered in the branches above as birds circled overhead. But not a trace of humanity anywhere. Despite the surrounding beauty, she felt a chill run down her spine as she wondered what lurked unseen beyond the bush. She felt ill at ease within the wide expanse of the unknown, even if she was slightly enjoying the peaceful sounds around her.

"Why take her back then?" she asked, her movements stopped as his blue gaze left her momentarily stunned. He grabbed her hand, and, before she could protest, lifted her over the tree.

"That's how she was, and for a while, I was fine with it. She'd get mad about something stupid, break up with me, go out with some young rising star, and post it all over social media. I'd apologize in some grand fashion, and she'd be back."

He was still holding her hand. She had known one side of West—the spoiled, standoffish, and selfish side—but she was seeing there was more, and that was bad, bad, bad.

His heat wrapped around her, and even after a night spent floating in the ocean, she could still smell his soap: crisp sage, pine, and something unique to only him.

He released her, and she walked ahead of him. "That sounds like an awful relationship." She forced herself to ignore how good he smelled.

"I realized it was, and I ended it officially when we were in Paris. That's why you haven't seen anything posted. She doesn't want anyone to know. She keeps trying to get me back, but I guess at some point you discover you want more for yourself." His hand reached out, pulling her back. "Let me go first."

"Why? I'm perfectly capable of going first," she said, crossing her arms. "I can find water, climb over logs, swim. And shocker—this little woman can move tree leaves just as good as you." She knew she sounded childish, but she needed distance between them. She didn't want sweet, nice West—the West she had worked with their first year together. The West that had made her believe in silly things, like rich rock stars could actually be nice guys. That might ruin her when this was all over.

West's eyes were smiling on his ridiculously tanned, handsome face, and for a moment, she forgot why they were even arguing.

"What?" she said exasperated. "Are you laughing at me?"

"No," he said, a slight chuckle in his voice. "It's just, right now, in this situation, you're so cute. And I know that's going to make you mad, but Kat, you don't have to be strong. We are lost on an island, dehydrated, hungry, tired. I have no shoes, my feet hurt like hell, and from what I can tell, this island is uninhabited. I'm not sure how we're getting out of here, so please let me be just a little bit helpful to you. Why struggle to get over the log when you can have help?"

He had voiced the fears she hadn't wanted to think about. The thoughts that she had pushed to the back of her mind. She had compartmentalized their problems into survival mode. First had been finding land. They had done that. She hadn't gotten to the "get off the island" or "get home" part of the plan yet.

"One step at a time, West. Water first," she said, willing the tears to stay back. How could he see right into her soul like that? He didn't even know her. She didn't need his permission to not be strong, and she wasn't about to crumple because big strong West was going to save the day. If she wanted to struggle over the log, then she'd fucking struggle to get over the log.

In what felt like hours of walking, they both had fallen silent, West's body aching for water and rest. He could only imagine how Kat felt. He saw a bead of sweat glide down her neck, and his imagination ran wild. What would she taste like there? How would she react if his tongue took the same path?

"You know this is all your fault," she grumbled, gesturing for him to walk ahead of her as they closed in on a large tree, shaking him from his thoughts.

"Didn't we just have this conversation? I'm pretty sure you could have found help, but fine. I'll bite. You shouldn't have tried to save my sorry ass at all. You should have just let me fall in."

"Probably." She shrugged. "In the immortal words of the esteemed Alanis, 'you live, you learn.'"

"Ah yes, now there's an album I had on constant rotation in my childhood." His tone was laced with sarcasm.

"I'm sure *Jagged Little Pill* was at the top of your list," Kat laughed, and West wanted to make her do it again, the sultry sound flowing through his entire nervous system, making him feel all his nerve endings. He didn't think he'd ever seen her so relaxed around him.

He turned around with his hand over his heart as if she had wounded him. "I have absolutely nothing against female empowerment rock anthems. I write love songs and praise every-thing about women, for Christ's sake. I love women."

She made a face as if to say *yeah, right*.

"So, what made you give a big fuck you to your old man's music? I mean, he can't love your choice of genre."

West's jaw clenched, trying not to let her see she'd hit a nerve. The subject of West and his father was a contentious one, one he didn't want to talk about. It hadn't been easy growing up in the shadow of one of the '80s biggest rock stars.

"He's not exactly proud," he said. "But I didn't quit music completely and become a fireman or something normal, so he deals with my 'girly' rock, as he calls it."

"I think you would make a great fireman. Is that want you wanted to be?"

West thought about it for a minute. No one had really asked him what he wanted to be. Everyone had just assumed he want-ed to be a musician. "For the longest time, I thought about every job I would do that wasn't being a musician. I wanted to be a pilot the most."

"So, what changed?" she asked. "You obviously became a musician, and I personally think you enjoy it."

West turned back toward her. "At first, I didn't have any other skills or training, so it was the only thing I knew how to do," West said. "I'm not like Luke. I needed something to do, more than just sit around and live off daddy's money. But after releasing my first album and going on my first headlining tour, I realized why my dad loved being a rock star so much.

The crowds, the people I met, the feel of a guitar in my hands, and the music surrounding me—there's no greater feeling than knowing I created that music."

"Then why quit?" West could tell Kat was trying to push at him, and he wasn't sure how much more he was willing to answer. He had never told anyone these things, and yet with her, it seemed easy. Something he didn't want to think about when it came to why he pushed her away all those years ago.

Not that he was going to tell her everything. "It's not enjoyable anymore," was all he offered her.

"But . . . it can be. You just need to—"

"Kat, that's enough. I don't want to talk about it," he cut her off.

"But—"

"Kat, please, not right now. I don't want to fight, and I don't want to explain myself. I just want to get you water and know you're safe."

She took a step back from him, annoyance on her face, and West felt bad that he had snapped at her.

Moving toward her he shrank the space between them. They had entered a clearing where the trees had parted into an open canopy. A single sun ray pierced through the leaves and shone on her like a halo. His fingertips lightly grazed her arm and moved down her skin, leaving a trail of goosebumps in their wake. She didn't move, and all West could focus on was how soft her skin was beneath his touch.

West could hear her breathing become uneven. His proximity unsettled her, and he didn't know why he felt compelled to touch her.

"I'm sorry, Kat," he said.

He wasn't usually one for apologies, but there was something about falling drunkenly off a yacht into the Indian Ocean that had West realizing he owed her one. "This situation is all my fault. I usually never get so drunk, although I didn't think I was drunk enough to fall off a yacht. I still feel like something is off about all this, but I'm going to take responsibility for our predicament. I promise I will get us out of this."

She blinked up at him in confusion, and he could swear he saw disappointment in her eyes. Whatever she was expecting to hear, it wasn't that. She shook her head and rolled her eyes before turning away from him, annoyed by something he said.

"You don't have to keep promising to save me," she called back over her shoulder as she continued walking.

"Kat, wait . . . where are you going?"

"Come look!" she cried from up ahead. He couldn't see her, but he could hear the excitement in her voice.

"What is it?" As he got closer, he saw she had found a small stream with a little waterfall and she was drinking the water eagerly, a smile on her face.

As he walked toward the stream, relief coursed through West's body. But his euphoria was short-lived as he felt something slimy and squishy underneath one of his bare feet. Before he could react, a searing pain shot through his foot and he stumbled to the ground, clutching it in agony. Looking down, he saw two puncture marks on the top of his foot and watched in horror as a snake slithered away into the brush.

"Shit!" he yelled, his heart beating wildly with fear.

"What happened?" Kat asked, her voice trembling with concern as she rushed to his side.

"I-I stepped on a snake," West managed to choke out between gasps of pain.

"It bit you?" Her face turned white with alarm.

West nodded weakly, feeling his vision blur and head spin.

"What color was it?" Kat demanded urgently.

"What does that matter?" West cried out, trying to stay conscious.

"Just tell me!" Kat's voice rose in panic as she moved closer to him.

"Green," West gritted out before succumbing to darkness.

Six

Weston Monroe, international rock star, would go and get himself bitten by a venomous island pit viper on an uncharted island in Indonesia.

She held his limp body in her lap. He would die, and it would go in the history books as all her fault. They would bury him in Bali, and everyone would flock to his grave like they did to Jim Morrison's. His headstone would read, "Here lies Weston Monroe, who died tragically young of a snakebite because Kat Brooks couldn't save him."

Kat's heart pounded against her ribs, the blood roaring in her ears. She fought to keep the panic at bay, but it threatened to consume her. What options did she have? He was going to die, and she was going to hyperventilate to death.

Kat had to pull it together. She wasn't some simpering person who caved under pressure. She could save him. She just had to think of how. Before Kat had left for college, she and her grandmother had spent a lot of their time learning about Native medicine; she had the knowledge, she just had to put it all together.

After hours upon hours on the tour bus, Kat, along with Cher and Lydia, had seen countless documentaries on animals when they hadn't been watching others on cooking or travel, and she racked her brain for any on snakes.

Knowing they were coming to Bali, they'd watched a travel series on the island, and if she remembered correctly the green snake was definitely the pit viper. Based on West's reaction to the bite, there was indeed poison coursing through his body. She had to make an antivenom and apply it to the wound, and she should have had it on him say . . . now, or West would die.

No pressure.

Once again, Kat hoped for a great creator, not just in the sky but all around her, as she needed all the help from the spirit she could get. Her family was staunchly Christian, but she preferred the old teachings of her people. These teachings had been effectively whitewashed out of her family. But ultimately, she didn't believe in much of anything. The problem with being a semi-atheist lost on a deserted island needing to save someone's life was that there wasn't anyone to pray to. Which meant she sincerely hoped she was wrong, for West's sake.

As the venom coursed through his bloodstream, his body twitched and writhed in her lap, his muscles spasming. With each quiver of his skin, concern churned within her. If she wanted to save him, she had to act quickly. She inspected the bite mark on his foot. Fortunately, it seemed the viper hadn't sunk its fangs in deep.

Stupid, stupid man, walking around the deck without shoes. Not that he knew he would be thrown overboard, but that was beside the point. If he'd had shoes on, he would be awake, still teasing her, frustrating her, and making this situation more bearable, and she wouldn't be holding back tears while racking her brains for how to make this antivenom.

Lying him down on the rainforest floor, water became her first inclination. She didn't have a cup and searched for the largest leaf she could find.

Her gaze fell upon a towering banana tree, its leaves swaying mockingly just out of reach. Kat felt tears prick at her eyes as she realized there was no way she could scale the tall trunk with West in tow. But then, a glimmer of hope appeared—a lone coconut had fallen from one of the palm trees above. Without hesitation, Kat rummaged through West's pockets until her fingers closed around the small pocketknife she knew he always carried. West now lay stock still, not a good sign, and Kat tamped down the sense of dread that reared its ugly head.

The coconut was going to have to wait.

Her grandmother had a distrust of modern medicine after losing her husband to cancer. Personally, Kat felt there was a place for both in the world, but she still loved learning about the old ways. Kat had wanted to be closer to nature and understand the ways nature provided for them. Closing her eyes, she thought about the story of a boy bitten by a rattlesnake; the remedy had been chewed tobacco, the milky root of *prenanthes alba*, the bark root of the *tulipier, spiraea trifoliata*, and because it was a serious case, they added sage for good measure.

Surveying her surroundings with a heavy heart, she knew the plants used in the remedy were native to North America and wouldn't grow here—except maybe the sage. There seemed to be plenty of different varieties of that growing in abundance here.

Kat paced back and forth, wringing her hands as she stared down at West. If only they were back in the States—in America, she knew exactly which plants to look for. Little blue and yellow ones with white roots that could save his life.

Kat tried to recall any knowledge she might have. What did they watch together? Hear about? Almost ten years of living in the city and being on the road had made her disconnected from the natural world.

Think, Kat . . .

She paused as her eyes fell upon a stack of tiny white flowers, resembling the *trifoliata*, and as she stared at the tiny little white plants, a voice played in her head—the tour guide from one of their visits while in Bali.

They'd gone to Tanah Lot, also called Snake Island, a Hindu temple surrounded by snakes. Come to think of it, maybe West should have chosen a different vacation spot that hadn't been so full of snakes.

The tour guide had assured them the snakes wouldn't bite, and they would all be fine. Then she remembered what he'd said. There was a hospital easily accessible, but that before modern medicine, locals used *Mucuna* leaves as an antivenom by grinding up its leaves or the purple beans found in the buds and applying it directly to the wound.

As she studied the delicate petals of the white flowers, her fingers rubbing over them, her thoughts turned to West. If she combined traditional healing methods from both cultures, perhaps she could save him.

Cringing, she knelt beside his infected foot. The first thing the people had done was suck the venom out of the wound in the story of the boy. Her stomach roiled at the thought of possibly poisoning herself, but she knew this step would be critical in slowing the poison. Kat placed her lips around the punctures and sucked, immediately spitting out the fluid that entered her mouth. West owed her big time for this. After a few more tries at sucking out the venom, she ran to the stream and rinsed her mouth out. She would go to her grave with West never knowing she sucked on his foot.

He'd never let her live that down—if he survived.

Next, she needed to find *Mucuna* leaves, or beans, and sage; this island had to have something close. It was uninhabited, and humans hadn't destroyed its ecology yet. She'd read that Indonesia had upward of six thousand uninhabited islands, so this one had to have something useful.

Grabbing the knife, she took one last glance at West. "Please don't die," she pleaded as she ran off, searching for the plants she needed.

Later, as the sun began to set, Kat felt a surge of adrenaline course through her body. With determination, she had searched for the specific plants she needed—*Mucuna* leaves and sage. She had climbed trees, foraged bushes, and even chased off a bird to get what she needed.

Finally, she found her way back to West and checked his pulse—it was weak but still there. She grabbed the coconut and tried to crack it open with her knife, but the hard shell refused to budge. Panic rising, she desperately searched for anything that could help her break through the tough exterior.

Then, out of the corner of her eye, she spotted a fallen tree with a branch jutting out. With one swift motion, Kat slammed the coconut onto the branch but only managed to scrape her hand against it.

"Dammit!" She continued cursing as she hit the stubborn coconut against the branch. West's life depended on it—she needed to break it open so she had a place to grind the herbs into medicine. Time was running out.

With trembling hands and aching muscles, she finally cracked it open. Without hesitation, she gulped down half of the precious milk and saved the rest for West. Time was of the essence—she needed to get the poultice on him. She quickly returned to her task, using the butt of his pocketknife to mash together various plants and herbs. She didn't have chewing to-bacco, but she remembered her grandmother's trick—spitting into the mixture for added potency. Every second counted as she searched for something to put it on, eventually settling on a piece of her own torn pants.

West was only in his shirt and shorts, while Kat had layers upon layers—linen pants, a tank top, and a hoodie.

Crawling over to West's injured foot, she gasped at the angry red wound. After tending to it, she knew they needed lemon balm or *chaparral* to properly clean it out and stave off infection. She wasted no time in cutting off the bottom of her pants and rushing over to the nearby stream to rinse it off. Time was ticking.

Kneeling beside West's foot, she desperately hoped he would stay passed out for this procedure. Inhaling deeply, she readied herself for the gruesome task of cutting off the pieces of dead skin from around the wound that had been killed by the venom.

Kat's stomach churned as she surveyed the red, angry skin. She steadied her hand and cut away the damaged flesh. Though West groaned in pain, he was still. Concentrating on the task at hand, Kat soon finished her work and applied her antivenom poultice, quickly tying her pants tightly around his foot.

She set his head in her lap and forced the coconut milk down his throat. He coughed and sputtered most of it out, but she managed to coax him into swallowing a decent amount.

Satisfied that she had done as much as she could for him, Kat set his head down on her balled-up hoodie, and laid her head on his chest, closing her eyes as she listened to the slow, steady rhythm of his breathing.

Hours later she awoke to the moon in the sky, the sun long gone, and the growl of her stomach.

She checked West's pulse, which was steady, but she was still apprehensive about trying to move him. On one hand, they needed shelter. On the other, if she moved him too early it could injure him further. She let the gentle rise and fall of his chest calm her nerves as she listened to the many sounds of the rainforest at night.

Birds chirped loudly, and land animals rustled the trees. Kat closed her eyes hoping to tune out the noises that left her feeling exposed. Were there bobcats or other large mammals on this island? Would she be eaten? Her thoughts strayed to the worst-case scenarios before she could tamp them down. This was why she needed West. He kept things light and fun.

Her stomach growled at her again, shaking her from thoughts of her demise at the claws of a tiger. It had been well over twenty-four hours since she'd eaten anything, and her gaze settled on the overripe papaya she had fought a macaque for, unsure if she should eat it.

She didn't have the first clue how to start a fire. She didn't even know how to fish, or cook one for that matter, so the gross looking fruit was her only option. She may have understood the healing aspect of nature, but when it came to the hunting and gathering part, she was a failure. The spirits, if they were out there, were simultaneously applauding and booing her as an Indigenous woman.

If West would just wake up, he could cook. Kat shouldn't even remember that about him, but she did. She knew so much more about him than she should, more than he ever cared to know about her.

Earlier, when he had put his hands on her arms and gazed into her eyes as if he was going to say something utterly romantic, Kat had been thoroughly disappointed when he'd simply promised to get them off the island.

She was so stupid to think he would ever have any romantic feelings for a woman like her. She had already been down this road and been summarily rejected. He dated sophisticated women, or he liked crazy, dramatic ones. She knew exactly what he saw when he looked at her. Average height, average brown eyes, average brown hair, a too-big butt, and thick thighs. Sure, she had nice breasts, but considering all the models he dated didn't have a chest to speak of, that likely wasn't something he found attractive.

She groaned, the noise probably alerting some predator to her location. "Why do I even care?" She dropped her head in her hands, knowing she shouldn't entertain any feelings for West.

He was far too attractive to ignore—his arrestingly handsome features made it difficult to look away. But it wasn't just his looks that made her heart flutter; they shared a common love of music.

The first album they'd worked on together had been truly collaborative. He had let her into the process, and working with him had been amazing. He played every instrument on his albums, and Kat, Lydia, and Cher had worked with him to create the harmonies. He even asked their opinions on lyrics.

Then feelings had gotten involved, and a wall had come up between them. But that hadn't stopped Kat from watching him create beautiful music, leaving her to daydream about what those talented fingers would feel like on her skin. The dexterity in each digit was enough to make any woman go mad.

She would watch in awe as he played his guitar. His head gently lolling backward, his eyes closed, his hair falling over his forehead. Every line of music played with complete abandon, and she knew that was exactly what he would look like in the throes of passion. Music was his great love, and she doubted any of the women he'd been with ever came close. Thousands of people each night saw more of him than those women ever did, and he probably didn't even realize it.

Kat had lost that in herself. She hadn't written a single note in years. She sat down at the piano plenty and played other people's music and sang other people's lyrics, but never her own. At this point, she wasn't even sure she could. Her creative drive had diminished or gone missing. It didn't seem to matter how much yoga, meditation, or grounding practice she did, she wasn't at one with anything. She was adrift in the universe, and now she was literally and not only figuratively lost.

Kat didn't like being alone with her thoughts like this. On tour they were never alone, always together doing something to keep the boredom at bay. She was going to miss everyone so much. A lone tear rolled down her cheek, and she realized that was the first tear she'd allowed herself since West had upended her life, deciding that he was done with music and with her. And then she thought about their current situation, and the tears started to flow so fast she couldn't stop them.

She was going to die alone. Whether on this island or back in Iowa where her family lived, it didn't matter, both were equally depressing. She had no future, no love prospects, no career, her life was a failure. Her fifteen-year high school reunion was already in the works, and she was absolutely not going to that. Her ex-best friend Peggy, with her four children and dentist husband in the 'burbs of Des Moines, was living a much better life than she was at the moment.

Not that Kat wanted a husband or kids right now. She loved her life: she traveled the world and met amazing people; she only wished she had been ready for the ending.

She felt betrayed by her mind and her own internal clock. Why did society make her feel like she was past her prime to start over?

Her stomach growled at her again, and she picked up the overripe papaya, the yellow skin now turning brown in places. It was soft to the touch and she was scared to open it, but she had to eat something. Using the knife, Kat cut into it easily, the fruit soft and squishy. As the papaya fell open, she tried not to gag at the putrid smell that emanated from it.

Taking the knife, she cut out a few pieces of fleshy fruit that seemed okay and swallowed, choking as she forced them down with some coconut milk. Her eyes watered, and she pushed away the urge to vomit the disgusting rotting fruit back up. Inhaling deep gulps of air, she repeated the process until most of the offending fruit had been eaten.

She might die from that rotten piece of fruit, or she might die of starvation, or she might die from lack of shelter, but one thing was for sure: at this rate she and West were both going to die within the night.

She moved West's head onto her lap, keeping her warm. His breathing was still an even pace, so maybe the snakebite wasn't going to be the death of him. She was going to wait another hour to change the poultice, and then she would try to sleep again. Maybe West would wake up in the morning and they could find better shelter. It wasn't like either of them had anywhere to be. Kat wondered if the rest of the group was searching for them, or if they had flown back to America by now. Then a thought occurred to her. Had they told her mother?

Seven

As the moon rose for her third night on the island, Kat's survival skills were improving. She had built a shelter using branches and fallen trees, providing some protection from the elements for herself and West. The dense tree canopy above had also helped keep them dry during the heavy rain that poured down earlier.

Despite her resourcefulness, Kat was still struggling to find food. All she had managed to eat so far was a mushy papaya and a brown banana, which she found unappetizing due to its overripe state. But with her source of fresh water and access to coconuts, she was determined to make do until they could be rescued.

Kat felt a sense of comfort in the continuous sounds of the jungle around her, even though some of the animals could pose a threat. They hadn't bothered her yet, and she was grateful for their presence because it reminded her that she wasn't completely alone.

For the past couple of days, Kat had been tending to West's injuries while he remained unconscious. He would groan occasionally, which reassured her that he was still alive and his body was trying to heal itself.

After an entire day of self-pity and wallowing, Kat realized that she couldn't just sit around waiting for life to come to her, but rather she needed to get out and find her new life. They just had to get off this island first.

He groaned again and she rushed to his side with a coconut full of water, carefully helping him sip it without choking or sputtering. Slowly but surely, and against all odds, Kat was nursing West back to health and keeping him hydrated.

Kat knelt beside West, her hand resting on his forehead to check for a fever. His eyes were open but dull, and he weakly gurgled as she tried to offer him water. She could feel her heart flutter with relief as he spoke, his first words in three days.

Joy flowed through her, not because she wanted West specifically, she told herself, but because she was tired of being alone and proud of herself for saving him.

"You have to drink," she said softly, lifting a coconut to his lips. "It will help you feel better."

He struggled weakly, trying to push her hand away, but eventually gave in and drank the cool liquid.

"What . . . what's wrong with me?" he asked, his voice barely audible.

Kat tilted more water down his throat. "You were bitten by a snake, but you're going to be okay. You can go back to sleep, I got you."

His eyes fluttered closed again, and Kat was left in silence once more. But this time, she felt a glimmer of hope that they would make it through this together. She knew working with West instead of arguing with him would be difficult, but not impossible. And for the first time since being stranded on this island, Kat allowed herself to believe they could get home.

<hr>

West's head felt like it was about to burst, his tongue a withered raisin in his mouth, and the slightest twitch of his muscles felt like daggers piercing his skin. His eyes protested as he opened one and then another. The slivers of light shining through the canopy sent a shock of pain through his brain. He tried to remember what had happened: thrown from a yacht, stranded on an island, and . . . bitten by a snake, that about summed it up. When he tried to sit up, his world spun, and he would have toppled back if not for two hands steadying him and guiding him down onto a lap that felt like clouds.

"What are you doing?" her angelic voice whispered in his ear.

He tried to speak, but his voice was stuck in his throat.

"Don't try to speak yet." She reached for something and helped him to sit a little, handing him what he now noticed was a coconut. "Can you hold it?"

He took it and lifted it to his lips. The liquid hit his throat, cool and sweet. His whole body seemed to quiver with life as the elixir rushed through him, giving him strength and vitality.

He gave her a weak smile in thanks, and she smiled back, encouraging him to drink more. He complied meekly, gulping down the rest of the liquid.

After he'd finished, she rose from her crouched position and walked over to the stream that ran nearby. She filled the empty coconut shell with fresh spring water and returned to him. "Here, you should probably have some actual water."

He took it and drank eagerly.

After a while of staring out at their surroundings, he felt his body slowly come back to life. The fog began lifting from his brain. "How am I alive? People don't survive snakebites without antivenom. Not that I'm not eternally grateful," he added for good measure.

Kat hid from him, a faint blush tingeing her cheeks. "There are quite a few herbs and plants on this island that can be used to create an antivenom, so I made one."

She stood up and went to fill her own coconut with water, not elaborating any further. West glanced down at his foot and noticed part of her pants wrapped around it, with a dark reddish paste smeared on it.

"And . . . how did you know those plants would do that? Are you a herbologist in disguise?" he prodded her for more information.

She returned to his side, a sweet jasmine scent trailing behind her, blending with the salty ocean breeze. Her wild hair was coming out of its braids in an unruly mess, but she didn't seem to mind. A smudge of dirt colored her otherwise perfect face and West had the urge to reach up and brush it away. But he remained still.

"It was just a simple mix of some plants, a little coconut milk, and my grandma's secret ingredient."

"Which is?"

She smiled, unable to meet his eyes. "Spit."

West looked down at his foot in awe, strangely aroused at the idea of her spit on his foot. He knew her mouth hadn't been on him, yet it felt oddly intimate all the same.

"My grandma swears by the healing powers of spit," she continued. "I figured it couldn't hurt."

"I'm alive, so she must be right." He admired her handiwork. "You still didn't answer my question. You're not a doctor, at least I don't think you are, so how did you know how to save me?"

"Stereotypes and clichés aside, I learned with my grandmother from our Indigenous ancestors," she said, almost with a sigh.

"What?"

"I'm Native."

"Like Native American?" He stared at her questioningly. "You don't really look Native."

She glanced up at him before averting her gaze. "It's not like you look Irish," she said sarcastically.

"Probably because I'm no' Irish." He smirked at her, speaking in his best Irish accent.

She pushed at him lightly, not wanting him to fall over from his precariously seated position. "That's why, right there. I got sick of defending myself because I could pass for White, or people thought I was Jewish, or Hispanic. It just became easier to stay quiet and not openly claim my heritage all the time."

For the first time, he truly studied her: the high cheekbones, the aquiline nose, the darker shade of her skin, and suddenly he could easily see her proud Native features, not that she needed validation from him, or anyone. "Why not? You are who you are. You shouldn't let others stop you claiming that just because you may not look the part."

She sighed, staring off into the distance. "That's easy for you to say. Too many people try to take ownership of a Native culture they know nothing about, claiming their great-great-great-great-whatever was some Indian princess, which isn't even true. We don't have princesses. Besides, I've spent most of my life feeling like an outsider looking in. I'm used to it."

"Why?" West slowly rotated his body and shifted his weight, bringing his face close to hers. It had been a long time since a woman had been open with him, not just being who they thought he wanted them to be. He was seeing her for the first time in all her vulnerability—something she had never done with him before. Not that he hadn't made their relationship more guarded in the first place.

"My grandmother was orphaned at a young age and was put into an Indian boarding school—those places were awful. If you've been paying attention to the news lately there have been a lot of mass graves found at those 'schools.'" She put her fingers in the air to make air quotes on the word schools. "Places that forced Natives to assimilate into White culture." Kat's voice trembled. "My grandma was young, and they whipped all the Native out of her. She still, to this day, is a mix of god-fearing Christian with a complicated relationship with patriotism, who occasionally prays to the Creator but, more often than not, can be found in church on Sunday. The only thing she ever fought back on at first was modern medicine. Together we spent years going to the reservation and learning about tribal medicine."

Kat nudged his shoulder. A mix of sadness and pride warred within her. "You're alive because she wanted to learn about the old medicine, and I wanted to go with her. That, and I sucked at the tribal softball tournaments, so medicine seemed the better bet for me."

She smiled wistfully as she remembered her past. "At first, we went to the powwows and I tried it all. Basket weaving, quilting, cooking, and dancing. I was too old to learn the ceremonial drums, so in the end, I took a deep interest in medicine with my grandma. She eventually found some cousins at a powwow, but she always struggled to fit in with them."

"She sounds like a remarkable woman."

Kat shrugged. "She could've been, but she married a White army man who drank too much and didn't embrace her true culture."

"What about your parents?"

"My dad met my mom in college at a person of color community event. I'm still surprised they even went. There was an entire population of five Indigenous people at their large university. Both are mixed with parents who grew up in boarding schools. My dad was raised completely in White society, so I know nothing about my paternal grandmother who passed away when my dad was two, and my dad died four years ago, so all of that culture is long gone, but I mean, it was the seventies. It was easier if you could pass White, and my parents just went with it, never realizing how both their mothers were just married off to these White men. I loved my grandfathers, but the older I get, the more I realize how complicated those relationships were."

West had never thought about his race or his background that much. He fully recognized that the music he played was rooted in Black culture and that his musicians were mostly Black. And although he enjoyed learning and developing musically with them, he thought little about the implications of race in his daily life. He acknowledged the world's problems, but as a privileged

White man, he didn't feel it was his place to take the lead on those issues.

The more he was with Kat, the more he was finding he was lacking in a lot of areas, and he didn't like it. While it may not be his fight, maybe he should be doing more.

"So, what about you?" he asked her.

"What about me?"

"You're not much different from them. Your parents, I mean. Seems like you're hiding who you are too."

"I am not," she said, anger in her tone.

"Yes, you are. Not once have I ever heard you embrace your culture or who you are. Sounds like you hide behind your Whiteness too."

"It's not like that. I grew up in a very blue-collar, middle-class family. I didn't live the rez experience. I may be that race, but I still don't grasp all the culture and have had to work hard to learn about a life I've missed out on, a life a lot of us have lost. I get weird looks from some people trying to figure out what I am, but to most people, I just always seem tan, have high cheekbones, and a prominent nose. I'm what they call racially ambiguous, and since I didn't get to grow up in my culture or experience it until high school, I just feel like an imposter. I used to be really proud when I was a kid. But year after year of being told I didn't look Native wore me down."

"I'm the last person who should say anything about this, but just be who you want to be, Kat. You've clearly worked hard to understand your culture and your people, to get back to your roots. You just saved my life with a bunch of plants, for fuck's sake, so next time you feel like an imposter, just remember that."

Kat looked down, and he lifted her chin. She'd mastered the art of hiding, and it had extended all the way to her culture. Hell, she had been hiding behind him for years. He just didn't know how to help her.

"Promise me you'll remember how badass you are," he said.

Kat nodded.

"Good girl." His hand moved up her face and cradled it in his palm. He was captivated once again by the swirling colors in her eyes.

He could do it. All he had to do was close the distance between them and he would be kissing her. Would she let him, or would she pull away? Her lips were slightly parted, and her tongue glided out to lick her bottom lip. He had the distinct urge to pull on her braids, bringing her even closer to him.

Every inch of her called to him, from the passion in her voice, from her story, to the sincere gaze in her eyes. She had just saved his life, and it all rushed through his mind. Every instinct in his body told him to move closer. The problem was he knew Kat would want more than he was willing to give. He couldn't bring himself to close the space between their lips; it felt wrong, manipulative.

His heart raced and his breath caught in his throat, the sensation of electricity prickling his skin as their eyes locked and he leaned closer to her.

The unmistakable screech of a monkey echoed through the trees, and his hand dropped away from her face. In an instant, she backed away.

"Have you heard a lot of those?" West pointed up into the tree canopy.

"Here and there. One tried to steal my papaya, which was rather a fun time."

He tried not to laugh.

"It's fine, you can laugh at my expense."

He let out the laughter. "Sorry, I'm picturing you chasing a monkey to get a hold of a papaya."

She stood up and put her hands on her hips, accentuating her waist, and West's mouth instantly went dry. "I didn't chase the monkey. I had to beat the monkey to it. Besides, it was a macaque."

"So you're a healer and a monkey expert now?"

She shrugged. "I guess you didn't watch as much mindless TV on tour as we did."

What else had they done all those years on tour? She was wrong about him though. Plenty of nights he had read books or watched pointless shows. He had partied, or been with women frequently, but that didn't mean there weren't other times when he wished for peace, wished to be alone. He went to tell her something to that effect, but as he looked around, she was gone.

"Kat . . . Kat . . . Kat!"

"Over here . . ." He heard her call out from around a bush. "I'm just grinding up more leaves. You need your bandage changed."

He tried to stand, but realized he was still too shaky on his legs and fell back down. Soon, she reemerged and sunk to her knees next to his foot.

"I'm glad you wore pants," he joked as she cut off another piece of them.

She didn't smile, only frowned as she took the bandage off.

"What's wrong?"

"It's redder than I hoped. I need to find more natural antibacterial. But you don't have a fever, so you're not infected. I guess it's just red. I'm going to clean this off a bit and then change the bandage. It might sting."

She set to work, and West felt the burn go through him as she used the knife to cut the dead skin away. She carefully added new herbs mixed with water, and most likely her saliva, and tied the new mixture onto his foot. It stung, but the pain wasn't too excruciating. She had saved him countless times now, and he felt a deep gratitude, and something else he couldn't quite name toward her, knowing that she was the reason he was still alive.

Eight

He'd been about to kiss her. Why hadn't he kissed her, and why was she so upset that he hadn't? She knew better. She really did. So, what was wrong with her? He didn't close the distance, and Kat reminded herself she shouldn't care. He had just woken up from being poisoned after all.

She sat back from his foot, looking at her handiwork. Her grandmother would be so proud of her—she was rather proud of herself. Maybe if music didn't work out, she would think about becoming a practitioner in Indigenous healing.

She wasn't against modern medicine. Hospitals were important and played an important role in society, but Kat believed there was also a place for the ways of Indigenous medicine. Look what she had done with what the earth had provided. Maybe she'd just avoid going back to society altogether.

She might be starving right now, but at least on the island she could breathe clean air, feel the breeze on her face, and the sand on her feet. She was living how her ancestors had—at one with the earth. Maybe that was what she needed to do when they got off this island— because at some point they would . . . right?—move back into nature.

Her family had land they didn't use. Maybe she'd build a tiny container home. The problem was there wasn't even a road to get to their parcel. It wasn't theirs originally. It was land her ancestors were forced on. After her grandfather had passed, her father had done some digging—god knew her mother had no urge to learn more about her background—and they had taken a trip to the southeastern states to see her ancestors' original land. It was lush with rolling hills and running streams, nothing like the arid, red, sandstone plains of Oklahoma.

Kat thought back to the emotion she had seen on her grandmother's face as they had toured the Trail of Tears exhibit at the Smithsonian. She had seen her reflection mirrored back at her. "So many of our people lost," she had whispered as she wept at the destruction of her people. Kat's people.

Her mind strayed to the current missing and murdered Indigenous women. So many were lost without a trace. Her grandmother's words swirled around in her head. Maybe West was right, maybe she was hiding behind her Whiteness, and she wasn't doing enough, but what weapons did she have?

Her stomach growled, and Kat felt her face heat up.

West smiled. "I'm starving too. What have you been eating?"

"Just the overripe papaya, and I haven't seen too many of those. I think it's past their season. We need a fire and a way to fish, or we need to find some nuts or berries. I know nothing about cooking fish though."

"Your grandmother didn't teach you anything about cooking?"

Kat laughed. "No, she's the worst cook ever. Thanks to government subsidies and canned food, a lot of Native communities have poor health and have lived off food from a can or package, especially those like my grandmother who have no familial recipes."

West looked away from her, taking a great interest in a beetle-looking bug walking across their path. She could sense he was uncomfortable. It was why, as a rule, she kept her heritage to herself, but at least West asked her questions. He may have been uncomfortable, but he still wanted to know more, and for that, Kat was grateful. She lived in a strange in-between world, with no clear sense of belonging. She was adrift in more ways than one.

Was she White, or was she Indigenous? Was she both, and would the world accept her for being both? Would she be able to accept herself? Was she going to be a musician, a singer, a songwriter, or something else? Was she going to fight for others like her, or was she going to escape? The questions continued to swim around in her head all while she should have been worried about finding food, but rather than thinking about eating, or even her future as an Indigenous woman in a White world, all she wanted to think about was West's perfect mouth, and how it had been so close to being on hers.

"We're not too far from the beach. I thought if we could catch a fish, we could eat something real."

"Do you have my knife? I noticed you using it earlier."

Kat searched the pockets of her pants. "Shit, it's somewhere around here." She dropped to where she had been making West's concoction of herbs for his antivenom, her hands raking across the dirt.

He stopped her, lifting one of her hands closer to his eyes, concern on his face. "What happened to your hands?"

She pulled it back, unwilling to let him get close again. "It's fine. I just couldn't get the damn coconut open. Your knife was useless in that regard."

He picked her hand up again, genuine worry in his eyes. "I'm sorry, Kat, I shouldn't have left you to fend for yourself. I should have paid attention to where I was stepping and avoided that snake."

She felt the warmth of his hands as he massaged her raw palms. She forced herself to break away from the mesmerizing sensation before she lost control.

"West, stop. I can take care of myself."

"Kat. You're missing the point. You don't have to. This whole situation is my fault. I do something stupid, and you end up in the crosshairs. Can you please let me take care of you for once? I'm not just a pretty face you know."

Kat knew he was more than a pretty face. She had always thought so. He was a brilliant musician and singer. He was good with people and was always kind and attentive to his fans, even when they could be overzealous. She didn't know how he dealt with it so well. He was a good person, just not to her. She had never thought he dealt with insecurities based on his looks.

She saw something silver under some brush and grabbed it, the cool metal soothing her hands.

"Here." She shoved the knife at West. "You want to do something, catch a fish and figure out how to cook the damn thing because I sure as hell don't know the first thing about making a fire without a lighter."

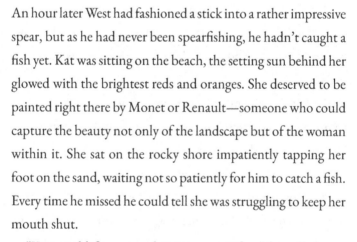

An hour later West had fashioned a stick into a rather impressive spear, but as he had never been spearfishing, he hadn't caught a fish yet. Kat was sitting on the beach, the setting sun behind her glowed with the brightest reds and oranges. She deserved to be painted right there by Monet or Renault—someone who could capture the beauty not only of the landscape but of the woman within it. She sat on the rocky shore impatiently tapping her foot on the sand, waiting not so patiently for him to catch a fish. Every time he missed he could tell she was struggling to keep her mouth shut.

"You could figure out how to start a fire," he yelled over his shoulder. He was knee-deep in the water, and even from a distance he could feel her fiery stare on him.

"I don't know how," she called back.

"Haven't you seen a movie? Take a stick and . . ." He took the spear in his hand and rolled it back and forth to simulate making a fire.

The action made him picture her hands gripped around a stick, stroking it back and forth, and it transported his mind to another shaft he'd like to see her stroking.

He had wanted to kiss her earlier, and now he was mad he hadn't. Fuck, she was pushing him off his equilibrium. He was always in control with women—they threw themselves at him, and he decided if he wanted to make their night. Conceited? Most likely, but the truth. He gave women what they wanted, and they always left satisfied. Except for Gia—she had kept him on his toes, making it interesting enough for him to come back again and again until her tantrums and pouting had lost their charm. Even if their make up sex was fantastic, West knew she wasn't worth the effort anymore.

Kat couldn't be more different. She wouldn't be fake with him; she had already told him more truths about herself than Gia ever had. She was real and raw and all the things he hadn't realized he had been missing, and he should have kissed her. But he couldn't shake the feeling that if he crossed that line, there would be no going back for them. Something had ignited within him when his lips had touched hers long ago, and if it happened again, he might not walk away from her this time.

"People don't start fires like that," Kat said, walking toward him, dipping her toes into the ocean. She stood still and let the wave pull her feet under the sand.

"Yes, they do." He just didn't know how.

She cocked an eyebrow. "Okay, Boy Scout, how?"

"I don't know . . . it's friction or something. You need a stick and to get some of that coconut fluff."

She looked at him with disbelief in her eyes. "Maybe I should try spearfishing."

"Seriously?" He flexed his biceps to make it clear who had the muscle power to throw the makeshift spear.

"You've been at it for over an hour. How about I try, and you go do your little friction thing." She rubbed her hands together.

"No, I think I can catch the fish."

"You made the spear. Don't worry, you're still just as manly if you make the fire."

West hadn't been paying attention, and before he knew it, she grabbed the makeshift spear from him.

He held on to it. It was a matter of pride now. "No, Katy, go make the fire." He said, using the name he knew she hated to distract her.

But she wasn't giving up. He knew it must hurt her hands and he was being an ass, but she could end this by just letting go.

"No, you tried, let me catch the fish." She pulled hard on the spear, frustration on her face.

"Stop, you're going to hurt your hands more."

"Then let go!"

"That's horrible logic. You let go."

His face was inches from hers, the tension between them palpable. He had to end this. With a swift movement of his leg, he unbalanced her, making her stumble backward into the water.

But she still refused to let go, and in an act of stubbornness, he kept his grip on it too. They both fell into the water. Her warm, pliant body was under him as he tried not to crush her. She pushed him to the side, grabbing the spear. Sitting up he used one hand to wipe the water out of his eyes; the other was still locked onto the spear's handle with a death grip.

"Exceptional work, genius." She stared daggers at him. "Now I'm wet and the sun is setting."

His eyes hooded as he watched her get up. "I can think of better ways to make you wet," he said under his breath.

A slight blush crept up her face, but otherwise, she made no sign that she had heard his comment.

"All the more reason to get a fire going," he said more loudly.

"West, please just let me try. Fifteen minutes, and if we both suck, we'll switch back." Her eyes glowed golden, and for the briefest moment, West stood still, utterly entranced, before looking away.

It wasn't the worst idea. He knew he wouldn't get a fire started in fifteen minutes, especially now that he was wet, and there was no way she was going to catch a fish. He suspected it would be a waste of time, but if it would stop their fighting he'd give in to her.

He stood up out of the water, dropping the spear. "Fine, we have no clock, so whatever fifteen minutes means, I'll be back."

He walked back to the rocky beach to find some tinder and a dry stick. Looking out of the corner of his eye he saw Kat as she pranced around the waves, searching for a fish. A few were swimming around in the shallow waters, but the spear was a crude instrument, and it didn't glide through the water like a true metal spear. He had struggled with brute strength; he had no idea how she would pull it off.

The stick was taller than her as she attempted to throw it like a javelin. It bobbled in her hands and fell into the water. He held back a laugh as she tripped, almost falling backward.

"Don't"—she yelled at him, putting up one of her hands as if to stay his reaction—"even say anything."

He held his hands up and clamped his mouth shut with effort. It wasn't as easy to spear a fish as they made it look on those survival shows on TV. West knew all about the smoke and mirrors Hollywood used when filming so-called "reality" TV shows.

He remembered when MTV had shot an episode of *Cribs* in his dad's house and they'd wanted them to look as natural as possible, without looking natural at all. They didn't go into West's room, and they felt his dad's cars weren't edgy enough for a rock star, so they had brought in a couple of classic cars to put in the garage.

His father hadn't cared all that much. MTV had been a big part of making his career so he didn't fight them. Now the channel was useless and did nothing for musicians, but back in the eighties and nineties it had been everything, and Tommy Monroe knew who not to piss off. It was a big part of why his career was a success. He had passed that on to West.

"The most talented musician can be singing in the subway tunnels," he would say to him. "It's about who can play the game."

The whole thing made West sick to his stomach most days, and Dec had taken care of the business side. He had played the game, let the label control his music, and it had morphed into something he didn't want to do anymore. Now, he saw that was a mistake. Taking the hands-off approach hurt not only his career, but Kat's too.

Shit, he had no music career left, and he didn't know what he was going to do next. He could do the whole acting thing, but deep down he couldn't decide if he was doing it because it finally removed him from his dad's shadow, or because he really wanted to try something new.

None of it mattered if they never got of this island.

<hr />

Kat tried not to look as West's long, powerful form walked across the beach, and wished she could ignore his presence. She couldn't help it. He had a magnetism that drew her into his sphere. His hair was wet and curling at his nape, and all she wanted was to run her fingers through it.

She should pinch herself for thinking something like that. Weston Monroe was an international pop-rock superstar. He was not interested in someone like Kat. Her eyes followed him as he bent down to pick up some dried leaves, admiring the way his swim trunks pulled across his muscular backside. He had toned calves, strong thighs, and perfectly sculpted glutes. Kat watched the rivulets of water drip down his muscles as she felt desire pulse through her. A truly unwelcome reaction considering their situation.

As West sifted through a pile of wood, every muscle in his legs and arms flexed. Even though she'd never found fit guys that attractive before, her mouth went dry. Why was she even looking at West like a piece of meat?

Probably because you're hungry.

The spear hung heavy in her hand, reminding her of what she was supposed to be doing. She was starving, and while the idea of eating West sounded appealing, she needed actual sustenance first. Later she could consider if she was willing to be his flavor of the week. West didn't allow feelings. Could she live with that?

Kat watched the fish swim near her legs; they seemed to have no fear. The spear was too long for her to throw like West had been doing, and its length made it quite unwieldy for her. No wonder he thought she couldn't do it, but if the fish would come up close to her like this, maybe she could get one from up top.

A small school of fish swam toward her and she eyed them carefully. They looked similar to the yellowfin tuna she'd eaten in Bali—since the snake incident her biggest worry was ingesting something poisonous—so if these were tuna they'd be okay. After this, Kat would never make fun of doomsday preppers or survivalists again.

All the reality TV and TikTok videos in the world could never have prepared her for this. To top it all off, she looked like shit. Her hair was a tangled mess, and no amount of braiding could make it look good. Her nails were torn to pieces, and dirt covered her from head to toe. All the while West took one swim in the ocean and looked perfect. Men sucked.

Focus.

Her movements were slow as she watched the fish. As soon as she thrust the spear into the water, she knew the fish would scatter and her opportunity would vanish. With the spear poised above the water, she waited for the perfect time to strike. Closing her eyes, she listened to the water lapping against the beach, the breeze in the trees, and felt her feet sink into the sand with each push of the waves. Taking a deep breath, she inhaled the ocean air, clearing her head of all other thoughts beyond the fish swimming around her.

Opening her eyes, she held the spear with both hands, tracking a fish that was slower than the rest; it had an injured fin—a pity for the fish, but this was a matter of survival. She stood perfectly still, holding her breath, waiting. Inch by inch, it swam closer to its doom as Kat braced her arms, the spear tip held steady on the surface of the water. When the fateful moment arrived, she thrust down with all her might, feeling contact as she pierced through the flesh of the poor, defenseless fish.

"Yes!" She lifted the spear out of the water, amazed that she had caught not one, but two fish.

She began jumping up and down, the fish wriggling on the spear. "Oh West . . ." She smiled lifting the spear in his direction ready to gloat for days.

He glanced up from the fire he had been trying to make, disbelief written on his face, that soon turned to relief. "How did you . . .? I don't even care, we've got something to eat. Great work, Kat!"

Kat couldn't believe it. He was so different to the man she was used to. There was no manly pride or bluster, just sincere praise for her success.

She walked over to where he was working on the fire and was surprised to see a flame coming out of the coconut fluff he had used as tinder.

"Did you just rub two sticks together?"

"Maybe." He grinned, looking guilty, and blew on the small flame, adding more tinder, allowing it to grow before adding the larger logs.

Kat set the spear down, glaring at him. "So, how'd you do it?"

He held up something that made Kat do a double take.

"Is that a lighter? Did you have that the whole time?"

She wanted to hit him! She had been starving and could have cooked some seaweed or something to tide her over. But she'd gone through all his pockets when he'd been unconscious, so where had he hidden it?

"No, no, I promise," he said, seeing the disbelief in her eyes. "I was searching for tinder and sticks and found it. I wasn't sure if it would even work, but it did."

She sat down next to him in the sand, the urge to collapse into his arms stronger than she wanted to admit. For days, she had been trying to survive. She pushed the emotions to the side. She was close to food, and, hopefully, a good night's sleep. She hadn't slept and had eaten only rotten fruit. For almost forty-eight hours, she had been keeping West alive. He was shaky on his feet, even if he wouldn't admit it. And Kat had to push back the sting of tears behind her eyes.

"Does that mean there are people on the island, you think?" They had covered little of the island, too busy trying to survive to explore.

"It's possible; maybe on the other side. But it could also just be trash that washed ashore."

Kat frowned, the weariness in her body sinking in. She needed to believe there were people. "Sad but true, but this is a big island. There could be people we haven't seen yet. We could be off this island soon!"

West stood. "I wouldn't get your hopes up." He walked over to the fish, looking at the spear, admiring her handiwork. "How'd you do it?"

"Patience."

"Mmmm," he said as the delicious sound of his deep voice reverberated through her body. "I think there's more to the story, but I'm too hungry to care. Lucky for you, my grandpa would take me fishing as a kid. I think I can cook these things well enough."

"Your grandpa meant a lot to you, didn't he?"

West shrugged the comment off. "He was the opposite of my dad. He loved camping and the outdoors and would never be caught dead in skintight pants."

Kat wasn't buying his nonchalance. There was a deep relationship there. "That's his knife, isn't it?" She nodded toward his pocket. "That's why you carry it with you everywhere."

West nodded. "He didn't have much, but he left me this knife. It's the one thing I have to remember him by."

West turned to prep the fish, and Kat knew the discussion of his family was over.

Two descaled, cooked, and eaten fish later, Kat couldn't believe how much better she felt. "That was the best fish I have ever had in my life." It had been crude and not pretty, but food was food at this point. All propriety had gone out the window for Kat.

"That's high praise, considering we ate at that Michelin Star restaurant in Paris a couple of months ago."

They were sitting by the fire, the sun now gone from the sky, the cool ocean breeze blowing across their skin. Kat pulled on her hoodie, grateful she had it with her. West was always emanating heat, but even he had goose bumps as the breeze kissed his skin. The fire was a welcome presence in the cool evening air.

"I'm sure I didn't have fish there," she said, amazed he had cooked two fish in the middle of nowhere.

"Are you going to miss it?" She'd been wanting to ask him since they'd been alone together.

He smiled, but it didn't quite meet his eyes, a hidden pain there. "Miss what?"

"Don't be difficult."

"I'm not, you're being unspecific. Miss making music professionally, miss touring, miss having every moment of my schedule micromanaged? Miss racking my brain for new lyrics and musical combinations that are fresh and that won't piss off music critics and fans alike? Which part do you mean, Kat?" His eyes bored into hers. It was dark, but his clenched jaw was apparent in the firelight. Kat didn't care if she made him angry. Too many people treated West with kid gloves, allowing him to get his way all the time.

"A little cynical, aren't we?"

"No, I've been doing this for a long time. I know the game, and I'm done playing it."

"Why . . . what are you going to do then?"

"Onslaught pictures offered me an acting gig for two CIA spy films."

Kat gaped at him. "You're going to act?"

"At least it will be different, and it will piss off my dad, so I get two for one."

"Ah."

He turned to face her. "What does that mean?"

"Nothing."

He raised an eyebrow, moving closer, his mouth inches from her ear. "What, Kat?" he whispered. "That was quite the loaded *ah*."

She pushed him back, refusing to let him get to her.

"So, your quitting music has something to do with your daddy issues, or whatever you've got going on there."

He straightened, backing away from her. "No, I just enjoy pissing him off."

"West, you're like thirty-seven years old. That's the definition of daddy issues."

He pushed himself up, dusting the sand from his hands, the muscles from his thighs and calves drawing her attention.

"I don't want to talk about this, Katy."

"Yes, call me Katy and walk away. That's what you're good at!" she called after him, jumping up to follow. "You are ridiculously talented, West. If I had even half the talent you do in my pinky finger, I . . . I . . ."

"What? What would you do?" He whirled around to glare at her.

She stopped in her tracks, and he took a step closer to her.

She lifted her chin in defiance. "I know I wouldn't give it all up."

He took another step closer until their chests were touching. He hovered over her, his proximity unnerving. "You don't know what you're talking about. You don't know what it's like being the one everyone is there to see, the one everyone wants the new album from, the one they want on tour. Fans stalking your home, women throwing their bras on stage, men hating you because their girlfriends wish they were me. Knowing that all you want to do is make fucking music! You constantly face the pressure of never living up to everyone's expectations, including record label execs who have never played a fucking instrument in their lives, criticizing your music as dated and providing suggestions for improvement. And now, throw in social media, and you tell yourself it's just a bunch of noise, to tune it out, but it's there, and unless you want to throw your phone into the goddamn ocean, you can't unsee some of the shit that's out there. So don't tell me what you would do, because you don't fucking know. You got to hang out in the back riding my coattails all these years, just like the rest of them."

His words caused her to wince and retreat as if he had stabbed her in the chest, reminding her of her inadequacy as a musician, her inability to be like him and create true art. She was just the chick who *hung out behind him*. To prevent herself from crying in front of him, she pinched the bridge of her nose.

He reached out, trying to pull her back, registering what he had said. "Kat . . . wait, I'm sorry."

She put her hand out to stop him. "No. You meant every word of that."

"I didn't, not the part about—"

"I don't see how Hollywood is any different," she said, cutting him off, trying to avoid how he had just shredded her self-worth. "Can you even act?"

"I don't know. The movie studio thinks I can. But listen . . . I'm sorry."

She ignored his apology. She couldn't bear it, or she'd cry. "Is that even what you want to do?"

"This conversation is done."

"But . . . how long did you know this? You didn't just decide this."

He ran his hands through his hair. "I thought maybe I could do both. But we're not talking about this."

She crossed her arms over her chest. "So, what changed?"

"Kat!" He stalked toward her, clearly feeling better and grabbed her by her upper arms. He wasn't rough, but he wasn't gentle either, pushing her up against one of the tall rocks.

She felt the air crackle with awareness as his face came close to hers. Deep in the pit of her stomach, she thought he was going to rip off all her clothes and have his way with her, which she was completely fine with. Or squeeze her until she stopped asking him questions. His eyes had gone wild. She had never seen him lose control like that. He seemed like a feral animal that needed to be released from its cage.

Then his face changed just as quickly as his anger had come, and he stepped back, dropping her arms, uttering a soft apology. His voice shook with an emotion that unnerved her more than his earlier lack of control.

She rubbed her upper arms, not because they were in pain, but because she missed his touch. Noticing her actions, his face turned angry—whether at her or himself, she couldn't tell. It didn't matter. Either way, she was done. He had made it clear he had no interest in confiding in her.

"I'm sorry. I shouldn't have pushed you to share. You don't owe me anything. You're my boss, who I, unfortunately, am marooned on an island with. We mean nothing to each other, and you've made that abundantly clear for a very long time." A tear slipped down her cheek, betraying her feelings.

She walked past him back toward the campfire, not daring to turn around as the tears continued.

"Kat . . . Kat, wait," he called after her.

Steeling her shoulders she kept walking, unwilling to let him know his words got to her.

"Sleep, I'll keep watch." His voice was gentle from somewhere behind her.

She paused for a moment before nodding and settling down close by the fire. Exhaustion tugged at her eyes as she drifted off into a not-so-peaceful sleep.

Nine

He woke up the next morning, groggy from lack of sleep and lack of a bed. This entire situation was killing his spine. He'd be living at his chiropractor's office if they ever made it back.

For hours he had listened to the sound of waves on the beach, and animals rustling the trees while she slept. The calm rhythm of her breathing was the only sign that she was even alive. She didn't move once, proving to West how tired she was. Guilt had taken over as he thought about the things he had said, the way he had treated her, and the fact she had been on her own caring for him the past few days. He was an utter ass, and if they hadn't been stuck on an island together, he wouldn't blame her if she wanted nothing to do with him.

He had made her cry. He cared about her. It might have been this situation they were in, or maybe he had always cared but had refused to admit it to himself. Watching that lone tear roll down Kat's cheek had made something hurt in his chest.

She had saved his life, and yet he couldn't admit to her why he had left the music business. She pushed him, pushed him to be better, to open up and talk about what was on his mind, and he'd told her more than he'd wanted. He'd told her all the thoughts that had been swirling around in there and it had made him angry.

West had told no one about the pressures he felt daily, what it felt like to be him. Now, to top it all off, he was stuck on an island with a woman he would love to fuck, but shouldn't. If he did he might develop feelings for her, and that wouldn't bode well for him because he didn't know what to do with a woman like that. A woman who wanted more from him than a physical relationship.

Toward the east, the first beams of sun were appearing over the horizon, telling him it was still early. He had never been so in tune with the sun's position in the sky in his life, but now it had become integral to figuring out what time of day it was. Looking around, he realized Kat was nowhere in sight.

Shit.

Rubbing his hands through his hair he groaned, cursing his stupidity. He had chased her off. She thought him an asshole, and she had every right to. It was imperative for him to find her and apologize.

One of the coconuts they had filled with water had disappeared. He didn't know if that meant she had gone to get more water, or if she was walking far away from him, and would need a drink. He hoped it was the former. Grabbing his own coconut, he took a drink and headed to the stream they had been filling from. She wasn't there, but he filled up his water, keeping his eyes peeled for snakes. Mostly, Kat had been the one to fill up their coconuts since she had shoes. West was paranoid and didn't want to tempt fate again.

He couldn't fathom where she would have gone without telling him. Even if she was mad at him, it wasn't like she could get away from him. He made his way across the rockier part of the beach, cursing his lack of footwear once again. If he ever made it home, he would never go barefoot again.

West replayed the words she had said to him about his "daddy issues" in his head. She was right, but that hadn't been the point. He hadn't wanted to talk about being a walking rich kid cliché with daddy issues. She didn't know the first thing about growing up with a famous father, the expectations to be just as talented, just as famous—the idea of doing anything different hadn't even been possible. Even worse, there was the worry of wanting to be like his dad but not being half as good. Sure, his label was done with him, but this movie deal was also a chance for him to prove that he could do something besides make music, do something outside of his father's shadow. To not fail at something.

She had asked if he was any good, and that was a question he asked himself all the time. He believed he had done quite well during his auditions. He was constantly training with his trainer, toning his body to perfection to play a CIA agent. Looking the part was half the battle, and he'd succeeded in that. Self-doubt crept in as he contemplated failing at another career.

When she had called him talented, it had taken everything within him not to ask her what she meant. Everyone had always attributed his talent to his father, not to his hard work or dedication to the craft. Kat on the other hand, saw him for his own person, saw his talent. Throughout all their years together he finally saw that she challenged him because he knew he had the potential to be better. Her love of music was clear, and he could see how much she hated that West was leaving it. It had been unclear to him whether her reasoning was because of their professional connection or her personal gain. He realized his foolishness for contemplating the former; his hurtful words had been uncalled for. He needed to find her and beg for forgiveness. She could be everything and more without him if only she'd take a chance on herself.

Coming around the corner he saw a shadow in the distance, silhouetted against the sun, and he realized it was Kat. Relief swept over him faster than the waves lapping at the beach. She stood on the flat part of the beach where there were no rocks. At first, he almost called to her, but then realized she was concentrating on doing yoga, dancing, or some kind of movement, soaking up the first rays of the sun.

Rather than interrupt her, he watched, mesmerized by the movement in her arms, waist, and hips. Her eyes were closed, and he could see her take deep breaths, exhaling in time with the waves. He wondered what she focused on. Her hair was down and flowing. She had been braiding it since they had been on the island, which gave him thoroughly lewd thoughts of roping them around his hands and yanking her to him, but now it was down and equally alluring as it fell across her back and shoulders.

He wanted to run his fingers through it. Her hips moved back and forth in time to the waves, her arms straight out to her sides now swinging side-to-side. A slight smile was on her face, and she looked so serene. West couldn't believe she was the same woman he'd known for almost a decade. Here in this space, she looked like a goddess soaking up the sun.

⬤

The rising sun had warmed her skin as she made her way to the flat part of the beach. Whenever they could on tour, Kat, Lydia, and Cher would have a morning yoga session. This morning, Kat had woken up and decided that sunrise yoga was just what her weary soul needed. But it had devolved more into a dance. She had started with meditation, but all she could think about was West.

His perfect eyes sparkled cobalt blue, and his perfect jaw that could cut glass was now sporting the most perfect stubble that she wanted to rub her hands through, and his stupid perfect hair that was graying on the sides making him all kinds of sexy, rather than appearing old, all called out to her. Then she hated herself for her excessive use of the word perfect when describing him. Never mind she was supposed to be mad at him for being a complete moron to her the night before.

It had been impossible to focus and meditate, so she had gotten up and tried some yoga poses and vinyasa flows, but she needed some music because she kept getting distracted with that too. West consumed her thoughts when she was supposed to be clearing her mind.

"Get it together, Katrina," she said to the vast ocean before her.

She sat staring out into the blue water, listening to the waves as they lapped in front of her and thought of a technique she had learned at one of the tribal gatherings called grounding. It was similar to grounding in yoga, but Native culture focused on the act of healing through nature, something she desperately needed if she was to survive their time on this island. Her shoes were already off, and she sank her feet into the sand, closing her eyes and facing the sun.

She emptied her mind of all thoughts, and with her arms hanging loosely by her side, she focused only on her senses, starting with the warmth of the early sun on her face and the coolness of the sand on her feet. Then she listened to the magic of nature around her: the waves gently sloshing against the beach in a rhythmic pattern; the breeze rushing through the leaves; the birds chirping in the trees, louder and more of them than she'd realized; the rustling in the treetops, from the macaques, perhaps. The sounds worked together in harmony, and soon she found music within them.

The vibrations through the ground moved through her feet and her body, causing her to move, and before she knew it, she was swaying to the music of nature. She started humming the tune she heard, and the music came to life. It was one of the most magical moments she had ever experienced, and she hoped she never forgot the music in her head that came from the beauty of this place.

She felt connected to the island and all its inhabitants. She could feel it pulsing through her. She breathed in the fresh air, and wished this moment would never end, that she never had to leave this place. She loved city life, but there was something so restorative about becoming one with the earth, despite the lack of comforts.

She felt a warm hand at the small of her back and a deep voice in her ear. "Don't stop, it's just me."

Kat should've stopped. She should have felt embarrassed—he been watching her dancing and singing in the breeze, with no actual music playing, for who knew how long. She probably looked like a crazy person, but she couldn't muster any embarrassment. She felt too calm, too at peace, and his touch sent further ripples of awareness through her. Her movements slowed and he grabbed her wrists, raising her arms back to where they had been.

"Don't stop moving." His lips grazed the shell of her ear. "What are you doing?" he asked, his breath fanning her neck, sending shivers down her spine.

She continued her movements, and behind her, his hands moved up her back and down her arms, holding onto her hands and allowing her to choose the movement as he moved with her. She backed against him, feeling every hard inch of him. Her senses had already been on high alert, but now his scent and touch overwhelmed her. His hand came around her middle, pulling her hips into his.

"Natives, like many ancient cultures, have a tradition of grounding," she started, her voice more breathless than she wanted to sound. "We use our connection with the earth to heal our bodies or souls. We are just one small infinitesimal speck in the universe. As humans, we try to control nature, but in reality, we are beholden to it. Being on this island has reminded me of how true that is. I tried to focus, but it devolved into me hearing the music of the island and dancing to it . . . Listen."

She placed one hand on top of his where it rested against her stomach, and he reached out to hold her other outstretched hand. They moved together in silence, listening to the sounds of the island, her back tucked tightly against him. She felt his breath on her nape, and she felt the electric current it sent all the way to her toes as they curled in the sand.

"This might be the sexiest image I've ever woken up to," he whispered in her ear.

Her eyes snapped open, the ocean coming into focus as they adjusted to the light. He didn't mean it, he couldn't. This man woke up next to models, actresses, and pop stars. Plain old Kat dancing to the ocean breeze was not a sexy picture. She was also still mad at him for what he said last night.

Right?

"I think the snake venom is rotting your brain."

He spun her around as if they were slow dancing at a school dance, and Kat's heart flipped.

"I mean it, Kat. You look so free and at peace. I don't think I've ever seen anyone be so alive before. The way your hips move, the way you hear sounds and feel the island as if it's alive."

Well, she couldn't stay mad if he said things like that.

"It is alive. This island is full of life."

She wrapped her arms around his neck as they swayed to nature's song—the music that only they heard made by the waves, the rustling of the trees, and the songs of the island's birds. It was their song.

"Do you hear music in your head a lot?"

She shook her head, looking out to the ocean. "No, not in a long time." She tried to hide the emotion in her voice but failed.

"When did you first fall in love with music?" he asked.

"When did you?" She tilted her head back, and gazed up at him.

"Now who's deflecting?" His hands moved up and down her back as they continued to sway. Kat thought back to her senior prom with Archie Llewellyn, the once thespian now finance guy for some hedge fund. Her first boyfriend, and the first guy to break her heart. The one who taught her it was easier to be alone. West probably never did pedestrian things like going to a high school prom. What would prom have been like with him if he had?

"Kat?" he asked, bringing her back to the moment.

"I don't think I have a single instance. It's always been a part of me. It controls my moods, it creates my memories, and it's the soundtrack for each stage of my life. I can go back and listen to different playlists from times in my life and it brings back memories as if they were yesterday. Music is just a part of who I am. I went to a"—she smirked at him—"Fall Out Boy concert when I was fourteen, and I decided that's what I wanted to do."

"What? Be in a band?"

"Yeah, make music for a living. Have people singing my music back at me. Make art, make a difference through that art."

His brow furrowed, and the look only enhanced his appearance. Kat needed to back away. "You never struck me as the rock type," he said.

She laughed, pulling away from him, her hand gliding along his arm before they broke contact. "Are you kidding? I was such an emo kid. Fall Out Boy, My Chem, AFI, Taking Back Sunday . . . the list goes on forever."

"That's not even close to the type of music you play."

"I won't lie and say I didn't have Something Corporate, Prince, Tori Amos and even Billy Joel on repeat too. I have eclectic tastes. I was even in an emo band with some friends for quite a while. I played the piano and sang backing vocals."

He pulled her closer again, his hands coming to rest on her hips, a confused look on his face. A look that was entirely too cute on him. Her heart flipped. "You are not meant to be playing keys in someone else's emo band."

She laughed, shaking her head at the irony of his statement. "I learned to play the piano at six, then I learned the flute and saxophone. I tried the guitar, but it was an epic failure, so fronting a rock band was a little out of the question."

"Guitar isn't that hard; you just have to stick with it."

"Easy for you to say. You're amazing at it."

"That's what four-hour music lessons a day will do for you."

"Was it all that bad though? You're an amazing musician. You have a talent people would kill for."

He buried his face in her hair, inhaling deeply. "How do you still smell so good? We've been on an island for like—what is this, our fifth day now?"

She pulled away, looking up at him, disentangling her hands from his neck. "Now you're deflecting again." He refused to let his armor down with her, and while it shouldn't annoy her, it did. He couldn't be the sweet man with the sweet words who danced and caressed her, and then turned cold whenever she asked him anything personal.

He ran his hand through his too-long hair, frustration written on his face. "What do you want me to say, Kat? That I didn't have a typical childhood? Of course I didn't. My dad was traveling all over the world. Tutors taught me everything from music theory to reading, writing, and history. But I barely know half the book smart shit everyone else knows, so I hope to never get recruited to *Celebrity Jeopardy!*."

"I wish my parents could have afforded all those music lessons." They'd worked hard just to get her piano lessons.

"You think I'm not aware of that privilege? All I wanted was a normal life. I wanted to go to school, play sports, and have normal friends."

Kat blinked, processing that information. She'd placed West in a box with the rest of the Beverly Hills scene he hung out with, but he continued to surprise her at every turn.

"Is that why you're giving it all up? Do you think acting is going to make you feel better or be different? It won't be a normal life, you know?"

"At least I won't be on the road seven to eight months of the year." He walked away from her into the water, letting the waves wash up onto his feet.

"You're the one who chose to go on these world tours like every other year. Even the band kept saying you needed to slow down, but you never stopped. It was like you were running from something. What was it, West? What have you been running from?"

He turned, glaring at her. "All of it. My dad, the label, the fans! Fuck!" He kicked an incoming wave. His tone softened. "We were talking about you, not me. Why are you so stuck on this topic of me retiring from my music career?"

"Because you love it." She didn't know how to convey to him that she still couldn't believe he would give it all up. She walked up to him, putting her hand on his chest, on his heart. "Right here, I know you do. For years, night after night, I've watched you play that guitar, watched you get lost in the moment. You leave your body, and your soul gets lost in the music. Your fingers move up and down of their own volition, they own the music, and you bend it to your will. I see it in your face. It's your one true love." She took a deep breath. "And it's the most beautiful thing I've ever seen."

His eyes softened, and before she knew it, his arms wrapped around her, his mouth inches away from hers. She had just revealed one of her deepest secrets, and rather than running for the other side of the island, he was holding her, their breaths mingling, with nothing but the sound of the ocean and the breeze in the trees surrounding them.

He bent his head, his mouth grazing the shell of her ear. "I never knew you were watching me."

"There's a lot you don't know," she said, her breath coming in short bursts.

His eyes darkened. "Clearly."

For a moment she froze. His eyes held hers, a promise that he would close that distance if she allowed it. And other than self-preservation, which was crumbling quickly, she had no reason to push him away.

She forgot everything else—the music, the tours, the lonely years of watching West pour his soul into his guitar. All that mattered was the way he held her, the way her body crackled through every nerve ending. His head lowered and she could feel the heat of his warm lips as they gently touched hers, but just as quickly as she had felt him, they were gone. Before she could be upset, recognition set in.

"Oh my god, West that's . . ."

"A motor," he finished.

He released her and they ran down the rocky beach.

She had fallen behind slightly, and West grabbed her hand to help her keep up. Instantly, she thought about what they had just been about to do, and she couldn't help thinking that if they were rescued she would never know how his lips would have felt on hers after all these years.

She was being ridiculous. Weston Monroe was not for her. He didn't do actual relationships, didn't do long-term, and for as much as he said he had wanted normal, she knew he would be bored. He didn't know what normal was. Normal was a novelty to a man like him.

As they rounded the corner, her heart nearly stopped. Two speedboats were racing toward them. The foam of their wakes sparkled in the sunlight, and for a moment it seemed like salvation, but it soon appeared they were going around the island.

"They're not coming this way," he said, his disappointment evident.

He started to yell and jump up and down, waving his arms to get their attention. "Come on, over here."

"Hey! Hey, over here!" she joined in.

For a while, they both waited desperately for the boats to spot them. Just as they were about to give up hope, the boats changed direction and were moving straight toward them.

West swept her up into his arms and spun her around. She could feel his heart pounding against hers as he shouted, "We're saved!"

She mustered up her most excited face. "Yay," she squealed as enthusiastically as she could. Deep within her she realized that as much as she wanted to be rescued this would be the end for them.

"Kat! Come on, we're getting out of here."

"I'll believe it when it happens."

"Skeptical much?"

She shrugged, unwilling to let him see the real reason for her mood. She was just starting to enjoy learning who West truly was, but once they got back to society it would be over. He would go back to being Weston Monroe, now apparently a movie star who dates other movie stars, and she would be unemployed, unmarried, unloved, un-everything. Boring old Kat.

As the boats drew ever closer, the hairs on the back of her neck started to stand on end as a feeling of dread filled her. A warning from an unknown source that something wasn't quite right. Narrowing her eyes, she squinted at the boats; something about the drivers sent a chill down her spine.

"West."

He was still waving his arms with excitement, trying to get their attention.

"West . . ." The men on the boat were grabbing something.

He wasn't listening, still flailing his body.

"West!"

"What?" He stopped, finally turning around to look at her."

"Run!"

"Wha—"

Her grip on his hand was viselike as she yanked him behind her, barely dodging the onslaught of bullets that went whizzing by. She darted into a dense thicket of brush and rocks, zigzagging around them, uncaring of the branches slapping at her face.

With every twist and turn, Kat had to check on West to see if he was still behind her. She staggered through the brush and flinched from the bullets that pelted the surrounding air.

The gunfire ceased for a moment, and she risked a glance behind her through the trees. The sight of the boats pulling up to the shore made her heart lodge in her throat.

"Shit, they're coming ashore!"

"Who is it? How did you know they had guns?" he asked her.

"I just had a feeling, and then I saw them lifting them."

"Fuck, why are they shooting at us?"

"I don't know, but we need to find somewhere to hide. How does your foot feel?"

"It doesn't matter," he said through gritted teeth. "Let's put some distance between us and them."

Bullets flew through the air and Kat felt something graze her arm, causing her to yelp in pain. They both dove to the ground, squeezing their eyes shut as they waited for their lives to end.

"I'm sorry, Kat," he said, gripping her hand to the point she couldn't feel it anymore.

"For what?" she said through gritted teeth, ignoring the pain searing her arm.

"Getting us into this mess. I will never drink on a boat again if we survive this."

"Can we worry about finding a better place to hide first and then discuss your drinking habits?"

The gunfire became quieter, and Kat realized they must have changed directions. As soon as it was quiet, West dragged Kat to her feet, and they were off again.

Questions raced through Kat's mind—who were these men? Why were they shooting at them? Maybe they mistook them for someone else, and they could just talk to them? She had little time to contemplate before West yanked her onto a different path, almost pulling her arm out of its socket.

After some time, she passed West. She could hear his footsteps behind her, heavy and labored. He was still wincing from the pain in his foot. They kept running, her lungs burning in her chest. Her body begged her to stop, and her legs felt like they might quit working at any minute. But she couldn't think about any of that. She had to keep pushing or she would be shot, and then she would never know the feel of West's lips again, or just what exactly was going on between the two of them. They ran until they reached a steep incline, blocking any further progress.

"Oh shit, we have to climb that?" West leaned against the rocky mountainside, looking up. Indonesian islands were anything but flat.

Kat put her hand on her hips, looking up the solid cliffside as she sucked in gulps of air. It was tall, but the incline wasn't super steep, and it had easy footholds; they could make it. "This is our best chance of losing them."

"I haven't heard gunshots in forever, and we've been running for at least an hour," West panted.

"That doesn't mean they're not searching for us."

The sound of raised voices floated to them on a breeze.

"Quick! We have to go up," she said.

"No, wait." He held up his hand, pointing upward. "It's coming from up there."

She stopped and listened. He was right, the voices were coming from somewhere on the mountain.

"We need to find a place to hide."

Kat nodded, and they crept back into the safety of the rainforest.

———◆———

After resting, finding some food, and hiding out in the bush, the sun was setting in the sky as they searched for a more permanent hiding spot. West noticed an opening in the rocks that seemed promising.

"Here." He motioned to Kat.

West stepped inside, flicking on the lighter.

"What if there's a jaguar or something in there?" she asked.

"Well, tell my . . . I guess tell Lina I love her."

She scrunched up her nose in confusion. "Who's Lina? A new girlfriend?"

He laughed at her apparent jealousy. "No, she was our house-keeper, the closest thing I had to a mom."

"Oh, sorry."

He waved her off. "I don't want to talk about it right now."

She didn't reply, although he knew it was killing her to keep her thoughts to herself. She was so eager to get him to be open, but there were some things he wasn't ready to talk about, es-pecially as he was walking into a dark cave on an island hiding from the men shooting at them. He'd rather not go there before death. He reached the back of the cave, which wasn't too deep, and turned around to walk back to her.

"It's empty."

"That's good." She walked in and plopped herself down against the cave wall. Her shoulders slumped and her legs stretched out before her. She looked pale, tired, and defeated. There was nothing he could really do, except . . . "How about I go find some water? I think I saw a stream not too far away."

She nodded, and it surprised West she didn't want to go with him.

"I'll be right back."

"I saw some fallen coconuts back there." She had dark smudges under her eyes, and West was worried at her look of fatigue. They had been running almost the whole day. She was devoid of all color in her face, and something seemed off.

Outside the cave, West searched his pockets for his pocketknife to open the coconuts and realized she must have it. Turning back around for the cave, he stepped back in and stopped dead in his tracks when he laid eyes on her.

"Jesus, Kat, what happened?"

He knelt in front of her, trying to remain calm despite the panic coursing through him. Her arm was coated with a thick layer of drying blood, and he could still see it oozing from the wound. He gently took hold of the fabric she had been trying to tie around her arm, and she flinched in pain as he pushed it down on her injury.

"Did you get shot?" he asked, his voice shaking slightly.

She tilted her head back and closed her eyes, her face absent of all emotion. "It just grazed my arm," she replied.

"You're still bleeding." He couldn't believe how calm she was about this. Her arm was practically gushing blood, and she was trying to bandage it up herself with nothing but what remained of her pants.

"Here." She handed him a torn piece of cloth. "Tie this one above the wound to slow the blood."

"Like a tourniquet?"

She nodded, and her eyes fluttered shut. He worried the blood loss was getting to her. What if she passed out and he couldn't wake her? He needed to keep her up.

"Kat. Kat! Wake up!" He pulled her into his arms. At the sound of his gruff voice, she opened her eyes, trying to focus on him. "What's your full name?" he asked, trying to keep her awake.

"Katrina Nicole Brooks."

The words rolled off her lips like a mantra and he smiled despite himself at the realization that he hadn't heard her full name in a long time, and just how beautiful it was. "Do you remember when we first met?"

She shook her head as it lolled back against the cave wall.

"You bounded into the recording studio with stars in your eyes. I remember thinking *this poor girl is about to get eaten alive by this industry*. And then you walked right up to me, your hand outstretched . . ."

Kat groaned. "Please don't remind me. I was so fucking weird."

West laughed. "I thought you were adorable. With your 'Hi! I'm Katrina, you can call me Kat, like the animal, but it's spelled with a K, just not Katy. Well, I guess you can call me Katy, but I don't like to be called Katy.'"

"Okay," Kat said, cutting him off, "I get the idea. How do you even remember that?"

"It just came to me when you said your entire name. I think I might have forgotten your name was Katrina. I always remembered 'don't call me Katy,' and then enjoyed doing it to annoy you."

She let out a slight laugh. "Ten years together and you forgot my actual name, but you remembered how to annoy me?" Her words were soft and slightly slurred.

"You don't know my actual name."

"What? Weston?"

"No, it's Thomas Weston Monroe, and now you're the only person besides my family who knows that. No surprise that my dad named me after himself."

"Well, I might die of blood loss so you won't have to worry about that secret getting out." She attempted a smile, but her body was sagging. West didn't find it funny; she was going to bleed to death if he didn't do something.

"Have you been running around all this time bleeding to death?"

"It wasn't that painful; I think adrenaline took over."

"You need more than a slip of fabric, even if it just grazed you," he said, quickly assessing their situation. "Are there some herbs or plants for a gunshot?"

"I don't think so. Considering that's how the White men killed all my ancestors," she said with a sardonic smile, trying to push herself to a sitting position.

"Not funny. We need modern medicine. There must be something at the top of that mountain. I heard vehicles and voices up there. I'm going to sneak up tonight and see what I can find."

She grabbed his arm in alarm.

"West, don't go up there alone. Please, you'll get killed and then I'll die anyway. We don't both have to die."

Her eyes pleaded with him, and for an instant, he almost gave in, but he had to do this for her. He had to save her. On top of that, they might have other supplies he could steal, including some way to communicate with the outside world.

"They won't even know I'm there."

"You know you're not actually a spy, right? You haven't even played one yet."

The corner of his mouth tugged up into a mischievous smirk as he gently tucked a strand of hair behind her ear, his fingertips lingering on the column of her neck. "What, you worried about me?"

Her eyes fluttered shut at his touch and her lips parted ever so slightly. After a moment, she opened them again, taking a deep breath before saying quietly, "Maybe a little." Her face softened, and it seemed like she was about to say something else but stopped herself abruptly. After a beat, she finally whispered, "Don't get caught."

If given the option, he would've sold his soul to find out what she was going to tell him.

"I won't," he said with a conviction he didn't buy. He was a man without shoes and a foot that throbbed like a bitch.

After making sure she was stable enough and the tourniquet was doing its job, he went to get her water, and found another overripe papaya. They forced it down as they waited for the early hours of the morning when West could go to try to find the supplies they needed. He settled her head in his lap and stroked her hair, enjoying the feel of her intimately tucked into him. They were two puzzle pieces that fit. She was fading fast, and he couldn't stop himself from thinking about a life without her and how empty that life suddenly felt.

Ten

Their first tour together was almost over. After nine months on the road, Kat was in love with the tour lifestyle. Some nights, Kat and the band would hang around the venue getting drinks with people who had attended the shows.

They had just finished a show in Cleveland and West had arranged for a private party with another band he was friends with at the House of Blues VIP lounge. Kat still had to pinch herself daily just to make sure she wasn't dreaming.

The lounge was full to the brim and the music was blasting. Kat could barely hear the surrounding people, so she spent most of her time feeling the bass flow through her body as she drank her vodka sodas.

One guy from a group she'd never heard of was sitting next to her talking about how awesome their band was because they were touring with so-and-so. Kat had lost track of the conversation as she nodded at his bragging. She didn't feel like pointing out that the venue she'd just sang in was twice this size.

She was on her fourth or fifth drink when Lydia flew by pulling Kat from the couch.

"Sorry, I have to borrow her," Lydia yelled.

Kat stood up, smiling at the guy, and walked onto the dance floor hand in hand with Lydia.

"Just in time, Lyd!" Kat yelled into her ear over the music.

"You looked miserable. Why didn't you just get up?"

"I don't know. I didn't want to be rude."

Lydia made a sound of disgust. "You don't owe any guy your time."

Kat just shook her head and started dancing to the beat. It was easy for Lydia to say things like that.

Song after song played while they danced and laughed. Eventually, a guy Lydia deemed worthy began dancing with her and she danced away from Kat.

She looked around for Cher and didn't see her. In fact, she didn't see anyone she recognized. The rest of the crew must have gone back to their trailers. Kat decided it was time for her to go too, but a hand grabbed her wrist, pulling her back.

Her body ran into a very solid object. She looked up, realizing that the object was . . . *gulp* . . . Weston.

What was he doing out on the dance floor? He rarely came around the crew, he was usually in the super VIP—as Kat called it—with his entourage.

"Where are you going?" He leaned down, his breath fanning her neck.

"Back to the trailers," Kat managed to spit out.

It wasn't that she had a hard time talking to Weston, it was just that he made her nervous, and then she became awkward, spewing out the first thing that popped into her head. Word vomit was what Lydia called it. She wasn't the best at being social but throw in an incredibly attractive rock star and she was the worst. Alcohol helped though.

It was when they talked about music that they had their best conversations. They would go back and forth for hours about compositions or lyric changes. She had been a big part of the album they were currently touring, and she felt a lot of pride in that.

Weston pulled her body closer to his as his hands moved down her sides to the beat. "The night's just getting started. Why would you do that?"

Her jaw dropped. Was he flirting with her? No, that was impossible because Kat wasn't his type. Or did Weston even have a type these days?

Then again, there was no harm in dancing with him. Right?

She placed her hands on his chest and moved them up slowly, testing the feel of him under her skin. He felt entirely too good. "Is there a reason I should stay up?"

Where the hell did that come from? Kat didn't have a flirty bone in her body and here she was flirting with *the* Weston Monroe, while somehow their hips had fused together, moving to the beat of the music. His hand moved from her side and splayed across her lower back, holding her possessively.

"Shit, sweetheart, I can think of a lot of reasons to stay up tonight," he drawled.

Kat was doomed. She shouldn't do this. She would still have to work with this man the next day, and it would be weird because there was no way he would want anything beyond tonight. She would not fool herself into thinking he would ever want more. Kat was already awkward as hell around him, and this would make it worse. She had never excelled at the one-night stand thing.

"You know, you always run around in these tight little black skirts after shows and it drives me wild," he whispered in her ear. His hand roamed down her hips.

Kat couldn't breathe. When had he ever paid attention to her like that? He was always in the back room with much more beautiful people than her. She looked at him, uncertain where this was coming from, but also too tipsy to fully work out if she cared. Weston fucking Monroe just said she—boring, plain Kat—drove him wild. She inadvertently licked her lips and heard him groan.

The song ended and his finger traced up her arm and over her shoulder. "What's it gonna be?"

She nodded, and he stepped back, pulling on her hand. She followed him to a darkened hallway, and he pushed her against the wall, his tall frame caging her in, blocking out all semblance of light.

"I need to hear a yes, Kat."

She bit her lip. This was it. If she said yes, their relationship would never be the same.

She gazed up at him, at the hunger in his eyes, and desire shot through her. Kat couldn't even have imagined this moment in her dreams.

"Yes," she said, more confidently than she felt.

His hand fisted in her hair, pulling her mouth to his, and then Kat forgot to think. What was she supposed to do?

Kiss back, you dummy.

She opened her mouth with a moan as his tongue pushed past her lips. He was warm and strong and made her body light up as the music pumped loudly around them. She felt like the main character in some ridiculous movie where the rock star falls for the fan in the crowd or something.

His hand moved to her jaw, adjusting the angle. And holy hell. He kissed Kat so thoroughly that she had experienced nothing like it before. The hand not igniting every nerve in her scalp slid down her body, and she had never wanted her clothes off so badly.

His tongue played with hers, and Kat pulled back, nipping his lip, eliciting a low groan from him. Emboldened by his praise, she moved her hands up his chest and around his neck, finally digging her nails into his thick hair, reveling in its softness. She thought about his hair way too much and would die happy knowing it was as soft as it looked.

"Fuck, Kat, you taste so good," he murmured in her ear and Kat almost took off her underwear that second.

A noise sounded from behind them, making Kat jump and West groan.

"What, Dec?" he growled out.

"Can I talk to you for a minute?" Kat heard but couldn't see Declan.

West looked like he might commit murder, but his eyes softened when he turned back to her. She felt embarrassed to be seen like this, especially by Declan.

"I'll be right back. Don't go anywhere," West told her.

With one quick kiss, he turned, leaving her in the dark hallway.

He never came back.

Kat awoke with a start realizing she had been dreaming about that night. The night that had changed her and West's relationship. The night he had left her in a dark hallway with nothing but the taste of him on her lips and a broken heart. Not because she loved him or anything, but because he had rejected her for no reason other than she was apparently not good enough for him.

She was feverish, and while a lot of that had to do with the oozing bullet wound in her arm, she couldn't deny that her dream had been way too realistic. She didn't even like West, and yet all she could think about was his lips, and how they would feel if they had truly kissed again on the beach. What the hell was she thinking? Years ago, he'd walked away from her, making it clear that he didn't see her like that. The only thing that had changed was she no longer worked with him. He was not going to care about her. He didn't even know how. He didn't even know what love was.

Oh god, where did that come from?

She should never even put the word love in the same stratosphere as Weston Monroe. They didn't go together. He probably never even remotely thought about the term, but Kat did all those nights when she was alone in bed. Someone who would be with her until the end of her days. Someone who would love and cherish her and put her above everyone else. It was why she had remained single. She wanted it all, not some one-night stand while they were on the road. West didn't do love or commitment. He lasted a year with Gia, but that was a toxic shit show of a relationship.

Kat dropped her head between her knees, groaning. The echo reverberated around the cave and through her. "Why are you so helpless?" She had never considered herself a romantic. She had forgotten what it was like to be cared for by someone other than herself. She had forgotten what it was like to have someone else wonder what she was thinking or feeling. But West was only doing all those things because they were lost on an island. It was like Stockholm syndrome or something adjacent to that.

Before he left to sneak into whatever was on top of the mountain, he had forced her to lay her head in his lap and sleep, stroking her hair. She had never felt so safe in her life, and she had slept easily. It was those little things, like holding her while she slept, that had her falling for him just as easily as the sparks that flew through her body every time she felt his skin on hers. She was dying to touch him again, and he had only been gone for maybe an hour, risking his life for her. The problem was she knew if she let him touch her more intimately, once would never be enough, and in the end, she would be the one left broken.

Her wound had stopped gushing, but she had lost a lot of blood and couldn't sit up straight without falling back down. She tipped over rather ungracefully onto the cave floor. Her body tingled from head to toe and then suddenly went numb as the world plunged into darkness.

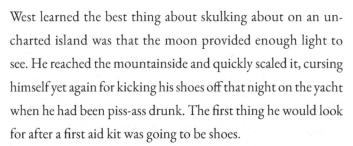

West learned the best thing about skulking about on an uncharted island was that the moon provided enough light to see. He reached the mountainside and quickly scaled it, cursing himself yet again for kicking his shoes off that night on the yacht when he had been piss-ass drunk. The first thing he would look for after a first aid kit was going to be shoes.

His feet were torn up beyond recognition at this point and would probably never look the same again. He could hear his dad in his head telling him to stop worrying about his prissy feet. There was nothing wrong with a man taking care of his feet in West's mind.

Finally, he reached a plateau and, muscles screaming in protest, walked shakily to the other side. Terraces had been cut into the mountainside and it was clear that some sort of crop was being cultivated. That answered one of their questions. The island was definitely inhabited. People were farming on it. He walked up to the plants and looked at them closely. It was dark, but he saw the little red buds that were unmistakably the coca plant that was used to make cocaine.

Christ! No wonder the men had been chasing them. What the fuck had they stumbled into?

There were a series of huts that he assumed were where the workers slept. He didn't want to go near those, but he wanted a pair of shoes. He also noticed a large structure that he hoped would be their main supply area, where it might have items like first aid. Two guards walked by the door and he cursed his bad luck. They were on a deserted island, who did they think would come around trying to take their cocaine?

His eyes scanned the rest of the compound, noticing a few smaller buildings and some Jeeps, which must mean there were roads on the other side of the mountain. The dock had to be on this side of the island too.

Sticking to the shadows, he inched his way to the largest building first. He watched the guard turn the corner, and then West snuck through the primitive wood door. It was a large room that looked like a mess hall with a kitchen at one end. He made straight for it and, grabbing a canvas bag off a hook, he opened the pantry and had to stop himself from completely emptying the shelf. He couldn't carry everything.

As soon as he laid eyes on a jar of peanut butter, he praised the gods above. He took hold of it along with a package of crackers. Noticing a cluster of bananas, he swiftly tossed them into the bag. He opened the fridge and saw a container of water. It was a gallon and going to be heavy to carry down the mountain, but it would be useful, so he took it. He opened a drawer and grabbed a spoon for Kat. She deserved at least one utensil.

The building had nothing else to offer, so he crept to the door and peered out. He looked through the window to see where the guard was. It was all clear, so he flitted over to the next building. It had no windows and was in almost complete darkness. When his eyes adjusted, he realized why. This was where they turned the coca plant into cocaine. Thankfully, the building was empty.

Looking up, he noticed a mezzanine floor with what looked like a manager's office. If there was any kind of first aid kit, it had to be up there. He stalked slowly up the stairs, wincing as they creaked under his weight. He reached the office just as he heard the door open.

"Who's here?" a voice barked into the darkness. "Show yourself."

West ducked into the office, finding a closet to squeeze himself into, barely fitting the bag with him, and closed the door quietly behind him. The sound of footsteps echoed on the stairs, and even though the sound was muffled, each footstep seemed to thud through him almost in time to the thundering of his heart. The light from the man's flashlight gleamed under the crack of the door, and West held his breath, praying the guard wouldn't find him. But then the knob turned, and West pushed himself back as far as he could.

"What are you doing in there, Salinas? You know you're not supposed to be in the office."

The other voice seemed to come from a long way away, but it was enough to distract the guard, and the knob stopped turning.

"I thought I heard something in here." The voice was so close, merely inches from him, and West held his breath, willing the man to leave. His heart beat so loudly that for a moment he was convinced the man would hear it.

"It's probably that damn monkey again," the other man said.

Salinas laughed, and to West's relief, the light moved away. "You're probably right but can't be too careful. I heard they saw two randos on the beach this morning."

The other man grunted. "They'll be taken care of before they make it up here."

West held his breath as he listened for Salinas's footsteps on the stairs and for the main door to close.

He waited, listening for any sounds outside the closet. After a few moments, he released the breath he had been holding and let out a sigh of relief. His mind raced with thoughts of getting back to Kat as soon as possible.

He scanned the shelves in the closet, searching for anything useful. His eyes landed on a large first aid kit, marked with a bright red cross on a white box. He grabbed it and quickly opened it up, revealing bandages, Neosporin, and a needle and surgical thread.

As he stepped out of the closet, he took in his surroundings and spotted an office desk covered in stacks of cash and shipping documents. They were clearly running a drug operation. West carefully sifted through the paperwork, making sure not to disturb anything. He grabbed a handful of incriminating documents and stuffed them into his canvas bag.

The next thing he needed was shoes. He left the manufacturing building and crept to the first bunk room, nothing was sitting out. He moved to the next one. Opening the door a crack, he spotted a backpack and a pair of shoes—they were size eleven and he was a twelve, but he'd take what he could get.

He gingerly picked both items up and slid them outside, slowly closing the screen door. He slipped on the shoes and transferred everything into the backpack, then took off at a run back to the edge of the mountain and to Kat.

Eleven

The sun had risen by the time West made it back to the cave. Kat was fast asleep on the cave floor, and he wished he had grabbed a blanket, a fresh set of clothes, or something else to make her more comfortable.

He knelt next to her, checking to make sure she was still breathing. When he had left, she had been pale from blood loss and breathing slowly. He was extremely worried that if he didn't get her to a hospital she'd get an infection and die out here. He looked at her arm, the blood staining the fabric of her pants. She needed stitches. The bullet wasn't lodged in her body, but it wasn't just a slight graze either. It had taken out a significant chunk of her arm.

He felt her move next to him, and his body thrummed to attention.

"You're back," she said, her voice still groggy from sleep. He smiled, happy to see her conscious.

She sat up, staring at him expectantly. "What did you get?"

"This first." He handed her the jug of water and she gulped it down.

"Ahh, that must be what heaven feels like." Her eyes rolled in the back of her head, and West immediately threw the backpack on his lap in an attempt to hide his ever-growing erection. This woman was driving him crazy. She couldn't make faces like that and expect him not to want to throw her down and screw her on this cave floor here and now. Not that he would.

But Kat was more than that. She made him want to be more than that. She looked at him with those amber eyes, and he wanted to be that guy for her, the one that would be her constant.

He opened the bag, pulling out the jar of peanut butter. "I have something even better." He held the jar in front of her with the spoon and her eyes widened into saucers.

"Wha . . ." She reached out slowly, as if worried the jar would disappear. "Where did you find this?" She took the jar from his hand, and dug the spoon in, eating a bite of the peanut butter. She made a sound of pure ecstasy.

"Here, you know you want some," she teased, offering him the spoonful of peanut butter. He opened his mouth and sucked the spoon clean. His spine tingled as they locked eyes, her cheeks flushed, and West attributed it to her heightened awareness of their situation. The connection between them was tangible enough to make him shudder with need.

He handed the spoon back to her, and she winced in pain as she took it back.

Shit, her arm. She was still bleeding to death, and he was thinking about screwing her on a cave floor.

"I'm such an idiot. Your arm."

The moment hung between them, but her pain doused him like cold water.

West broke the silence by grabbing the backpack. "I found a first aid kit."

"Whose bag is that?" she asked as she unwrapped her arm, inspecting her wound, unwilling to meet his eyes.

"Not sure. There were a bunch of sleeping cabins up on the top of the mountain."

"What's up there?"

"I think it's some kind of drug operation."

Her eyes went wide as she let the information sink in.

"What does that mean, exactly?"

West rubbed his face. He didn't want to worry Kat and debated telling her about what he saw. They had stumbled upon an operation where the people in charge would do anything to protect it, including murder interlopers. They were not going to offer them a way home, but he caved, wanting to be open with her.

"It's some off-grid cocaine operation, from the planting to the manufacturing. The farm has all the coca plants, but there is also a small factory up there as well, so it looks like they do it all on this island."

"Fascinating." Her eyes lit up with excitement.

"Fascinating?"

"Yeah," she said animatedly. "We land on an island, and it has a full cocaine operation on it! It's just fascinating, like a real-life true-crime documentary."

He gave her an incredulous look. "Are you romanticizing our situation? These aren't nice men. They will kill us if they find us; they don't want word of their operation to get out."

She bit her lip, and it instantly drew West to her mouth. He suddenly wished he had finished their kiss earlier.

"Nothing interesting ever happens to me," she said, interrupting his thoughts.

"What do you mean? You are on tour around the world half the year."

She frowned. "I know, and I fully appreciate the life I've lived, but it gets repetitive. Every day is sound check, sit around the tour buses waiting for the show, watch the opening acts, then do the show, maybe have a drink or two, and then go to sleep to do it all again the next day."

"Sure, it's repetitive, but think of all the cities we went out in. The cities we've explored and people we met."

She glared at him. "You mean you and the male members of the band?"

He racked his memory. That couldn't be right. He remembered the girls going to see the Alamo with them in Texas and basking on Waikiki Beach in Hawaii. "No, you did stuff with me."

She shook her head. "Not the past few years. Lately, we've been left to our own devices, and since we were just your boring backing singers, without you, we had to pay for everything. That gets expensive for people who don't have a ton of money. We usually just hung around the buses. So, I should have said 'interesting things don't happen to me lately' if that makes you feel better."

He ran his hand through his hair. He had a lot of making up to do to Kat for the past eight years. He'd wanted to keep their relationship professional, especially after taking advantage of her, but he shouldn't have pushed her so far away. Not that she had made things easy.

But as he saw the stunning woman across from him, he wanted more than a professional or friendly relationship with her, and that should have scared the hell out of him. Yet, it didn't. She still deserved so much more than a degenerate like him, but he was starting not to care.

When he'd left her in that hallway, it had been because Declan had reminded him that bandmate one-night stands were a bad idea. It had been on the tip of West's tongue to tell Declan he was open to more than one night with Kat. It was that feeling, wanting something more with Kat, over anything Declan had said, that had had him running for the hills. He had put up a wall between them faster than she could blink.

He didn't even know where to start. How would he tell her she made him feel things years ago, feelings he wasn't ready for, so he pushed her away like an idiot? But now he just might be ready to face them.

Instead, all he said was, "I'm sorry, Kat, I didn't realize you were so unhappy."

"I wasn't unhappy, it was just repetitive, especially as the partying got old. Some days we watched a lot of true crime or documentaries, and other days we did a little exploring. I loved my life, but now looking back, I'm thirty-two and have no purpose. I add no value to this world, and that's just something I need to figure out." Emotions played across her face, and West became angry at her words, because she did add value. "I'm not an idiot. We could be murdered, and I am aware of that. I just find the whole situation fascinating. That's it."

"You do add value, Kat."

She looked away from him. "I don't really see how."

He wanted to wrap her in his arms and tell her all the ways she added value to him, but he knew she wouldn't listen right now.

"You saved my life, you're kind, you care about others, and you want equality for everyone in an industry that doesn't know the meaning of the word. I'd say you add a lot of value."

She gave a slight smile. "Oh goodie, I've continued to bless the world with Weston Monroe."

"I suppose we can add taking down a drug ring, if you're so inclined," he joked.

"Seriously?" She perked up.

"No."

She slumped back down, staring at her toes. "I think we should go up the mountain. I want to see it myself. Maybe we could find a way off this island."

Was she crazy?

"No, absolutely not. They messed your arm up. You won't even be able to climb."

She picked up the backpack and rummaged around inside, pulling out the first aid kit and setting it next to her. She reached her hand back into the backpack, pulling out a glass bottle of golden liquid, and raised an eyebrow in his direction.

"That must have been in the backpack," he pointed out.

She laughed and read the label. "Ah yes, heaven forbid you leave the rum."

"Damn, it's rum?"

She held the bottle of Captain Morgan up to his face and he took it, removing the cap and taking a drink straight out of the bottle, making a face as it went down.

"Not whiskey, but it will do."

"It has to be like six or seven in the morning."

"Doesn't matter. It's been six days on this island. I think we deserve a drink. Fate left this booze in that backpack."

She laughed again, and West wanted to bottle her laughter and save it for every time he was feeling sad so he could drink it to make himself feel better. He didn't even need the rum; he just needed her laughter and smiles. She dug in the first aid kit, finding what she needed.

"Here." She handed him a needle and medical-grade thread. "Can you sew?"

"Uh . . . no."

"Can you at least thread the needle?"

He took the needle, feeling more helpless than he had ever felt in his life. He hadn't been kidding that his education had been rather lacking. There were many basic things that he didn't know. He could play the shit out of musical instruments, and he had learned a lot from Animal Planet and the cooking channel, but past that, he was helpless.

She noticed his reticence. "Just push the thread through that hole. It will be easy. That thread is sturdier than sewing thread."

It took him a few tries, but eventually he got the thread through the needle. "Now what?"

"Just set it down for a minute." She nodded to the lid of the first aid box. "Now can you grab the alcohol and pour some on the needle, then pour some on my arm, and then make sure I don't pass out."

Was she about to do what he thought she was going to do? "Kat, you're not going to-"

"West," she cut him off. "You can't sew, I can, so yes, I'm about to sew my arm up, but I need to clean the wound first and that's going to hurt like a bitch."

If West hadn't already thought this woman was the strongest, most amazing woman he'd ever met, she was once again about to prove to him she was well out of his league.

"Shit, I'm so sorry. This is all my fault."

"West." She looked straight into his eyes, annoyance written on her face. "No offense, but right now, I need you to shut up and help me. This is going to hurt, and I need you to stop blaming yourself. We can get back to doing that later. 'Kay?"

He nodded, wanting to worship the ground she walked on, his goddess. "Now, pour the alcohol on me." She took a deep breath, steeling herself against the pain she was about to endure, and then nodded for him to continue.

***

The alcohol burned at her skin like acid and an unearthly scream emerged from her throat as it washed away dried blood and filth.

Fighting her tears, she shook uncontrollably until finally, the worst was over. Her arm stung like a thousand fire ants had taken up residence beneath her skin.

When she got a chance to better examine the wound, she could see it was deep and the blood was still oozing out. "I'm going to have to stitch this up, and I'm going to need you to hold my arm down."

He looked ill at ease, and she wasn't sure if it was his disbelief in her abilities, or just stitching in general.

"Have you done this before?"

"What? Stitched up human flesh? That would be a no."

"Well, that's great. Sweetheart, are you sure we can't just put one of those big gauze bandages on it?" He said it in one of his most soothing tones, and while she knew she shouldn't like the endearment, her stupid heart betrayed her, fluttering in her chest.

"It's too deep. It needs to be stitched. I can weave a mean basket or sew a ribbon skirt. What's the difference?"

His eyes went wide, his mouth gaped, and it would have been almost comical if the situation hadn't been so dire. Kat held back a smile. She knew this was nothing like basket weaving or sewing up the hem of her skirt for her tour costume, but she had to do it. West shook his head as he examined the wound. "I'm certain there's a big difference. Not to mention sewing your own flesh."

"That's why I need you to hold me down." This man was not being helpful. What part of she needed to be stitched up or she might bleed to death did he not get? She was on borrowed time as it was. The bleeding had slowed, but it hadn't stopped and that was concerning.

"Christ, Kat, this is a horrible idea." He poured the alcohol on the needle and held it up to her, grumbling in disagreement. He moved to her uninjured side so his arms could wrap around her in a big bear hug.

She trembled as she held the needle. A bead of sweat trickled down her face as she drew closer and closer to the wound. With a burst of courage, she pierced her skin, stifling an agonized scream as she felt each tug. Forcing her eyes open, she bit her bottom lip hard to distract her from the pain.

With steady hands, she continued sewing the gaping wound shut, feeling sick at the numbing sensation that came with pulling the thread through. Each stitch was a reminder that this was what she had chosen to do—there was no going back now. After the final stitch, West applied antiseptic before bandaging it up. Her stitches were sloppy, but they would have to do—a reminder of this experience forever imprinted onto her skin.

She collapsed into West's arms when he was done bandaging her, the exhaustion of stitching herself up racking her whole body.

"That was incredible," he said, stroking her hair. "I can't believe you just stitched yourself up like that."

"Maybe I should go to med school," she joked, her voice sounding distant and not her own.

"That would be a waste of your talent."

Kat felt a tear burn its way down her cheek, the warmth only fueling the questions running through her mind. Did he really think she was talented? Despite what he'd said, his actions over the past decade seemed to suggest otherwise.

"You don't have to lie to me, West."

His hand glided lightly against her back and brushed the sensitive skin of her neck as he said, "I'm not." He roamed over her body, and she relished the easy intimacy between them. "I seem to be a bit of an idiot about what was right behind me for quite some time."

She felt a blush creep up, unsure what to say to that. Confusion clouded her thoughts as she tried to make sense of his unspoken words. Was this an apology for all the times he had pushed her away when she'd tried to collaborate musically after their hallway tryst? Or was there something more romantic at play here?

"We're going up the mountain," she said, deciding to change the subject.

He looked down at her. "You're exhausted. You don't need to risk your life by going up there."

"I want to see what's up there. It's our only way off this island."

"And arguing with you is pointless?"

"I'm glad you've figured that out sooner rather than later." She reached up, spreading her fingers through his beard. She had never thought facial hair was that attractive, but on West it made him more ruggedly attractive, no longer the "pretty boy" rockstar.

His hand covered hers, and he closed his eyes. Kat knew there was something between them, but what happened when they left the island? When this experience was over, and they went back to real life, all of this would go away, and they would be themselves again. West would still be the international superstar who left Kat alone in a dark hallway and would easily do it again.

"Penny for your thoughts?" he asked her.

Her eyes narrowed, her hand dropping. "I'm pretty sure you can give me more than a penny."

"Is that all it takes? What's your price for you to tell me what you were just thinking?"

She couldn't tell him. She didn't want him to know all the insecurities that flowed through her. She knew it sounded whiny and ridiculous, but he did that to her. For now, they were in a fantasy land.

"Getting off this island."

He let out a long whistle. "That's a high price."

"That's when I'll tell you what I was thinking."

He sat silent for a minute, and now she was the one wondering what he was thinking, but she was unwilling to ask. "I guess we better go up the mountain and see if there is a way to get home. Rest a bit and we'll go up in a few hours."

His strong arms enveloped her, and at that moment, Kat knew she never wanted to leave his embrace. It was where she belonged. A dangerous longing filled her, knowing it could never be her reality, but desperate for it nonetheless.

Twelve

Scaling a mountain after giving herself stitches was a horrible mistake. Kat's arm was on fire and begging her to stop. Throughout the climb, she feared that she might have popped her stitches, but by the time they reached the top, she was relieved to see the bandages had held. The cliff wasn't straight up, thankfully; it had a gradient that made climbing easier than it could have been. Granted, the last time she'd rock climbed she'd been in her twenties and securely tethered to the rocks with a harness, so of course she was nervous.

"Please tell me there is an easier way down."

West pursed his lips, and Kat groaned, knowing the answer was not the one she was hoping for.

"At the risk of being an ass, I told you your arm wouldn't be able to handle that climb."

"It's fine." She held up her arm to prove it and almost cried out in pain.

He lifted one infuriating eyebrow, and she hated he could read her so easily.

Although the sun was still high in the sky, their shadows had lengthened slightly, and Kat judged it to be around three or four o'clock in the afternoon. She was getting good at telling time by the sun, her ancestors would be proud of her.

Tucked away behind rocks at the highest point on the hilltop, they peered out onto the expanse of coca plants below. Men were scattered among the fields, their hands busy plucking off leaves, which they tossed into baskets.

"Is the coca plant legal in Indonesia?" she asked.

"I highly doubt it. Even weed is illegal. They're pretty big sticklers about all mind-altering drugs."

"Then why would these people choose Indonesia for their operation?"

West scanned the fields. "You're the one who said there are six thousand uninhabited islands. They found one and started an operation under everyone's noses."

"Smart."

West gawked at her. "Did you just compliment a drug ring?"

"I didn't say they should do it. It's just smart."

"Where do you think all these workers came from?" West asked.

"Wouldn't be the first time White men exploited people of color to make a buck."

West stared at her like she had five heads, and she shrugged. The scene was eerily similar to pictures of slaves working in the fields. The Indonesian men were pulling the leaves, while two White men surveyed their work. She hoped the workers were at least getting paid well, but she doubted it.

"Maybe we can blow the whole operation up."

"Jesus, Kat, you are crazy."

"Isn't cocaine combustible?"

"That's meth." He watched the workers, searching for something.

"What are you looking at?"

He pointed to the second largest wooden structure in the distance and said, "There is an office in there. There must be a phone or some way to communicate with someone. We just have to figure out a way to get in there without getting caught."

Kat looked down at the long stretch of ground that separated them from the office building, scanning the area for any sign of guards or surveillance. Her brows furrowed in frustration as she realized how slim their chance of making it without being noticed was.

"Maybe you could create some kind of distraction, set their field on fire or something, and then I'll run in and search for a satellite phone. They have to have something." He was talking animatedly with his hands, and Kat couldn't help but get wrapped up in his plan. But it was a fool's mission. She knew it.

Grabbing his hands, she brought them into her chest, as they crouched behind a rock.

"That sounds like a first-rate plan CIA man, but remember, you're just thinking about playing one in the movies. We at least need the cover of darkness, and I think we can add to your idea."

He glanced down at their intertwined hands then back at her. "And what is that?"

"First, if you could stop leaving me behind, that would be terrific. I like the setting their field on fire idea, but we both need to do it. Then we need to see if there is a satellite radio somewhere."

He released her hands and tucked an errant strand of hair behind her ear, an intimate gesture that made her want to melt into a puddle on the ground. His hand was now cradling her jaw, and Kat felt her heart leaving her body and heading straight to him. A fact she didn't want to think about at the moment. "Kat, I'm not trying to leave you behind. I just want you to be safe. But you're right, we can come back under the cover of darkness and see what we can find."

He dropped his hand, and they crawled through the tall grass back to the cliff's edge.

"Shit," West whispered under his breath.

"What's wrong?"

"Look." West pointed down the cliffside where two guards now stood. "Get back," he whispered, pulling her back into the long grass before the guards had a chance to glance up and see her.

"Can we take a different way down?"

West shook his head. "With your arm, this is the easiest path I know of. I think we should wait here. Maybe they'll move on."

<hr>

After what felt like hours of waiting, Kat plopped down next to him, her frustration evident. "So now what? I don't know how long it's been, but they haven't gone anywhere."

West reached out, his hand running down one of her braids, a smile on his face. "I can think of a way to pass the time."

"Nice try," she laughed, her face betraying her with a blush. West felt the tension between them, and wasn't sure he could fight it anymore.

"Then what are we supposed to do? Talk?"

Kat glanced over her shoulder, the sun setting behind her. "Yes, West, that's what people do. They talk. Why don't you tell me something real about you, something the rest of the world doesn't know or wasn't made up by the tabloids?

"Fine, but only if you do too."

"I've been an open book."

"So? I want to know everything about you."

He heard her breath hitch, and he wanted to lay her bare then and there, but he'd promised to tell her something, and he truly did want to know everything about her.

He pulled away, giving himself some space or he wouldn't be able to tell his story.

He took a deep breath and looked out at the ocean in front of him. The view from the top of the island was unparalleled, and he would have appreciated it more if their situation hadn't been so dire.

"I didn't retire from music, the label, well . . . they dropped me."

He heard her sharp intake of breath, but she said nothing, allowing him to continue.

"My numbers aren't what they used to be, my style isn't hip anymore, Zoomers don't buy records anymore, and whatever other excuses they wanted to make. They said they wouldn't record any more of my music if I didn't change my sound to what they wanted."

He gave a slight laugh devoid of humor. "Record sales have been down for a while. I suggested going back to my old stripped-down sound. They didn't like that idea, said I'm old, washed-up—whatever term you want to use. The label was done. So, they said to do it their way or walk. I walked."

Her hand found his, and she squeezed. The comforting gesture almost undid him.

"I'm sorry, West, I had no idea. I mean, this tour was a lot smaller, and I guess that should have clued me in, but I didn't think they would ever drop you."

"No one else knows, not even my dad. The label let me have the out."

"Did they think they were being generous?"

He gave a cynical laugh. "No, there was a catch. I can't sign with any other label for at least two years."

She shook her head, her thumb stroking his finger of its own volition, and West realized how much he enjoyed having someone just sitting there holding his hand, stroking him, comforting him. "Why can't you go to a new label if they say your music isn't worth it anymore?"

"Control. I keep control of my public image, and yet they keep control of my career. That's why Declan worked to find me the acting gig. It was something I could try and still make money. So now you see why I'm considering acting. What else am I going to do?"

"What worries you more? The world finding out you're not so perfect after all, or your father finding out?"

West tried not to flinch at the mention of his father; it was a question he had pondered more than he should have. Why did he care so much? His father's band only had four studio albums; West had seven. He'd been on far more world tours than his father ever had, and yet it still drove him mad he had failed.

"You know this business: one day you're in, the next you're out," he said, trying to brush off her question.

She placed her hand on his arm, her fingers long and firm, burning through his skin. "West." His name on her lips gave him pause as he saw the depth of emotion within her eyes. It almost did him in. That emotion was for him. "Tell me the truth. It annoys you that you didn't stay on top forever, doesn't it? That you couldn't beat your father."

He sighed, annoyed she understood him better than he understood himself. "Growing up, he always pushed me to be the best," West started, surprised he was willing to open himself to Kat like this, but he wanted to tell her.

He swallowed audibly. "He said I could be the best out there, that I had a legacy to continue, but then I made my type of music. I didn't want to make the harder rock like him, and he hated it. It was his fault for taking me to a Prince concert at such a young age. He said I would go nowhere, that no one would buy it, that I would be a failure.

"As my popularity grew, he eventually caved, but he still says I'll never have the lasting impact of his band, that they won't make documentaries and movies about me like they do him. But the funny thing is I never wanted any of that. Through all his pushing I found that I just wanted to play my music, and maybe a piece of me still does, but the joy of it is gone."

"Your dad was wrong," she said softly. "They'll make documentaries about you plenty, and who cares if they don't? You blended genres and experimented with sounds. There are people out there now who try to emulate you. So what if the new generation isn't on board?"

"Well, the label seems to care. They asked me to add a synth to my new album. A fucking synthesizer, Kat."

"So, what did you do?"

West gave a humorless laugh. "I'm done changing who I am for those guys. I told them to go fuck themselves."

She sat up and looked straight at him, a smile on her face. "They said you couldn't go to a different label, but they didn't say anything about starting your own."

"What?" He furrowed his brow, confused.

"Your own label!" She was getting excited as she moved to sit on her feet, her breasts bouncing in front of his face, and West decided he should be anointed as a saint for not grabbing her that second.

"My own label. Why would I do that? I don't know anything about production. I write the music, play the instruments."

She stared at him as if he was truly a dimwit. "Okay . . . you learn, hire people who do know what they're doing, learn from them. You'd get to make the music you want because it's your label. You're a millionaire. If I had your kind of money, I would do whatever the hell I wanted."

He scratched at his chin, his week-long beard growth beginning to annoy him as he thought about her idea. It wasn't a bad one. He could go back to making music the way he liked, without all the over-the-top production. Just guitars and drums and his voice—not that he hadn't enjoyed having her and the other girls on his tracks, he just enjoyed his stripped-down sound more.

He could sign acts that were overlooked; musicians like Kat, who probably wouldn't make a ton of money but had talent. "I'll think about it . . . What would you do?" he asked her.

"What would I do?"

"If you had my money," he clarified. "You said you'd do whatever the hell you wanted, so what would you do?"

She pursed her lips, and it immediately drew West's eyes to them. Her eyes sparkled as she thought about her answer. "You know how you always think about what you'd do if you won the lottery?"

"No."

She cocked her head, taking in his confused expression. "Oh right, you wouldn't. You've always been rich. Well, I do, and one of the things I would do is open a series of music schools across the US that are free to students who don't have access to music lessons but want them. They always cut the music programs when money is tight. That's how you got Cher. She lost her first teaching job because they cut the entire music program."

How did he not know that?

He really sucked, not bothering to know much of anything about the women who'd sung for him throughout the years.

"I would focus on a lot of folk and Indigenous music," she continued. "Especially in a lot of Native, Hispanic, and Latin communities. I would want teachers who teach cultural music so that the kids are exposed to their ancestral music. I always wished for more exposure to my culture in school, or for a place to learn more about our music. I chose to play the flute because of a book I had called *The Love Flute*. It was full of beautiful Native imagery and was the first time I saw myself reflected in a children's book. Turns out a White English dude wrote that book and it is full of stereotypes."

West watched the play of emotions across her face: the excitement she felt wanting to help those like her, and the disappointment she felt at not getting to experience her culture as a child.

Leave it to Kat to have millions of dollars and her first thought is to start a music program for others. She was so selfless and caring, and West did not deserve her. And yet he wasn't sure if he'd be able to give her up when they got off this island.

"But you give money to that charity that donates instruments to kids," she added, as if reading his thoughts and trying to make him feel better.

His head snapped up, his gaze searing into her. "How do you even know that?"

"I told you, Cher worked in a school; her students got some of those instruments."

It wasn't because he was embarrassed, but rather because he didn't want or need praise for it, that he tended to keep a lot of his charities quiet.

"That's a lofty goal," he said, changing the subject away from him.

"I know, it would probably be a lot, but I imagine I could do quite a bit with millions of dollars."

"You would think, but it's not that easy. I'm responsible for the livelihoods of a decent amount of people—it's partly why I'm even considering acting. Starting my own label and getting out there with my music sounds fantastic, but I have so many people who depend on me, and money has to come in somehow. I thought I'd made good investments, but my accountant says I need to keep bringing money in or I won't be able to continue living my lifestyle, so they clearly weren't as solid as I thought."

Kat blinked up at him. "You're going broke?"

He made an affronted sound. "Why does everybody immediately jump to broke? I just don't have as much money as I thought. Something's wrong with my accounts, or rather who's been running my accounts. I want to make sure I can still employ the people who depend on me. That's why I'm more inclined to take the sure thing, rather than open a label that may not generate much income, or even worse, be a complete money suck."

"I'm sorry, West, I had no idea." She pulled his hand into her lap, both of her hands resting in his. "I don't mean to minimize what you're going through. Do you think someone might be stealing your money?"

He looked down at her hands cradling his, and suddenly that was all he could think of. He didn't care about the money or what he was going to do next. "I don't know if someone is skimming off the top, or if it's just being mismanaged, but I know I'm not that big of a spender. I just need to inspect my books better—if we ever get off this island. As much as I find your idea appealing, I need the sure thing right now."

She scrunched up her nose, not particularly liking his answer.

If anything good came out of this experience, his record sales had most likely picked up because of his disappearance, hopefully bringing in more money. Declan was most likely having a field day.

"Now your turn." He needed to change the subject.

She blinked. "For what?"

"Something real. Your turn to tell me something."

"I did. You asked what I'd do with millions, and I told you."

He shook his head. "No, that was just an extension of mine. I want to know something else, something different. A true secret. I bet plenty of people know you'd do that if you had the money."

She huffed and moved her legs out from under her, releasing his hand. "Fine. I shouldn't even tell you this, since you already have a super-inflated sense of self, but I might as well."

He flashed her a smile. "Now I'm even more intrigued."

Kat couldn't believe she was about to tell him this, but somehow their stories had intertwined long ago. Something like fate had led her here, lost on an island, with a bullet wound in her arm, her body aching to be touched by this man like some nineteen-year-old, rather than a woman just over thirty.

She took a deep breath and looked at him. His eyes were dancing with laughter as the last rays of the sun filtered through his hair.

"When I was a sophomore at UCLA, I went to a show at The Troubadour, there was this new up-and-coming jazzy, folky, sexy, smooth-voiced artist playing that night whose fingers played the guitar as if his life depended on it. He sang of love and sex, and women, and boy was my little nineteen-year-old self sexually awakened by the middle of that show. Stupid college boys didn't hold a candle to the sensuality of the man on that stage."

West's head whipped up, staring at her, his tongue wetting his lips, and Kat couldn't help but notice his perfect mouth, hating that she wanted it on her.

"And . . . who was it?" He knew he had to know what she was about to say.

"Hmmm." She held her finger up to her mouth as if thinking hard, and West leaned closer. She could see she was driving him crazy, and she loved it. For once she held the power over him, and she couldn't believe it.

He did that; he empowered her, and he helped her see the power in herself. And all it took was being stranded on an island and hiding from murdering drug lords.

"I think it was Fleet Foxes. You know Robin Pecknold was really sexy back then. Still is."

"Kat!" He pulled her into his lap, and she went willingly, giggling like a teenager.

"Of course it was you! Weston Monroe, on his first headlining tour." Her hands threaded and wrapped around his neck, and it wasn't lost on her how intimate the position was.

"Mmmm, and how did this Weston Monroe sexually awaken you? Were you wet for him?" he asked, his voice suddenly deeper, more gravelly. That delicious sound rumbled through her body, sexually awakening her right at that very moment.

"West!"

His hand moved up her body, and she shivered at the sensation. "You started this, tell me. What happened when you saw my show? I remember that tour. It was my first major album before adding all the production value."

"Like me." She turned away, realizing how much he must have hated having her around.

He turned her head, making her look at him. "Kat, listen, I wrote those songs. I knew I wouldn't be able to do them all on my own. I know things went sideways with us, but I don't regret it for a minute. Besides, I can't play the piano for shit. You always did so much better on tour than me. Remember that. Now, what happened at that show?"

She could cry at his tenderness. He had never once expressed an opinion one way or the other on her talent, or on vocals on his tracks. After their kiss in the hallway their dynamic changed, and Kat was convinced he hated having her there. He was lying about the piano. He was amazing, but the fact that he would say that to her meant more to her than he realized.

"After moving to L.A. I had seen plenty of concerts, but there was something about that venue, and about you on that stage, that made it this ethereal experience for me. It was almost as if I was no longer existing in reality—it was just you and me. Every note seemed directed at me, and I felt a connection so strong it took my breath away. I was just a couple of people back from the front, and I could swear our eyes met; your face lit up as if to say, 'You are the only one here.' You winked at me before turning away and I thought, 'He's singing this song for me.' Now I know you can't really see the crowd that well, but at that moment, I truly believed something special had happened. I was a stupid girl, like all the other stupid girls in the crowd who think you're singing directly to them. Who think they're somehow special out of the thousands of faces you see."

West laughed, as he ran his hand down her side. "I bet I did wink at you, how could I miss such a beautiful face in the crowd?"

"West, I've literally been by your side for ten years, and you've barely noticed me." She felt her face heat up as a blush grew across her face. "Besides that one night," she whispered.

His eyes darkened. "A night I'd like to revisit."

He what?

"Were you hanging out backstage after the show? I always came out back then to greet fans," he continued.

Now it was her turn to laugh. "No, don't flatter yourself. But when the label said who I would be singing for I was so excited. I jumped at the chance to work with you. I wanted to learn so much from you."

West made a sound of derision. "I wasn't a very good mentor, was I?"

Kat looked away, unsure if she was ready to go down this path. "You were until . . ."

"Until that night."

She nodded. "The House of Blues. You never came back. I wasn't good enough for you, and it really hurt that the man I had looked up to for so long didn't want me. I was mad at you, but really, I was mad at myself. I should have known better. You weren't for me."

His hands grabbed her, his face inches from hers. "Listen to me, Kat. I wanted you so badly that night. Dec got on my case about sleeping with band members. He said it was a bad idea, especially later if you said I took advantage of you. He made sense to me that night. I went back to the trailer."

"Alone?"

West nodded.

A hiccup mixed with a gasp escaped Kat's mouth as she contemplated West's words. All this time, she thought he had just decided she wasn't worth his time. She had been wrong.

"Why didn't you just come back and tell me that?"

"Young, dumb, and drunk, I guess. I wasn't ready to have that conversation with you. You were different. We talked about my music. You were the only one who would push me when you thought it sounded bad, or notes didn't fit together, or lyrics were off. You weren't scared to tell me how you felt. But I fucked it up. I let my dick do the thinking, and I pressured you that night."

Kat shook her head. "No, you didn't. I knew what—"

"That's just it," he said, cutting her off. "You didn't know. You were what? Twenty-two? I saw the stars in your eyes, they're what drew me in. I hadn't disillusioned you yet. You just loved the music, and it was so attractive to me, but I should have

known better. I knew it would change our working relationship, and it did."

"Because you left!" Kat pointed out. Why was he being so
dense? It had nothing to do with him making out with her
in a dark hallway. She had enjoyed that part. "You left me in
that hallway on my own, and for the longest time, I thought
there was something wrong with me." She felt moisture build
up behind her eyes as she recalled the humiliation of that night
as she stood there waiting for a man who never returned. Her
heart had broken, and it had never really healed.

His warm hand brushed across her face, pushing away one of
the tears. "I'm so sorry, sweetheart. I thought I was doing the
right thing. That if I came back, I wouldn't be able to say no."

"You could have told me the next day." Kat sniffed, wiping
away another errant tear.

"I tried, remember?"

Kat racked her brain for any conversation between her and
West the next day, but nothing came to mind.

West smiled at her blank look. "You probably don't. I walked
up to you and asked to talk. You looked at me with those big
golden eyes like I'd just shot your dog or something. Then you
walked away, and I knew then you were mad at me for kissing
you."

Kat had to keep her mouth from hitting the ground. "I was
mad at you for abandoning me. Not even mad, just hurt."

"If you had talked to me, you would have found out it had
nothing to do with you."

Kat tried not to roll her eyes. "I was upset, West; you don't just give up after one try."

He shrugged. "I know, but I think in the end it was better we kept our distance."

"Why?"

He shook his head, staring off at the ocean for a minute before finally answering her. "I kind of agree with Dec. Band relationships or hookups don't end well. We may have had a strained relationship, but at least we still functioned. I've seen too many horror stories of bands falling apart because of sex."

It rendered Kat speechless. She was still stunned by his admission. It was hard to change what she had thought was her reality for so long. She crept her hand up his arm, feeling the coiled strength of his bicep under her fingertips.

"What about now?" she whispered as she repositioned herself on his lap, straddling his hips, both her hands moving up and down his sinewy arms. She felt emboldened, knowing he hadn't left her all those years ago. Not that she was his type today.

"Now?" He looked at her, his eyes glazing over. "I'd really like to pick up where we left off."

Kat sucked in a breath at his words. Was he attracted to her, or did being trapped on an island together still have something to do with it? She didn't care anymore. Kat was done fighting it.

"I'd like that too," she whispered into his ear, nipping his earlobe.

"Jesus, Kat." He grabbed her hips, his fingers digging in hard, and she could feel his self-control on the edge of detonating.

She licked a path up his neck, biting down hard, and loved the sound he made. Some part of her brain was telling her she could be reckless, let it all go, make him beg. She wasn't even thinking about the drug lords mere feet away. She was bringing *the* Weston Monroe to his knees, and she felt the intensity surging through her veins.

"No interruptions this time," she said as she ground her hips down on his arousal.

She felt West's self-control shatter as he tugged her face to his, their tongues tangling as their teeth clashed. It was an urgent, passionate kiss meant to possess her, and it did. She was his. Her hair fell out of its braids around her face, and West brushed it out of her eyes, drinking in the sight of her with a hungry gaze.

"Dear god, Kat," he whispered against her lips. "We're stranded on this island, surrounded by a drug cartel that wants to kill us, and somehow I've never felt luckier."

And then his lips were back on hers, and she felt her entire body ignite. He engulfed her in his warmth, his powerful hands roaming all over her body, and yet it still wasn't enough. She wanted him closer. They had too many clothes on, never mind that they were feet away from getting caught; she wanted to feel all of him. He broke the kiss and moved down her body, and Kat felt like he was worshipping every inch of her.

Typically, she was self-conscious. Her physique was curvy, with generous hips and a full chest, not petite by any of today's standards. She should have been embarrassed to be anywhere near West's fit, athletic frame, and yet he made her feel beautiful and admired.

Who was this man and where had he come from? This wasn't the Weston Monroe the world knew. Dragging his teeth down her collarbone, she sighed with contentment as his hands slid under her clothing with one hand coming around to cup her breast.

Leaving a trail of fire, he planted burning kisses all over her body, as he layed her down. His touch tantalized and teased her, building up the pleasure until she became an excited, trembling mess beneath him. His fingers moved over her with agonizing slowness, stopping just short of her panty line as he breathed across her skin. When he lifted his head away from her breast, she almost screamed in frustration at the loss of his seductive touch.

"Can I touch you, Kat?"

She nodded.

"I need to hear a yes, Kat. I don't want to do anything you don't want."

"Yes," she sighed. "Touch me."

His fingers teased their way down to the apex of her thighs, dancing over her panties before slipping underneath them. She felt one finger enter her, and her head fell back at the sensation.

West's voice dropped an octave, dark and rough. "You're so wet for me." He inserted a second finger and crooked his finger up. "Fuck, sweetheart, you're so tight."

Her breath hitched as he grazed her sensitive inner walls.

His thumb pushed ever so slightly against her clit, and sensations shot through her body like lightning. Her hips writhed beneath him.

"There?" His deep voice coursed through her veins like electricity, sending shocks of desire throughout her body.

He pushed again, harder and faster this time, and circled his thumb on her clit while moving his fingers in and out of her with masterful precision.

Kat felt like she was being sent into oblivion and might never come back. She had never experienced sensations like this before and wanted more.

West abruptly removed his hands from her. She let out an anguished cry of protest as the sensations disappeared.

In a flash, he ripped away her panties and hoisted her legs over his shoulders, his eyes wild with the promise of pleasure.

"West . . ." she stammered, her eyes wide in disbelief. "What are you . . .?"

He cocked his head, locking his gaze with hers. "Kat," he purred, as if savoring her name on his lips. "I'm about to taste pure heaven—but I can stop if you want me to. Just say the word."

Raising herself onto her elbows, she could see him now, his dark golden hair dipping between her trembling thighs and his face aglow with anticipation. Heaven indeed. "No," she answered, arching her back in silent invitation. "Carry on."

"You're entirely too calm. I think I'm losing my touch if you can think straight." He tickled her side, making her laugh. She reveled in the dark intensity between them, transitioning from sexual to playful and back again within seconds.

His finger probed deeper this time, making her moan with desire.

"You are also far too quiet. We're on an isolated island. I should hear your voice echoing off its shores."

"That's not true," she groaned with desire as his tongue explored her seam, licking its way from the bottom to the top, now dipping inside of her. "Did you forget about the murdering drug lords just a few feet away?"

Her words were barely audible as her body quivered in anticipation. It was hard to concentrate when an incredibly attractive man was busy manipulating her most sensitive parts.

He circled her throbbing clit and she drove her fingernails into his scalp, urging him on, never wanting him to stop. His groans reverberated through her body, sending wave after wave of pleasure coursing through her.

"I don't care about them, lose yourself," he said, as he added a finger, and she purred in appreciation.

"Like that," he said, satisfied.

His fingers worked in unison with his mouth to tease out every moan, every feeling. She felt her fear dissipate, replaced by raw emotion as her nerves unraveled beneath him, and Kat could feel it building inside her, all the pain, and frustration, all the times she had held back, all the times she hadn't gone for what she wanted and had played it safe, all the rejections, she let it all go.

"You taste so good," he murmured from between her legs. "Now let go."

The sensations built up in intensity with each movement of his hands and mouth until she felt the walls of her mind shatter, sending shards of ecstasy throughout her body. She screamed out his name into the twilight as wave after wave of pleasure washed over her, pushing her further and further until all she could feel was pure bliss.

The sky lit up, and a crack of thunder shook the ground. West had just given her an orgasm so strong she felt the ground shake.

West's hands moved up and down Kat's legs as he licked and kissed her in a place no man had been in years. He moved up her body, worshipping each breast with delicate kisses before his mouth crept up to her neck, leaving a trail of barely there kisses that had Kat entranced. His tongue tasted of the pleasure they had just shared, and she reveled in the sweet sensation.

He adjusted her clothes, putting her back together. Looking down at his shorts, she gestured toward him. "You don't want me to take care of that?"

He kissed the top of her head. "Trust me, sweetheart, I want nothing more, but we need to get back to the cave. It's getting dark, and it's raining. I'm going to check for the guards."

So, she hadn't imagined the lightning. She felt the drops of rain on her scorched skin as it fell.

Thirteen

At first, it was one raindrop, and then another, just as rain tends to do, and then it was as if someone who was holding a bucket of water had decided to dump it over Kat and West's heads.

"Watch your step," West yelled over sound of the rain as they slowly made their way down the side of the mountain, each step slicker than the one before.

Kat couldn't see as rain pelted her, hair whipping around her face. "Stupid guards, we could have been down here before this tsunami."

"I'm not going to complain."

She attempted to give West a sardonic look but was too scared of falling off the side of the cliff, so she went back to staring at her feet.

West descended and she sighed in relief. Now she only had to focus on her footing, but as she went to step, her foot gave way and she groped for support. Plunging downward, she braced for impact, but in a flash, she was caught by sturdy, embracing arms. "You should pay attention to where you're going," he said, smiling down at her.

"I was. It's just soaked," she said, pushing off him to stand up.

"It's not the only thing." He grinned.

She felt her face heat up, which seemed impossible considering how much cold water was pouring down on her. But thoughts of what he had just done to her body raced through her mind.

"Are you going to speak in sexual innuendos for the rest of the evening?" she asked, trying to ignore the heat growing in her core.

He leaned down, his arms still around her. "I don't plan on using any innuendos, I plan on finishing what we started if we can just get out of this rain."

Her body felt his words as they wrapped themselves around her, a promise for more, and as much as she would regret it later, she couldn't deny herself today.

The rain pelted down on them, and then Kat heard it, the sound she had been dreading. The sloshing of incoming boots and shouts couldn't be drowned out, even in the rain.

"Hey! Stop!" the voice rang out.

"It's them!" another voice called out.

"Fuck," West said at her side.

"Run." Kat took off at a sprint, West's large hand wrapped around her wrist to keep them together.

They dodged raindrops, trees, and brush as they heard the guards running after them, their voices yelling at each other to split up and cut them off.

"They're not shooting at us," Kat noticed.

"They must not have their guns with them."

"What were they still doing down here then?" Kat wondered aloud.

West pulled on her as she slowed down. "It doesn't matter right now. We need to get to safety first."

"We need to split up."

That made West stop dead in his tracks. "No."

"Look, they can get one of us or both of us. At least if it's just one, the other can do some kind of rescue attempt. Let me distract them while you get away, then you can save me."

The muscle in his jaw jumped. "No, Kat, that is the dumbest idea I've ever heard."

They heard voices, and he grabbed her wrist as they took off running again, but Kat pulled free. "Go! I'm going to run this way and get their attention. You go hide. I'll be fine. This is the best way, or we're going to be running all night. Go, West, I'll be fine. And who knows, maybe I'll get away and meet you at the cave."

She jumped into his arms, kissing him with more confidence than she felt, but she knew if she didn't do this, they were both guaranteed to be caught and then where would they be? This way, they at least had a shot.

Before West could protest further, she twisted from his grip and ran toward the guards.

"Here we go," she whispered to herself, then more loudly said, "Yo, assholes! You looking for me?"

Two twin flashlight beams turned on her and she took off running. West would probably be mad for a while; she'd deal with it if she actually survived this.

Each breath was a struggle, she could feel the oxygen rushing through her veins as she pushed herself forward. Her arm throbbed with pain, but she couldn't stop now. She crouched behind a cluster of rocks, her heart pounding in her chest. In the distance, she could see the beams of flashlights sweeping back and forth. They were getting closer.

Sitting very still, Kat held her breath, hoping that if she just sat there in the dark, silent and still, they would walk right by her. The lights moved past her, and she sagged slightly, relief filling her system. She might find her way back to West and the cave after all. She sat without moving, waiting for the light and voices to completely disappear, and then she waited even longer.

After a time, she felt the coast was clear and came up and around the rock, trying to get her bearings. The rain had finally stopped, and the moon was out, lighting the rainforest floor. Kat wasn't entirely sure where the cave would be from where she'd been hiding, but she had a vague idea of which way to head.

She walked in the general direction of the cave, hoping she would see West soon, but just as she was beginning to feel she was going to be okay, a powerful hand grabbed her, hauling her into their body.

"Gotcha," a male voice sneered.

She screamed, "Let me go!"

"No one's gonna hear you," the man said. "I thought you were still around here."

Kat cursed herself for being so stupid. He had probably just turned his light off and waited for her to reveal herself. She had played right into his hand.

Stupid. Stupid. Stupid.

"The boss is going to be happy to have at least one of you," the man continued as he hauled her toward his Jeep parked a few feet away.

"Although, he'd rather have both of you. Can't have anyone knowing about what goes on here," the man said.

"You mean your little drug operation?"

The man laughed. "This ain't no little operation, darling. Brings in millions of dollars a month. They can't have you and your boyfriend messing it up."

"He's not my boyfriend," she grumbled, more to herself. Her arm screamed in pain as he tied her hands and feet, before throwing her into the back of the Jeep.

"Well, I got one of ya. Maybe the boss'll give me an extra day off."

"To do what? Sit on this island some more?" Kat spat at him. But truly, what did a drug lord do on a day off on drug island?

"No, but there's something to be said about a day to read and drink a good rum."

Kat laughed. "Yeah. Bet you and Hemingway are great friends."

The man smiled as he jumped in the front seat. "Nah, I'm really into Kafka right now, but maybe I'll try him next."

Kat rolled her eyes as the Jeep took off to drive her back up the mountain. She sure hoped West was back at the cave.

West was furious at Kat. The cave was empty, and she was nowhere in sight. She wasn't supposed to be the one to sacrifice herself for him. He dug into the backpack, taking a quick drink of what was left of the rum. The familiar burn warmed his body, which was chilled from the rain. He pushed his wet hair out of his face as he sank to the cave floor, contemplating his next move.

He was going to kill her. That was his next move. First, he was going to save her, and then he was going to kill her. What crazy nonsense made her think she needed to sacrifice herself to save him? He felt an odd pang go through his body as he contemplated what the men might be doing to her right now. They wouldn't have killed her already, he hoped. But there was no guarantee of that.

Kat had sacrificed herself for him to get away and West couldn't grapple with what that meant—for him, for them.

Did she care about him? Because he was wishing the idea had come to him first; he would have sacrificed himself for her in a heartbeat.

On this island, she had come into her own, and yet she was still very much the same Kat, and West was kicking himself for never really noticing just how great she had always been. But now she was showing her confidence, showing her strength, and showing who she really was, and West wanted more.

He wanted to strip her bare in literally every sense of the word. To find out everything that made her tick. To know what would make her truly happy. His mind roamed to thoughts of her coming apart on his mouth, the throaty sounds of her moans as he'd made her come. He'd wanted nothing more than to push himself inside her, but the rain had ruined that, and now who knew if he would ever have the chance to truly feel that connection with her? One he no doubt knew would be unforgettable.

West took another drink, shaking the memories of earlier out of his head. He needed a plan. It wasn't too late. She was alive, and he was going to go save her or die trying.

Fourteen

The room smelled of wet wood, and humidity permeated the air. She could feel the oppressiveness of it as she tried to take a breath. Kat opened her eyes, but all she saw was darkness, as she was blindfolded. Her mind searched for where she was, panic flooding her senses. She remembered being grabbed by the man in the woods and had fallen asleep after being tied to the chair. Kat wasn't one to fall apart in a crisis, but she also had never found herself gagged and bound to a chair on an Indonesian island either. She felt her heart beating in her chest at a frantic rate as the panic grew.

She was going to die; they were going to kill her; she knew too much about their operation, and no one would know, and really, who would care? Her mom would be sad, and probably her younger brother Cam would miss her. Caleb her eldest brother might be a touch sad, even if he didn't know how to show a single emotion. Lydia and Cher would be sad, but they were all about to go their separate ways anyway, or at least it appeared they were. They hadn't talked about what their futures held.

Would West even care? They weren't anything to each other. Sure, he had just given her the best orgasm of her life, but that didn't make them anything. He hadn't professed any feelings for her, and even if he had, she wasn't sure she could believe him. West wasn't capable of long-term commitment.

She groaned, and it echoed in the vastness of the dark room. Her head ached; her body hurt. She should be worried about getting out of this situation, and yet all she could think about was him. She wanted him to run away, to get the keys to a boat and flee the island as they had planned. To leave her and not try to save her. But deep down, she knew better. He wouldn't leave her here, and he would get caught. They were both screwed.

Moving her wrists, she could feel the rope digging into them, making it impossible to get free, her arm protesting at the sharp angle. She discovered they'd tied her feet just as tightly when she tried to pull them away from the chair.

"Stop your struggling." A voice rang out into the silence, making her jump.

She saw light from beneath her blindfold. Contrary to what she'd thought, it wasn't night. She was in quite a predicament. Heavy, booted footsteps stalked closer to her, and she tried to push herself farther back into the chair. A hand touched her head, ripping the blindfold off. Light flooded her eyes and she squinted. A man she hadn't seen before stood in front of her.

He leaned down so his face was right in front of her. He smelled of weed and something else. She guessed it was cocaine, although she was unsure of what that smelled like when someone smoked it.

"So, you're the pain in my ass my guys found on the beach?" He smiled, and she saw he was missing a couple of teeth. Her head drooped, and she wondered if they had drugged her, causing her to sleep through the night. He pulled her head up by her hair, and it took everything in her not to wince in pain. She wouldn't let him see he was hurting her.

"You better hope your little lover boy shows up soon, or we're going to sprinkle breadcrumbs to help him find his way." He looked around at her tied-up hands. "You don't need all your fingers, do you?"

Pure terror enveloped her as she instinctively tried to pull her hands loose. The man laughed, let go of her, and backed away.

"You're dying either way, darling. Boss's orders. I can make it quick or slow, that's up to your man." He eyed her up and down, a lascivious look in his eyes. "Although it's such a shame to let you go to waste."

That hadn't been the news Kat was hoping for and she tried to scream, the gag blocking the sound. She knew it was a waste of time, and no one would hear anyway. They had locked her in what appeared to be a storage warehouse for their finished product before they shipped it out. Even if someone did happen to hear her, no one would save her. But that didn't mean it didn't make her feel better. She screamed again for West, but of course he didn't come.

The man chuckled, the sound unsettling her. It was nothing like West's laugh, which wrapped her in warmth. This one made her feel like she had a rock in the pit of her stomach.

"You keep screaming, girlie, you'll just wear yourself out. Might help your guy find you quicker though." As if he had just had a brilliant idea, the man stepped up to her and took the gag off. Kat sucked in huge gulps of air, on the verge of screaming for West again before realizing that was exactly what he wanted her to do.

"You want him to find me?" Her voice was raspy and not her own.

"Well, of course, we got to kill you both. The boss knows he snuck up here a few nights ago, and now you've seen the operation, so you both gotta go."

She cocked her head to the side, realizing this man liked to talk. Maybe she could get him to confess. Isn't that what all villains did? Well, maybe in novels and soap operas, but maybe she could get something useful out of him if she played to his ego.

"I thought you were the boss," she practically purred, batting her eyelashes.

He puffed up his chest, and she bit back a smirk. "On the island, I'm the boss, and you best remember that. But it's a global operation. There's a group of bosses. My boss answers to those guys, so it's got a big hierarchy."

"How fascinating." She pretended to practically swoon. She looked around the large warehouse. "This is quite the operation. It must be a lot of work. To keep it all going, you must be rather skilled." She gave her most radiant smile.

He walked closer to her, and for a moment, she had to suppress the urge to shrink away from his touch. She wanted him to untie her, and if flirting got the job done, she could push aside the massive icky feeling it gave her. His hand came out, and he grabbed a strand of her hair, wrapping it around his finger.

She had decently long hair—it was one piece of her culture she had tried to keep. After going through a phase of cutting and chemically altering her hair, she now wore it more naturally. It was much healthier and smoother, and her natural waves gave her the perfect beachy look every day.

But now that this rough-looking man had his grimy hands on it, she was rethinking the no-cutting. She felt gross and defiled as he wrapped the silky strands around his finger. West had done something similar, but she had allowed him to, had wanted him to. How starkly different the two situations had been.

"You have no idea how much work it is, darling. A man could definitely use a reward for his hard work."

She tried not to throw up in her mouth as she thought about what reward he was alluding to.

"Lock . . . Mr. Lock, are you in there?" she heard another voice call from around the corner. Thankfully, he dropped her hair, turning around to greet the newcomer who appeared at his side.

"What do you want, Williams?" he said gruffly, annoyed they had been interrupted. Kat made a mental note to thank Williams at her earliest convenience.

Williams was no more than nineteen, maybe twenty, years old and nearly shook in his boots. He was about five-foot-ten, but reed thin. He was American, like Lock, with greasy blond hair and obsidian eyes. Kat was curious how this boy had ended up on a remote island in Indonesia, but that would be a question for later.

The boy stood there wringing his hands, his eyes averted. "There's . . . there's . . . a . . . a . . ."

Lock crossed his arms over his chest. "Out with it, kid." His patience was clearly being tested.

"There's a fire in field four."

"What? Why didn't you say that right away?" Lock ran to the desk and grabbed a gun, handing it to the boy. "Don't let her outta your sight. I know this is the work of her man. If you see him, shoot first, ask questions later."

The gun looked comically immense in the boy's skinny hands. He weighed it in his palms, and Kat sincerely hoped he didn't scare easily. One little sound and she had a feeling he'd be shooting that thing off.

Her heart leaped into her throat as she realized West was coming. That had been their plan—start a fire in the field—and he had done it. Why he had done it in broad daylight while everyone was awake, she had no idea, but he was coming to get her, and she felt entirely too giddy for a girl tied to a chair. She was also worried about him. This Williams kid was standing there with a gun he did not know how to use, and in her mind, that was more dangerous than someone who did. West wasn't going to just walk through the front door, and if he spooked Williams, he was going to get himself shot quicker than he would if he had faced off against Lock.

She was formulating a plan to distract Williams when a blur of something raced across her peripheral vision.

It was West.

He was crouching behind some of the boxes that had been packaged to be shipped. His blue gaze struck her where she was, and relief and dread inundated her whole being. He was in danger if the boy caught him. Williams would shoot on sight, she was sure of it. She subtly shook her head, trying to get his attention, as she motioned toward Williams, in hopes he would see the gun in the kid's hand.

West peered around a crate, and Kat saw he had the pocketknife in his hand.

Who brought a knife to a gunfight?

He wasn't going to be able to do much with that. She had to distract the kid, but he wasn't looking at her, and seemed not to have the same interest in her as Lock. A cougar, she apparently was not.

"Hey, Williams," she said in her most sultry voice to get him to turn around. If West could sneak up on him, he could get the gun from him. He could easily overpower this scrawny boy, of that Kat had no doubt, but he was skittish, and that made

her cautious. Williams didn't turn around, and barely acknowledged her. "Shut it," he yelled over his shoulder. He wasn't the
most intimidating, but he tried.

"How old are you?" she asked. "You can't be more than,
what, twenty?" She saw his jaw jump as he turned around, gun
raised at her head.

"Old enough to shoot you. Didn't I say shut it?"

West moved, inching closer to Williams.

Okay, that struck a nerve. She leaned on his anger to give West
a chance. "Yes, you certainly are man enough to do that, so why
don't you go ahead and do it?"

He looked at her, confusion written on his face. "You want
me to shoot you?"

"Lock said I'm dead either way, might as well go quickly.
You'll be merciful, right? Or maybe you're not man enough to
do it?"

She saw the anger return to his eyes as he cocked back the
hammer on the gun. "Oh, I'm man enough. Lock will probably
thank me for getting rid of you."

He leveled the gun at her head, and Kat, never one for prayer,
closed her eyes and prayed to the spirits of the earth that West
would get to her in time before she had her brains splattered
across the walls of this makeshift warehouse.

<hr/>

If she wasn't about to get herself killed by some incompetent idiot who didn't know the first thing about holding a gun, he might have killed her himself. Kat had lost her mind, and West was watching in slow motion as she stared down the barrel of a gun. He wanted to roar and make his presence known, but he knew he had to be stealthy about his attack. He had a perfectly good plan to disarm the boy, and then Kat had gone and pissed him off, causing him to turn the gun on her.

Now West was going to have to tackle him and save her rather than his original plan of sneaking up on the kid. He gripped the knife in his hand, and watched as the boy closed in on her head. Then he lunged at him, slipping his finger behind the trigger before he could pull it.

"What the . . .!" he yelled out as West used the pocketknife to stab the kid in the side. It wasn't playing fair, but he had felt his heart pulled out of his chest and trampled the moment he had seen that gun pointed at Kat. He'd seen red and would kill him if he had to. No one would ever put her in that kind of danger. She was his. She just didn't know it yet.

Surprisingly spry, the kid's elbow sprung back and knocked West in the nose, sending him backward, his knife flying across the floor and landing behind Kat's chair. West wiped at the blood trickling out of his nose as he regained his equilibrium. Losing to some snot-nosed kid half his age was not an option, but the gun was still securely in his hands.

West was a boxer and enjoyed sparring with his friends, but he had never been one for hand-to-hand combat, and he was not trained to disarm anyone. Seeing where he had cut the kid with the knife, West punched him in the wound. He cried out, and West lunged for the gun. They both grappled for control, and it went off. For a moment West stood still, worried Kat had been shot. It felt like his heart was lodged in his throat as he prayed that she was fine. Relief swamped his senses when he saw she was fine, more than fine. She had grabbed his knife and was trying to cut herself loose. Her face contorted in agony as she worked to cut herself free.

That had been a mistake, because Williams, the name Kat had called the kid, punched him in the face while he was distracted, and it wasn't too shabby a hit. West's head recoiled on impact; he stood, and the room went in and out of focus. He lunged for the gun and pulled, but Williams's grip was stronger than he'd expected. With all the strength he had left, he pulled on the gun, but because of the awkward angle, it went flying across the floor. They both went after it, but Williams stopped him, punching him in the side. West doubled over in pain, and as Williams paused to celebrate his hit, West grabbed him around the waist and flung him to the floor.

West's fist connected with the boy's nose, with a bone-crunching punch that had to have broken it. The punch made his own hand hurt. It's a good thing he wouldn't be playing the guitar anytime soon because his fingers wouldn't work right for a while. The boy cried out in pain, gripping his face and crying out as he grabbed his bleeding nose. With all his leftover strength, West gave one last punch, and the kid was out cold. West jumped off him and lunged for the gun, but just as he was about to get it, the older man showed up. Before West knew what was up, he was sucker punched in the face, sending him flying to the ground.

The pain sent sparks through his head, and he saw fireworks. He had been so close and had failed in the last second. The older man picked up the gun and pointed it at him.

"I should make you watch me shoot your girl first, but I'm not vindictive. It's just business." He pulled back the hammer, and West searched the room for Kat. He wanted to see her one last time before he died. That was all he wanted. One last gaze upon the woman he realized he was coming to care for, because at this moment, if he had one regret, it was that she didn't know he was falling for her, and falling hard.

The man pulled the trigger, and the shot rang out. He felt nothing. West searched his body realizing he had no injuries. He sat up as the large man crumpled next to him, blood pooling under him.

West scrambled to his feet, searching for the shooter, and there she was.

Kat.

If there had ever been a woman who looked more like a warrior queen in that moment, he had never seen one. Her unbound hair was cascading down her shoulders and back, her clothes were dirty and disheveled, and her eyes were spitting fire.

He ran up to her, taking the gun and cupping her face in his hands. "Fuck, Kat, you saved me."

She stared at the man crumpled on the floor, and he pulled her face to look at him. "You saved me, Kat. I'm alive." He kissed her, making her focus on him and not the man on the ground bleeding to death.

"Is he . . . is he dead?" She was worried she had killed a man, and West didn't understand why she would care about that piece of crap.

The man made a groaning sound that made them both look at his prostrate form. "Apparently not," West noted, grabbing her hand. "Let's move."

She nodded, and they took off running to get into one of the Jeeps parked in front of the building. He jumped into the driver's seat and searched for the keys.

"Shit, I'll be right back."

"West, where are you—"

He didn't hear her as he raced back to the warehouse, searching the man's pockets for the keys to the Jeep. His hand wrapped around the key fob and pulled it from the still man's pockets—he was no longer groaning in pain, not a good sign for him—and ran back to the Jeep.

They weren't out of the woods yet though. While he had set the fire intentionally in the farthest field, someone had to have heard those gunshots. The Jeep roared to life and West drove like a madman, intent on getting them to the boats. Kat sat in silence, staring into space, holding her arm close to her chest.

West noticed her wince in pain and frowned, she was now holding her not sewn up arm. "What happened to your arm?"

"Nothing, just drive."

He didn't like her evading the question but didn't pry. She was right; they had to focus on escape first, and then he could take care of her.

He took the tight turns of the switchback too fast as he drove down the hill. He could hear cars behind him but didn't dare glance back for fear of taking his eyes off the road or the steep cliff they could plummet off of any moment. He saw Kat look back, worry on her face.

"How close are they?"

"I don't see anyone, just drive. Look." She pointed ahead, and West saw the marina. He skidded the Jeep into a small parking area where there were five boats docked. Jumping from the Jeep he ran to the other side to help Kat, who was struggling to get down with only one good arm. They took off running across the dock, jumping onto the first speedboat docked on their tiny marina. West saw a Jeep coming down the switchback out of the corner of his eye.

"Here." He shoved the keys into her hand as they ran onto one of the speedboats. "Get it started."

He stepped off the boat onto the dock.

"No, West, get back on the boat," she protested.

"Just get it started!" He took the gun she had used from his waistband as he saw one man aiming. He had an assault rifle and West was outgunned, but he would not let them hurt Kat. She was going to get the boat started and get herself off this island.

He heard her fumbling with the keys as she cursed while trying to get it started.

"It's not the right boat!"

"Then try another," he called back to her, preparing for a fight.

She jumped onto a neighboring boat, and then to his ever-lasting gratitude he heard the engine rev, and Kat screamed for him to get on the boat.

A stream of bullets sprayed across the deck as he jumped on, and Kat pulled away from the dock as fast as she could. West held his breath as the island shrunk in the distance, the bullets bouncing off and spraying the water, but not quite able to reach them. She turned the steering wheel and pushed the throttle forward as hard as she could, sending the boat flying across the water, almost knocking West off his feet.

"You think they'll come after us?" she yelled over the noise from the boat.

"Probably. We better find a place to hide."

As much as West wanted her to drive straight to an inhabited island for safety, he didn't want to risk them getting caught and shot by these people. They drove through the open water for what felt like hours, circling an island or two, before he saw a small cave and motioned for her to pull the boat in there. The sun was setting anyway, and they didn't want to be out on the ocean in the dark.

She maneuvered the boat in, dropping the anchor when the boat was in deep enough. Ivy and brush were hanging down around the cave entrance and they used it to cover the boat as much as they could. Once the sun went down they would be completely covered, and in the morning they could hopefully find an island with people on it.

Plopping down on the bow of the boat, West found a water bottle and handed it to Kat. She took a drink and handed it back, prompting him to finish off the bottle and savor every drop. It was getting dark in the cave, but he could see something was wrong with her. She was quiet, too quiet considering they had just escaped certain death.

"You're decently good at driving a speedboat, especially one-handed," he said, breaking the silence.

She lifted her head, still holding her arm against her chest. "I grew up in the Midwest. Not a whole lot to do. The lake is a big summer activity. We didn't do much else growing up, like vacations, eating out, or expensive Christmases, but we had a boat."

"I'm grateful you did. You got us out of there, Kat. That's the second time today you saved me."

He looked at the blue and purple bruise growing on the arm opposite of her stitched-up one. He had to get her to a doctor. Between her amateur stitches and potentially broken arm, she needed a hospital.

"How'd you get out of your binds anyway?" he asked.

She glanced down at her arm. "It hurt, I can tell you that." She gave a slight self-deprecating laugh. "When you lost your pocketknife it slid near me, and I thought if I could just get to it

I could get free, so I tried my feet at first, but they were tied tight. I tilted the chair to the side and fell on my arm." She frowned, and West wished he could take her pain away.

"I'll heal," she said, as if reading his thoughts. "I just wanted freedom. I had to wriggle a bit, but I got my hands on the knife and cut my bindings. You kept that Williams kid distracted, and that was all I needed to cut myself free."

West touched her arm and Kat let out a stream of air. "Babe, I wish this was over. I don't know how many times I can say I'm sorry." He kissed the top of her head and wrapped his arm around her.

She nuzzled in closer. "Where did you find the gun?" he asked.

She stiffened. "There was a cabinet sitting wide open. There were a bunch of them in there. Do you think I killed him? I know he was a bad man, but . . ."

"Kat." He stroked her hair, so smooth it still felt like silk across his calloused fingers. It was a simple and intimate gesture that he had never done with other women. "I saw him move. I'm sure he's alive, but even if he's not, he tried to kill us. He deserves whatever happens to him."

"I was aiming for his shoulder, but I've only shot a real gun once. I guess I'm not a very good shot."

West chuckled. "It was an excellent shot to me."

She snuggled in closer and sighed, and West continued to stroke her hair and her arms, his mind reeling as he contemplated the sheer terror that had come over him when he thought he'd almost lost her. How he had almost torn that entire compound up bit by bit to find her. It had turned his stomach sour as he saw her flirt with the boss to get him to untie her.

She was his and only his, and as medieval and antiquated as that thought was, he didn't care. Feelings were bubbling beneath the surface he couldn't quite name when it came to Kat, and he wasn't sure what he would do if she didn't feel the same.

He listened to the sound of her even breathing, glad she could fall asleep. They would have to find a way to Jakarta tomorrow. It was time for them to get home.

Fifteen

T he next day, Kat saw the sun rising through the vines covering their hiding spot. In the full morning light, she could see how close they were to the rock wall, as the boat barely fit in the small space. She had a blanket and a pair of muscular arms wrapped around her, and it took everything within her to not sigh in contentment. Where West had found the blanket, coarse as it was, she had no idea.

They slept reclined on the bow of the boat, where one would usually lie to sunbathe, and he had tucked her into his side. Somehow, he had moved her without her noticing. He looked so angelic as he slept. His dark blond hair, slightly graying at his temples, practically glowed as the morning sun showed through, bouncing light off his head. She was loath to wake him, but it was time for them to get home. They needed to get to safety. As much as she wanted their time together to never end, for it to be the two of them lost to the ocean forever, they were being hunted by drug dealing murderers and needed help.

Her mind was still reeling after shooting a man. Kat had never felt comfortable with guns or considered them a means for solving problems. It had been one reason she had left the Midwest. When every neighbor, classmate, and even friend seemed to think guns were the answers to problems, she felt like she didn't belong. It was going to take her a while to process the fact that she might have killed someone. The more disturbing part was that while she aimed for his shoulder, she hadn't cared if she had killed him in the moment.

When she had seen Lock level the gun at West, her heart fell out of her body, and she knew instantly that she would do anything to save him, even throwing herself in front of the bullet, which she had almost done. For a split second, she had almost yelled out to Lock to take her instead, to do what he wanted with her and to let West go, but then she had seen the gun cabinet and grabbed a gun instead. While she had aimed for his shoulder but had hit him in the chest, and in that split second, she hadn't cared. West didn't deserve to die, and she couldn't imagine her life without him.

She couldn't tell him she might have feelings for him, of course. What if he said it back? What if he didn't? Kat couldn't decide which scenario she preferred because either way it ended with her brokenhearted.

She felt him stir at her back, and turned in his arms as he opened his eyes, entirely too blue and even brighter against the backdrop of the ocean.

"Mmmm, good morning, sweetheart," he grumbled, his voice still gruff from sleep, the sound instantly sending shock-waves through Kat's body. He gripped her tighter and pulled her close, his mouth coming down on hers, his tongue slipping between her lips. She sighed and he took advantage of the invitation as his tongue met hers, and she felt warmth instantly pooling at her center. He had given her the orgasm of her life a day ago, and yet she wanted more. His large hand cupped her nape, pulling her closer as he sat up so that they were now face-to-face. He explored her mouth with his, while his hands explored her body, cautious of her injured arms. Kat wanted nothing more than to keep this going, but she knew they couldn't. They had to get back. She couldn't let her heart win over her head this time.

"West," she said into his mouth, pushing his hands off her, pulling herself back. "West, we have to go."

"Go?" He looked surprised.

"Yes, go." She gave him one quick kiss on the underside of his jaw. "We have a boat. We need to get to safety. It's time we got home and alerted the authorities about those men."

He looked down at his crotch and back at her. "We're not going to take care of this?"

Kat laughed. "West, come on!"

He grimaced and adjusted himself. "Fine, Kat, but we're not done with this conversation. You can't let me taste heaven and not let me have the whole meal."

She smiled, but inwardly she knew it couldn't be. She, too, wanted to give him everything. It was better she ended this now before she became even more attached.

"What are you thinking?" He always seemed to notice when she was deep in thought.

"Nothing," she said quickly.

"Liar." He smirked. "But we might as well get a move on, so I'll make you tell me later.

Before she could respond, he gave her a quick kiss, then stood to pick up the boat keys, jingling them in front of her. "Are you driving or me? You did such a good job getting us out of there, but I'll let you decide."

West could feel her mood. She didn't know how he did it. He knew her better than she knew herself. He knew she didn't want to drive, but also knew to ask. When did he become considerate? A single tear rolled down her face, followed by another until it all came flooding out of her.

He didn't run away—not that he could—or ask her what was wrong. He simply pulled her into his arms, wrapping her in his warmth, and rubbed her back in soothing circles. He spoke softly, telling her how amazing she was, that they were almost to the end of all this, and his kind words made her cry even harder.

She wasn't sure how long she stood there, crying like a fool. Eventually, the tears dried, and she wiped her eyes on his already dirt-stained button-down. She stepped back, looking into his eyes, and the care and compassion she saw reflected in them made her almost break down again.

He cupped her cheek and smiled. "Let's get home."

———◆◇◆———

Eight hours at sea, driving in what felt like circles, and they were almost out of gas. West looked over the bow of the boat at Kat as she watched the waves pass by. She had been quiet and not herself. Being kidnapped and shooting a man would probably do that to a person, but he felt it was something else, like she was distancing herself from him. He didn't like it.

As they moved closer to society, West couldn't tell what was going on in Kat's mind. He wanted to see where this went. To see if they could be together in the real world. It would kill him to let her walk away, but if that was what she wanted, he would never stop her. Deep down he knew she cared for him too.

He had opened himself up to her. Came almost too close to revealing his feelings for her, but since her tears that morning, she had been almost silent. He was worried he had said too much.

In the distance, he saw another island but was unwilling to get his hopes up. They had seen multiple islands, and each time they had driven around only to find them uninhabited. As they got closer, the island grew in perspective, looming larger in front of them, the trees growing from the craggy hills sticking out above the surface. Kat was standing on the bow of the ship pointing excitedly toward her left. He looked, almost falling to his knees as relief swamped his every last nerve.

A group of fishermen was working off the beach while other men sat at the edge of a dock. There were multiple boats floating in the water. The island wasn't large, but it was large enough. There were people here! Now, hopefully, they could find a way to get to Jakarta. West pulled the throttle back, putting the engine in neutral.

"West, what are you—" Kat asked, stopping mid-sentence as he prowled toward her. He was in front of her in two steps, pulling her into his arms and kissing her. He didn't know if it was from the relief of ending this nightmare, or if it was because he needed her to know that even if this was the end of their predicament, it wasn't the end of them. Either way, he needed her lips on him.

She nipped at his lower lip, and he reveled in the feel of her. He pulled her closer, feeling her breasts pressed against his chest. He wanted to rip her clothes off and finish what they'd started this morning, but they had an audience. A boat didn't just sail up to an island and not draw attention.

Stepping back, he broke the kiss, a deep sense of longing overtaking him. He wanted to pull her back into his arms, but instead, he walked back to the steering wheel, pushed the throttle up, and steered the boat toward the dock. A man directed him where they wanted him, and he docked their vessel. The men jumped onto the deck and started inspecting it. West did not know what they were looking for, and he grabbed Kat as they both got off.

The men started asking him questions, but he didn't understand them. They most likely spoke Indonesian or a dialect of their own island. They pointed at the boat, and then at him and Kat, and he shook his head, gesturing that he didn't know what they wanted.

"It's not our boat," he said, hoping someone might understand him.

One of the men looked at a kid of maybe ten or eleven who took off running.

They talked, and Kat looked at West, concern etched on her face. He wanted to smooth away the lines on her forehead and make her forget all her worries. They were going to get home; they were too close not to make it. He squeezed her hand, and she leaned into him.

The boy ran back with someone new who looked to be in his forties, maybe his father, and was wearing Western clothing.

"Hello," he said in clear English.

"Oh, hi, you speak English?" Kat asked him.

"Yes." He nodded to the boat. "Where have you come from?"

Kat and West spoke at the same time, saying that it was a bit of a long story. They looked at each other and laughed, and West could feel his heart swell for the woman at his side. He couldn't even think of the last time he'd just laughed with a woman without pretense.

The man across from them didn't seem amused.

"You tell him," West said, looking at Kat.

"Is this your boat?" he interrupted before Kat could say any-thing.

"Oh . . . well . . . no, we stole it," Kat admitted, as her feet began drawing pictures in the sand that had built up on the dock.

Dear god, Kat!

They were going to Indonesian jail now. He elbowed her in her side.

"What? It's true. Might as well be honest." She gestured to the man, who raised his eyebrows at her declaration. "You see, we washed up on this island with a bunch of men growing coca plants and manufacturing cocaine, then we escaped on their boat, ended up here, and now we need to get to Jakarta so we can fly back to the United States."

He looked at her and blinked a few times.

"I know it sounds crazy," West added, "but—"

He put his hand up. "I believe her. We thought you were with those men. We see these boats drive by, with their motors day and night. These White men with no regard for our customs or our waters. I am glad you are not one of them, but we can never be too sure."

Then he smiled. "Welcome to Sawu Island!" He opened his arms wide, gesturing for them to follow him off the dock. "Let's get you cleaned up and get you some food."

Kat smiled up at West. "Did you hear that?" Her eyes sparkled.

"What? We're going home?"

She laughed. "No. Food!"

He laughed and kissed the top of her head as they followed him off the dock; she would finally be safe.

———————◆———————

A few hours later, Kat had showered, and had eaten real cooked food for the first time in what she had estimated to be ten days. Her whole body relaxed and felt slightly normal—aside from her aching arms—for the first time, and she sat on the bed, looking out at the ocean finally able to appreciate the beauty of her surroundings.

Sawu Island was small, not a destination for tourists, but thankfully had a place for them to stay. West used the man from the beach's phone to call his father, who in turn said they would be picked up in the morning.

It wasn't as spacious or gorgeous as her room in Bali, but there was a beautifully carved bed, a small powder room, and half of the space opened to the ocean breeze. The moonlight streamed in, and Kat thought she might never go back home. What was she even going back to? She still didn't have a career. Her family loved her, but they all had their own things going on, and she couldn't face seeing West with someone else, which would inevitably happen. Here she could toss her phone into the ocean, write music, and live a nice peaceful life.

You'd be lonely.

She pushed her intruding thoughts aside and sat at the edge of their room on the steps. She watched West as he walked up from the bathhouse and crossed through the moonlit clearing to reach her. His tanned skin glistened with water droplets. A towel was draped around his neck, and he had a new pair of shorts on, but no shirt, and it took everything within Kat's power not to start drooling as she watched his muscles bunch and flex as he walked toward her.

He smiled as he saw her watching, and her body felt like a live wire buzzing with anticipation.

"I thought you'd be asleep by now," he said, his deep voice wrapping around and warming her.

West leaned his arm on one of the columns that held up the *rumah adat's* roof, looking the perfect picture of a relaxed male, his crisp clean scent floating all around her. Kat had to get away or she was in serious trouble. Who was she kidding? She was already in trouble.

She uncurled herself from her seated position, and as she rose, her arm grazed his bare chest. She heard the catch in his breath and stumbled back a step, desperately searching for something to say. The noise of crickets filled the silence between them, but their eyes remained locked.

He grasped one of her hands, pulling her into his arms and started swaying back and forth.

"Dance with me," he whispered in her ear.

Kat leaned her head on his shoulder, listening to the crickets chirping around them, and the wind rustle through the trees.

"There's no music," she said breathlessly.

"Aren't you the one who hears the music all around you?"

She nodded against his chest, inhaling his scent. "I hear it. I wasn't sure you did." She looked up into his eyes, half shadowed in the dark, and he smiled at her.

She couldn't handle the emotion she saw, so she rested her head back on his strong, warm chest.

And then he started to sing. A song she had never heard before. One he had just made up, or one she just didn't know. Either way, her legs were failing her.

His voice was soft, but his deep sultry tone still wrapped itself around her body. If there was ever a fantasy she'd had over and over growing up, this was it. The sexy rock star, singing a song just for her. This had to be a dream. Famous stars did not sing love songs to women like Kat. She jerked her head up, surprising West.

"Is that a new song?"

"Yeah. Something about being lost on an island has been rather inspiring." His deep voice reverberated in his chest and warmed Kat's body.

"That means you're going to forget the acting then?"

He was silent for what felt like an eternity. "Nice try, sweetheart."

Kat pulled away, moving across the veranda, annoyed with his answer. "So, you write a new song, but won't do anything with it? I don't get it. Acting just seems so superficial for you."

Was she purposefully picking a fight with him?

Most likely. He was breaking down all her defenses, and her heart was becoming a puddled mess in his hands. If they crossed the line tonight there would be no going back for her. He would own her, body and soul.

A corner of West's mouth quirked up, and Kat backed up farther into the room, feeling her pulse pounding with fear, or maybe it was something else, as his gaze bore into her. He pushed away from the column and moved toward her slowly and deliberately, like a panther stalking its prey.

She felt rooted to the spot and couldn't move, even if she wanted to. In just a few short strides, he reached her. He leaned in close until his breath tickled her ear.

"Kat, what the hell are you so afraid of?" His voice was low and intimate, sending shivers down her spine. He saw right through her, and Kat hated him for it.

Wrestling out of his grip, Kat walked across the room. "Me? You're asking me what I'm afraid of?" She let out a sardonic laugh. "How about you? You're going to take the easier route simply because you can. God forbid you take a chance on yourself, on others in this infernal industry. You have a chance to make a change in alternative music, but you're too worried about your bottom line, about your cushy lifestyle, about failure. It would be a shame if you couldn't get into those rich-kid clubs anymore."

It was a low blow; she knew it, but she had to put distance between them. Kat turned away from him, placing her hands on the dresser in front of her, willing the stinging in her eyes to go away. She wanted him to be more than he was. Deep down she had continued to hope that if he was willing to do the right thing and stand for something in the music industry, maybe he'd change in other ways too. Ways involving his love life. Ways, dare she think it, involving her. The wishful thinking was stupid on her part.

A firm hand turned her around and pushed her back into the dresser, his heat and powerful body igniting all her nerve endings.

"Fine," West ground out, anger and something else glowing in his eyes. "You want me to start an indie label? I'll do it, and guess who my first signed artist will be?"

Kat glared at him, both hating and loving the feel of him.

He tipped her chin up. "Take a guess, Kat."

"I don't know," she said more breathlessly than she wanted.

"You." He dipped his head, and his tongue blazed a scorching trail from her collarbone to behind her ear. Her body betrayed her with a shudder.

"I don't want it," she said through clenched teeth.

He bit her earlobe, and she turned her head away. His teeth raked up her neck.

"Now who's scared?"

"I'm not scared. You're not even serious, you're just trying to bait me. You won't do it. That would require giving a fuck about anyone besides yourself."

He let out a guttural sound that sent a shiver through her, his powerful arms lifting her off the ground with a single movement. Kat yelped in surprise as West held her close to his body, their faces inches apart in the pale moonlight.

"Oh, trust me when I say I give a fuck," West said, pinning her against his body and the wall, his face shadowed. "I give such a fuck that all I've been able to think about is you. About your smile. About your laugh. About how much you care for everyone else over yourself. About what you taste like, and what you'll feel like coming apart on my cock, the sounds you'll make as I push that pussy to its breaking point."

Kat's head spun. She was supposed to be mad at him, not falling to pieces in his arms with her legs wrapped around him, her panties wetter than if she'd just jumped in a swimming pool.

He pushed his arousal against her. "You feel that, sweetheart? You do that to me and trust me, it wouldn't do that if I didn't give a fuck."

"I'm the only woman you've seen for days," Kat reminded him.

"Dammit, Kat." West spun her around, laying her down on the bed. "At some point, you're going to have to trust me. God willing, I hope that moment is now because I'm about to take all your clothes off and fuck you until the only name you can remember is mine."

Kat searched his face for any hint that he was just using her, but all she could see was the same intensity and passion that had been building up in her for days. "I trust you," she whispered.

His lips crashed into hers, claiming her with a kiss like no other. Their tongues intertwined, tangling together as West explored her body with his hands. All conscious thought faded away, and Kat allowed herself to be swept away in his passionate embrace.

West pulled back, lifting her shirt over her head. She winced at the pain in her arm.

His eyes softened. "Sorry, I'll watch out for your arm," he said, leaning down to rain kisses on it. "Now," he said, a mischievous glint in his eyes, "you're going to be a good girl and do what I say tonight."

Kat's heart raced and she opened her mouth to protest, but West placed one finger to her lips, silencing her. "No, tonight you're going to do as you're told."

Kat's body became incendiary, her mind racing as she thought about what West had planned. He may sing sweet, sexy love songs, but this was a completely different side of Weston Monroe.

He grasped her hips, his fingers digging into her sides, and flipped her onto her stomach in one swift movement. She felt a strange mixture of fear and anticipation as he reached for the waistband of her shorts and pulled them down with her panties, leaving her feeling exposed and vulnerable on the bed. He licked up her spine and skillfully unhooked each tiny eye hook of her bra, seeming to savor every moment.

"Holy fuck, Kat, how have I never seen this tattoo?"

Usually covered by her bra was the Indigenous Thunderbird; it spanned across her upper back, a symbol of power and protection in her culture.

Kat laughed. "My brother and I got them at a powwow when I was nineteen. I knew my mom wouldn't approve, so I put it in a place most don't see."

"It's so fucking hot." He moved his hands over the tattoo, and she moaned, turning her body to look at him.

His eyes were full of fiery intensity as his hand found her bottom, delivering an expertly sharp smack that left a burning sensation. "Good girls do what they're told," he said into her ear, "and I didn't tell you to turn over."

Her ass cheek burned, and she verged between being insanely aroused and utterly shocked. She had never been treated this way in bed, and her body felt utterly delicious.

"West, what are . . ."

"No girl who bites like you do likes it soft and gentle." He spanked her again. "Tell me, Kat, you want me to give it to you soft and sweet?" He smoothed where his hand had just forever imprinted on her ass.

Kat bit her lip and shook her head as waves of pleasure crept up, and she arched her back into him. His arms were like pillars of strength, holding her in position as he allowed one of his fingers to push deep within her, a moan escaping her lips.

"That's my good girl," West said, his voice rich with satisfaction.

Men had never really asked or been in tune with what she wanted, and she had never really felt comfortable voicing how she enjoyed both the pain and pleasure of sex, but West knew.

He knew exactly what she wanted because he had bothered to notice her.

Kat twisted her fingers in the sheets beneath her and pleaded, "West please . . ." He wrapped his large hands around her ankles, pulling her to the edge of the bed and flipping her onto her back so that she could see him.

"What do you want, sweetheart?" he asked, his hands roaming up her body and his hand lightly gripping her neck.

Kat let out a long sigh as she felt herself melt into the mattress. "You."

He sent shivers down through her toes as he tore her bra off with a growl, and his lips descended over one breast. His tongue moved in languid circles around the contours of the sensitive flesh, and she scratched down his back at the sensation, eliciting a moan from him. His exploration continued to the other breast, his hands beginning to venture lower.

Kat felt her breath catch as he reached inside of her, his expert fingers working their magic with practiced ease; it was almost too much for her, the feeling of him everywhere making her mind spin. His touch lit a fire inside her that seemed like it would never be quenched.

West's mouth let go of one of her breasts, kissing and licking his way down her body. Landing at the seam of her pussy. His tongue circled her clit, sucking it into his mouth while he ran a hand up her thigh. His fingers worked in tandem with his tongue as he held down her hips, forcing her to take all the pleasure.

"Yes, Kat, come for me. Scream my name. Who's making you feel this good?"

"Y-you are," she said between hurried breaths.

"No one else will ever make you feel as good as I do," he said as his fingers and tongue continued their assault on her body. "Scream for me."

Kat dug her nails into his scalp and did as he commanded, screaming out his name and coming apart on his mouth. She felt every sensation of pleasure rush in, like the tide coming in on the coast. Her legs shook with need and desire, and her entire world caved in at his touch.

West continued to kiss and lick her as she breathed through the last convulsions. He stood, taking her in.

He bit his bottom lip, and Kat almost came again at the sight of him. She had no business being with a man who looked like this.

He pulled his shorts off, and Kat's eyes widened at the sight of him. She had expected . . . well, she didn't know what she had expected, but what she saw might not fit.

He smirked knowingly, bending down to kiss her. "That's my girl, you came so hard for me." Even in his state of undress, West managed to exude a powerful confidence that aroused Kat even more.

Kat sat up on the edge of the bed, emboldened by his dirty talk. Two could play this game. She licked her lips and reached for him eagerly, wrapping her hand around his hard shaft and pumping it up and down.

His eyes rolled back in pleasure, and a moan escaped his lips. "Fuck, Kat, you have no idea how long I've been waiting for you to touch me there."

She laughed. "Ten days?"

He pinned her with his eyes. "I think it's been more like ten years."

Kat swallowed. He didn't mean it, he couldn't, he was just lost in the moment. His hand shot into her hair, wrapping it around his fist and he pulled her toward his straining cock. She licked him from the base to the tip, swirling her tongue as she reached the top. He groaned as she took the whole of him into her mouth.

While he was the one who held her head, moving her up and down his hardness, she was the one who felt powerful. As West moaned and cursed into the darkness, Kat knew she was the one giving him such pleasure.

"Fuck, Kat, you have to stop or I'm going to be done before we start." His fist pulled hard on her hair, sending delicious waves of pleasure through her as she released him from her mouth.

Before she knew what happened, West lifted her up and she was straddling him on the bed.

"I want to watch you," he said, and while she would normally have felt self-conscious, he made her feel powerful. "Protection?" he asked her.

Kat gave him a sardonic look. "You're going to ask that two seconds before you're inside me?"

West fingers dipped inside her. "I promise I'm clean, but it's up to you."

She arched her back, pushing into his hand. "I have an IUD and haven't been with anyone in a couple of years. I'm clean."

West was going to bust if he wasn't in her soon. He groaned at the confirmation and with one swift thrust buried himself deep inside her, impaling her with no gentleness. Kat gasped at the sudden sensation and West feared he had hurt her; yet the grip of her perfect tightness around him told another story entirely.

Her head tilted back, and he ached to change their positions so he could bite and taste the column of her long neck, but first, she was going to ride him until she cried out his name again to the universe. The world would know that Kat was his.

He moved his hips and she moved with him, and then his entire plan to take her multiple ways went to shit. His fingers dug into her hips and moved her in time with his thrusts, slow at first, but he couldn't maintain his relaxed tempo. He wanted her too badly.

"God, sweetheart, you feel like pure ecstasy. I never want this to end!"

She looked down at him through a veil of velvet hair and West could barely contain himself. The emotion in her eyes was raw and real. A passion that seared through his very soul and lit up every inch of his body with desire. He thrust deeper into her as he pressed his finger to her clit, needing her to come with him as he lost all control.

Kat's cries echoed around them, quickly followed by West's throaty roar of pleasure as they both came together in a frenzy of blinding bliss.

With a final powerful thrust, West spilled into her with a force he had never experienced with another woman. A feeling of complete connection and fulfillment.

Kat dropped onto his chest, her body radiating heat and comfort. His heart burst with warmth when she pressed her lips against his skin, sending shockwaves through his body. He was used to being the one who put in the effort, always taking care of women and seeing to their needs, so this newfound connection made him feel both uneasy and content all at once.

She slid beside him on the too-small bed, his feet dangling off the mattress. West had rarely opened up to another person enough to cuddle after sex, but as Kat settled into the curve of his arm, he felt as if he would fight the devil himself for this moment together.

Kat kissed his neck and looked up with a smirk. "That was . . . surprising."

He returned her smile. "Surprising?"

"I thought you were more of a 'Your Body Is a Wonderland' John Mayer-type than"—she gestured vaguely toward the disheveled state of their room—"the whole dominating, spanking thing."

West gave a soft laugh. "I told you; I just knew what you'd like." With a gentle touch, his hand traveled along her arm like a feather, and he asked with a sly raise of his eyebrows, "Was I wrong?"

He saw a blush spread across her cheeks. "It would seem you were right."

They both laughed and West pulled her into his arms. "Should we try again? I can be 'Your Body Is a Wonderland.'"

"Mmmm, I don't think I'd like that as much," she said.

His hand moved lazily on her back. "So, do you really hate actors that much, or is it just the thought of me being one?"

Kat yawned. "I dated one once. Archie Llewellyn played the lead every year in our school musical. He was such a diva, but we dated for one year. I'm never dating an actor again."

"You're judging all actors from a high school relationship?" He laughed, nipping her shoulder.

She nodded and whispered. "He broke my heart, and I have a feeling they're all the same." Her eyes fluttered shut as she fell asleep.

West was unsure if she was talking about him or Archie, but the feel of her body wrapped in his at that moment was the most natural thing he'd ever felt in his life. He had to convince her that he had every intention of taking care of her heart.

Sixteen

One call to his father—the only number West had memorized—and a helicopter was landing in the middle of Sawu Island the next morning. Begrudgingly, West left the warm bed and the comfort of Kat wrapped around him as she slept. He had admitted a lot last night and hoped she had believed him.

It was becoming increasingly clear to him that he had strong feelings for her, and the second he had released himself inside her he knew there could be no one else. He needed her to challenge him when he was being an ass, and to comfort him when he was feeling low. And he wanted to be there for her. She deserved to know just how perfect she was every day, and that was exactly what he intended to do.

West ran out to meet the helicopter as he contemplated how to get Kat to stay with him when they got back to the States. She had a tough armor that he was slowly chipping away at, and yet, he could tell while she had given herself to him, she wasn't quite ready to give him her heart.

"Mr. Monroe?" the captain yelled as West reached the helicopter, its blades spinning above loudly.

"Yep, that's me."

"Fantastic! Your father is going to be happy to see you."

"My father?" West asked. This was a military helicopter and an American one at that. West had no idea what his father had to do with the military other than alerting the officials to his location. Their conversation on the phone had been short, as service had been spotty at best.

"Wouldn't take no for an answer," the captain said. "We didn't have a transport at the ready to get you until tomorrow, but your dad must have friends in high places because I was woken up in the middle of the night with orders to come get you."

"Oh . . . sorry about that." West almost felt bad for making this poor guy fly through the night. His dad was, of course, a force to be reckoned with, and he didn't even want to think about what favors he had called in to get West. They would have been fine on the island for another day, but Tommy Monroe would only expect the most expedient exit for his son.

"Don't be. If I could just get something signed for my wife, all will be forgiven."

West supposed it was the least he could do. "Yeah, sure of course," he said with more excitement than he felt.

He covered his eyes from the sun and stared back at the *rumah apat* where Kat slept. "Let me get Kat and we can get out of here."

A few hours later they were airborne and on their way to Jakarta. The whirls of the blades drowned out all other sounds, and West wanted nothing more than to comfort Kat as he watched her nervously wring her hands in her lap.

Being on the same channel as the pilot, he was unsure if he should ask her what was wrong. If it was about him, he knew she wouldn't answer—and he wasn't sure he actually wanted to know.

Giving in to curiosity, he grabbed one of her hands, pulling it into his lap. "What's wrong?" he asked into the microphone of his headset, the only way she would be able to hear him.

"I don't know. I know I should be excited to get back to my family and friends, but for some reason, I'm kind of sad it's over. Does that make me crazy?"

West let go of her hand, wrapping his arm around her shoulder, their heads resting on each other, the headphones impeding the closeness West wanted. "No, that's not crazy. It was nice being just the two of us in the end; it was our own little paradise, if we forgot about the murdering drug lords."

"Yeah, it was nice. I guess I'm kind of nervous to see my mom too." West's dad had told him that Kat's mom was at the hotel in Jakarta waiting for them, and when he had told Kat he was surprised she hadn't reacted with much excitement.

"You don't mention your mom very often, is there a reason for that?"

She exhaled audibly and glanced up at the pilot. "Uh, captain, can you just ignore us for a minute?"

"Sure thing, miss." He saluted her and Kat looked visibly more at ease. Of course, the pilot could still hear her, but maybe he'd tune her out.

"My mom and I don't get along very well," she started, her hand tightening on his. "I was always daddy's girl, and she adored my brothers."

West searched his brain for what he knew about her brothers but came up blank. She really hadn't talked much about her family other than her grandmother.

"Caleb is older than me and is an accountant. He's married with two girls, and my mom can't get enough of her grandchildren. Then there is my younger brother Cameron, he's the baby of the family. He just had a kid with his new wife. They both have their shit together."

"You have your shit together just fine," West said loudly through the mic.

She rolled her eyes, a smile finally creeping across her face. "You know that's not true. I still have no idea what I'm going to do when I get back to the real world, and I know that's going to be the first thing my mother asks now that she knows I'm alive and fine. She was okay with me doing music, but in her eyes I'll never be fulfilled until I'm married with children."

"Do you want kids?" he asked, unsure if he even knew his own answer to that question.

"Someday, with the right person, but in her eyes my internal clock is ticking and soon it will be too late."

West waited for her to continue, and at first she didn't say anything. An array of emotions played across her face, and he sat there just holding her hand, wanting her to know that he was there for her.

"My grandma, she and my mom always fight. The more my grandma pushes away White assimilation, the more it angers my mother. My brothers, well at least Cameron and I, really loved getting to know that side of us, and yet my mom pushed back on it all the way. Every time my grandma would tell my mom she was raising us wrong it became a fight. I think I remind my mom of my grandma, and that brings up a lot of bad memories. My dad had always been the barrier between us, he would talk my mom down when she'd go off on one of her supposed well-meaning rampages. I just never feel like I'm quite enough for her."

West knew that feeling all too well and lifted her hand to kiss the back of it. "Why are you just now telling me this? You know how I feel about my father, you didn't think I would understand?"

She shrugged and smirked. "Honestly, I had hoped you'd never meet her. I love her, I do, but if you think my self-image is low now, just imagine what it was like in high school."

"It's okay, Kat; thanks for telling me now. Maybe she'll be so happy just to have you alive she'll never criticize you again."

Kat laughed. "Doubt it, but she might just be a little more understanding."

"Hey, she's spent a week with my dad, if that doesn't make her more open and understanding, I don't know what will."

———— ◈ ————

After arriving in Jakarta, a black town car picked them up at the small private airport. Kat tried not to squirm in her seat, but her nerves got the better of her. Soon she would be with her mom and the myriad of questions she would pose. Questions Kat just didn't have any answers for.

Her future plans? Nonexistent.

What happened on the island? Who knows. Kat sure couldn't put into words everything she had just been through.

Her relationship status? Kat couldn't say.

She wasn't ready.

But as they pulled up to the hotel's front door, she knew she didn't have a choice.

West slid out of the car, offering her his hand, and in any other situation Kat would have felt like a princess with her prince leading her into a ball. But alas, she was just about to be assailed with questions left and right, and she had very few answers for anyone.

The doors opened and they walked into the flashing of cameras and a crowd of people waiting for them. Cher and Lydia were the first to practically jump on top of her, causing her to let go of West's hand, her one anchor in the storm.

"Oh my god, you're alive!" Lydia screeched, jumping up and down. "You look so tan," she added, causing Kat to laugh.

"You really do look amazing for someone who spent ten days on an uncharted island," Cher said as she gripped Kat for dear life. "I'm so happy you're okay," she added as a tear slid down her cheek.

Before Kat knew it, she was crying because she hadn't expected such a homecoming, and because she had indeed missed her friends. Her lifeline over the past ten years. They hugged and cried for who knew how long before Kat's mom finally pushed through.

"Katy, I'm so glad you're okay." Her mom pushed away a tear, a rare show of emotion. She had barely cried at her husband's funeral.

"I'm happy to see you too, Mom," she said, and surprisingly, she meant it. On the island they had been *go, go, go*, and survival had been their main goal, but now her thoughts caught up to her, the idea that she could have never seen her loved ones again.

Out of the corner of her eye, she caught West and his dad deep in conversation with the press surrounding them.

Just as she suspected, they weren't especially interested in her.

"You're going to have to tell us all about that," Cher said, motioning toward West.

"There's nothing to tell."

"Liar."

Of course she was lying. The last thing she needed was her mother thinking she was on the verge of getting a rock star son-in-law anytime soon. While Kat realized she was hopelessly in love with the man, she had no idea if he remotely felt the same.

"Sorry, I need to borrow her," West said, grabbing her elbow. *When had he even made it back to her?*

"Take her forever," Lydia quipped, causing Kat's eyes to grow huge. Damn Lydia, always opening her mouth.

West just smiled as he pulled her from the crowd. "The doctors and the cops need to see us," was all he said, maneuvering her through the room. "Don't worry, I'll be with you every step of the way."

Kat wasn't sure what on her face had given her away, but his words instantly calmed her nerves as she followed him into the conference room.

The warm water from the shower fell on her tired muscles, soothing Kat more than she knew she needed. She was beyond exhausted from all the excitement around their return.

West had been right; everyone had still been waiting for them. Kat had been convinced that they would just go to the police and that no one they knew would still be in Indonesia. How wrong she had been when they had walked into the hotel.

Besides her mother and her friends, it had all been for West, of course. The media frenzy that had exploded the moment he walked through the door had been astounding, reminding Kat of why they could never be together. She couldn't live that life, always fighting the media when they were out. What kind of life would that be? West's father had placated them, promising a full-on press conference later that evening, after they had had some time to see the doctor and get cleaned up. Tommy Monroe's ability to keep the press at bay impressed her.

After they had seen the doctors, who were rather impressed at her stitching and antivenom-making abilities, they were questioned by the police, which had been exhausting.

They didn't know where the island was. They had boated in what felt like circles, so they could only give a vague explanation of where they thought they had escaped from in relation to where they ended up, which was Sawu Island.

It wasn't much to go on, but the Indonesian police said they would start hunting for the operation and the men responsible. It didn't make Kat feel much better. Once the news started to show West's face, the drug operation would figure out who he was, and they could easily retaliate or send someone to kill him. West blew off her concerns, telling her not to worry. Kat wasn't convinced.

Clean for the first time in dyas, she stepped out of the shower. She felt like a whole new woman with all the grime and dirt finally off. She would never take a hot shower or a toilet for granted again.

She was meeting West and his father for dinner, along with her mother. Her stomach was full of butterflies. It wasn't real. She and West weren't dating, and this was not a meet-the-parents dinner, but it still felt significant. She worried Tommy Monroe wouldn't like her. West had said some harsh things about him, and she was worried she wouldn't live up to his standards.

Kat wiped the steam from the mirror, her raw, reddened skin staring back at her. She was back in civilization; she should have felt happy. Despite being alive, clean, and well-fed, all she could focus on was her purposeless life and a future that may or may not include West. Not once in all their lovemaking had he expressed any desire to continue after they returned home.

Cocaine island, as she now referred to it was looking better and better with each passing day. West's father had booked their flights home, but when West had been busy talking with Luke and Declan, Kat had asked him to book her flight to Iowa with her mother and not tell West. He had given her a close inspection but hadn't pried into why. Kat had been thankful for his discretion.

She needed to go home for a while, and not home as in L.A., but home to her family. She wanted to talk with her grandmother and to see what her ancestors would say to do when feeling blocked and out of sync with the universe.

Kat wrapped the towel around her body and went to her luggage, the one thing that hadn't gotten lost on her journey. She dug through the pockets, pulling out a bracelet with a turquoise pendant.

"I should have been wearing you," she said, slipping it around her wrist. Turquoise was meant as protection, and tonight Kat's heart needed as much protection as it could get.

She had to tell West that this was the end of the road, that when she got on the plane in the next few days she was going to Iowa to figure things out, and that he needed to do the same. To work some things out with his father, maybe try acting if that's what he needed to do to feel fulfilled. To make decisions about who he was, just like Kat.

Who was she kidding? Her heart was already breaking into a million little pieces just thinking about it, but she had to do it now before she became even more attached. What life did Kat have with him? She knew she would never be happy lounging around his large house living off him. She had to do something with her life, and the appeal of being her own recording artist had begun to fade away. But if she didn't have that dream, what did she have?

She had loved writing music with West when he had allowed her to. Maybe she could partner with some other artists or be an agent, Creator knows she'd be better than Declan. She could actually help women looking to break into an unforgiving industry. Not that Kat knew the first thing about being an agent, but she wouldn't ask West for help. She knew it was pride keeping her from asking him, but she couldn't do it. She had always done things on her own, and she wasn't sure she could change her ways.

A knock at the door drew her thoughts away from West and her breaking heart. A welcome reprieve. She opened the door, and Cher waltzed into the room. She looked at Kat, still wrapped in her towel, and walked over to the closet, looking through Kat's dresses.

"I bet that shower felt good," she said.

"I already picked out a dress."

Cher looked at the dress laid out on the bed and frowned. "That is too subtle. You need something sexier."

"For dinner with my mother and West's father? I don't want to be sexy!" Kat lifted the navy dress with the higher neckline. "It's at least form-fitting. What's the problem?"

"The neckline goes for ages. Come on, Kat, show off your assets." She looked pointedly at Kat's chest.

"I'm not trying to impress anyone. What makes you think anything happened in the first place?"

Cher pulled out a black bodycon dress with a plunging neckline that thankfully had mesh to hold her chest in. It was sexy in a not-so-obvious way and would still be appropriate enough to appease her mother's sensibilities.

Cher scoffed. "Please, I saw the way you two reached for each other when you first showed up at the hotel. I know something happened on that island, and I get it. You didn't want to say what it was in front of your mother, but you can't lie to me."

Cher knew her all too well, and that's when Kat couldn't hold back the tears any longer. She threw herself across the bed, the tears coming unbound. "I think . . . I . . . I think I'm in love with him." And as she voiced it for the first time, she felt the reality of her words sink in. She was falling for him. For his charm, attentiveness, the way he now truly saw her as a legitimate musician.

Cher came to the bed, wrapping her arms around Kat, and that made her want to cry even more. Her friend held her for a while. No questions, no comments, and no recriminations because that's just how best friends should be. Eventually, Kat felt the tears abate and sat up, wiping her eyes.

"God, I'm going to be so puffy."

Cher chuckled and handed her a tissue. "I don't think West is going to care. I think he loves you too."

Kat wiped her eyes. "It's just some island version of Stockholm syndrome. Once he gets back to L.A. and his life of glitz and glamor, he'll realize how plain and boring I am and go back to his models and actresses."

"Is that what you're worried about?" Cher leaned in to look at Kat, her hand resting on Kat's back.

"Come on, you know West, it's a legitimate fear."

Cher contemplated her words. "Perhaps. But have you actually told him this?"

Kat was quiet for a minute. "We all start with good intentions."

"And why can't you trust him to keep those good intentions? If it's truly love, he'll never notice another woman again."

The air left Kat's lungs. There was the question she kept asking herself. Why couldn't she trust him? "It's just who he is, Cher. A tiger can't just change their stripes."

"Maybe, but that tiger can be slightly domesticated with the right partner. Remember, you fell in love with that tiger, and if he loves you, you have to trust in that love. He didn't cheat on Gia; in fact, it's been a really long time since I've seen him with a different girl every week."

Kat scrunched up her face. "You're not allowed to make sense."

She stood up and walked to the bathroom, grabbing Kat's makeup. "I always thought there was a strange spark between the two of you, even before that night. I wasn't sure what it was exactly, but it took long enough for you both to figure it out."

Cher was annoying her with logic. They had something, she just wasn't sure if that something was worth risking her heart for.

"Now, you're gorgeous without makeup, but since he's seen a hot mess for the past few weeks, let's knock him off his feet," Cher said, a mischievous smirk on her face.

West eyed Declan and Luke over his whiskey glass. Since he and Kat had arrived at the hotel that morning, it had been one thing after another, but now he was finally properly showered, shaved, and in his own clothes having a drink with his friends. Even if the term friends didn't really feel appropriate these days.

The two were talking about a party they had attended at an Indonesian billionaire's home. It had been "epic," and they bored West to death. His mind kept shifting to Kat. What was she doing? Was she showering? She was probably naked. He wanted to be in the shower with her.

Snap out of it, West.

He shook his head, adjusting himself and crossing his legs, forcing himself to listen to Luke.

"Gia's here."

His head snapped up to glare at Luke. "What's she doing here?"

Luke took a drink slowly, while West tried to school his features. He didn't care about Gia, he just didn't want her coming around him and Kat. She was good at making trouble.

"She's here with me. I told her you were missing and we were staying in Jakarta, but I asked if she wanted to stay with me, as two people who deeply care about you."

West rolled his eyes. "How thoughtful of you."

Luke laughed. "Let's say we've found ways to pass the nights in your absence. Why didn't you tell me she was so feisty?"

West didn't care that Luke was screwing Gia, but he couldn't figure out what Luke was trying to do. They were friends, so why was he trying to goad him into caring?

West smiled. "That's great, I'm happy for you, man."

Declan choked back a laugh as Luke's face fell.

What the hell was going on? They were acting strangely, but for the life of him, he couldn't figure out why.

"You call your studio agent yet?" Declan asked, changing the subject.

"Yeah," West replied.

Declan waited for him to elaborate; West didn't. He didn't want to. These two were acting weird. "Did you take the acting gig?" Declan finally asked.

West let out a long breath. He didn't want to tell them first. There would have been a time, probably even ten days ago, where they would have been the first to know, but now he felt like he owed Kat that answer first. But as two pairs of expectant eyes glared at him, he nodded, and they both smiled at him, clearly happy with his decision.

West wasn't so sure he had made the right one if these two were so on board. He tilted back the rest of his drink. He had talked to his accountant that afternoon, and after the tour, the trips, and all their expenses, his accounts weren't looking so good.

West had been right about his music streams going up thanks to his disappearance, but until he figured out where his money was disappearing to, he needed a large payday, and Onslaught Pictures was offering a lot of zeros to do two pictures, provided the first one did well at the box office.

Kat's disappointed face flashed through his mind, but he pushed it aside. He had to do something, and she just didn't understand this part of his life. This was the one time where the fact that they came from two different worlds played a role in their relationship. It would take time for her to understand that acting was a sacrifice for him, not the easy way out.

He looked over at Declan and Luke, sipping on their drinks, and was ready to leave them and get back to Kat. If he had learned anything after his time on the island, it was that he was done with shallow conversations and pointless parties.

"I have dinner with my dad and a press event later tonight. I'll see you guys later," West said.

"I'm flying back to L.A. tomorrow with Gia since you're safe," Luke said.

West left the bar realizing his longest friendship had completely changed forever, and he wasn't sure how he felt about it.

Seventeen

Why did he agree to dinner with his father and Kat's mother? He just wanted to be alone with Kat. He completely understood that Mrs. Brooks would want to be with her daughter, but he wanted to be with her more. He needed to tell her how he felt about her before they went back to L.A. in the morning. After everything they had been through together, he knew he would never find anyone who understood him as she did, and he wanted to be with her, preferably forever, in whatever capacity she wanted. He was thinking about marrying the woman. An idea that had previously felt so dated and old-fashioned now sounded like the perfect life if it was with Kat.

He sipped his whiskey and watched his father shamelessly flirt with Mrs. Brooks over the rim of his glass. He could tell they had spent a lot of time together over the past few weeks, and their conversation flowed easily. It didn't really bother him;

he was used to seeing his father flirt and tease women, although they were usually much younger than Mrs. Brooks. He must have said something funny, as she laughed, her eyes crinkling the same way her daughter's did, and West ached to see Kat. It had only been a few hours, and already he was missing her.

"Where is Katy?" Mrs. Brooks voiced his thoughts, as she looked around the hotel restaurant.

"I'm sure she'll be down momentarily," his father said, patting her hand reassuringly. West's eyes narrowed in on that small touch, wondering if the two had been up to anything else these past few weeks. He wouldn't put it past his father to take advantage of Mrs. Brooks.

Kat's mom turned to West and smiled. "I hear you're going to be in a movie?"

West almost choked on his drink. He didn't want to talk about this in front of his father, who had somehow found out—from Declan most likely. "I'm still considering my options," was all he could reply.

His dad scoffed. "Like some prancing pony."

"That's not very kind, Tommy," she admonished, and if West's eyes could have fallen out of his sockets they would have. To West she said, "You can call me Doris. I think after everything you and my daughter have been through there is no need for formalities."

"Uh . . . I haven't signed any deal yet, ma'am." West nodded, still stunned she had said anything to his father, and also not wanting his father to know what he'd actually decided.

"Well, whatever you decide to do, just make sure it's what you're truly passionate about. Everyone always gave me such grief for letting Katy go to UCLA for music, but I believed in letting her choose her own path. I told all my kids, whatever you do, you do it well."

She gave a pointed look at his father, who looked chagrined, and for a moment West wondered if this is what his life would have been like if he'd had a mother to keep his father in check.

His father cleared his throat, piercing West with his eyes. "She's right, of course. I'm sure if you put your mind to it, you'll be rather good."

West gazed longingly at the door and debated the merits of running away. Was he in the twilight zone? His father had just said something sort of nice to him. He brought the glass of whiskey to his lips and downed the rest of it, unsure what to say to a comment like that. Thankfully, he was saved.

"Oh! Here she is," Doris exclaimed, seeing Kat at the door.

She had been beautiful on the island, full of strength and courage. Her clothes had been torn apart, her body stitched up, covered in dirt, hair a mess, and he hadn't cared. To him, she was a warrior queen.

Now she stood before him in the doorway, and it wasn't the dress that hugged her curves in all the right ways, the makeup that perfectly accentuated her features, or her hair that flowed down her back that drew his attention. It was the confidence that flowed from her in waves that drew West to her. Without thinking, he rose from his chair and walked toward her, offering his arm.

She looked down at it and smiled, slipping her arm into his. He walked her across the restaurant and held out her chair. Sure, these were all antiquated male rituals, but after days on an island, she deserved a little pampering.

"You look beautiful, Katy," her mother said. "Even if that dress is a bit tight."

"Thanks, I guess," she said, dipping her head behind the menu. West saw firsthand how a compliment from her came with a backhanded comment. It seemed she hadn't changed much in the absence of her daughter. And yet, Doris Brooks had greatly affected his father. He was being nicer to West, and seemed more relaxed.

"Oh, I see you have your grandmother's bracelet on," her mother said.

Kat lifted her wrist, and West noticed the gold band with a turquoise pendant in the middle. "Your grandmother asked if you had it. Were you wearing it?" her mother continued.

"Not when we fell overboard."

"Hmmm, maybe your grandmother is right."

Kat ducked her head, avoiding her mother.

"And why is that?" his father asked.

"That belonged to my mother," Doris explained. "In many Native tribes, we believe turquoise protects us from evil. Unless you were Navajo or Hopi, turquoise is scarce and a precious stone. Some say if there is a crack in your stone, it has already

protected you from evil, but of course, that's just the old stories."

Her mom gave a slight laugh, and West saw what Kat meant
about her being uncomfortable with her Indigenous heritage.

His father looked at Doris but spoke to Kat. "Yes, Katrina, it
appears you should have been wearing such an amazing family
heirloom."

Kat swallowed, and West gazed at the long column of her
neck, wishing he could scrape his teeth up it. He needed her.
After last night, all he could think about was her body against
his. Her lush hips in the palm of his hands. He needed this
dinner to be over now.

⊷◈⊶

After the backhanded comments from her mother, Kat quickly
realized nothing had changed, and yet, her mom seemed calmer.
Less overtly critical, and more subtle. A slow change, but a
change nonetheless.

Kat stole glances at West, her mouth going dry just at the
sight of him. He wore a perfectly tailored gray suit with a white
shirt. He didn't wear a tie and had two buttons undone. She
had seen his chest plenty, but something about the V of the
dress shirt and the chain he wore around his neck made his chest
that much more alluring. His jacket fit him perfectly, and Kat
couldn't think of anything else other than sliding it down his
lean and sculpted torso. She was sitting right across from her

mother, and her mind kept wandering to stripping the man next to her naked. What was wrong with her?

Dinner went rather amicably. She was surprised by how easily her mother and West's father talked, and they carried most of the conversation. She never imagined in a million years her mother having anything in common with an eighties rock star, and yet the two laughed and joked as if they were old friends. Kat locked eyes with West and inclined her head toward their parents in question. He shrugged, just as confused about their relationship as she was. Then he gave her a dazzling smile. Not the fake one he gave fans after a long night of playing, but one that reached his eyes. It left Kat breathless. She was never going to be accustomed to how he took over her senses.

It was more than his looks though: his kind words, caring disposition, and the way he made her feel like she really was capable of anything meant far more to her, and she couldn't fathom walking away.

She glanced across the table, and Tommy Monroe raised an eyebrow in question at her. He had caught her staring at his son. What did he think of her? Of them? Did he know there was something between them?

He was a good-looking older man, and she saw so much of West in him. If this was how West would age, the world was certainly in trouble because he did not look like he was in his sixties. No wonder her mother was enamored. After being stuck with a blue-collar man like her father for over thirty-five years, having a man like Tommy Monroe give her any kind of attention was probably rather enthralling.

Same, Mother.

Kat held back a sigh as her mother talked animatedly with Tommy. They had finished eating, and she was ready to leave. Sensing her urge to get up, West cleared his throat.

"It's been fun," he said in his sardonic laid-back tone, "but I think Kat and I are going to hit up the outdoor bar if that's okay with you?" He smiled his most charming smile—the one she had seen him use on fans, but oddly enough, never on her. It did nothing for her, but her mother practically tittered out of her seat.

"Oh yes, of course. You two have fun." Her mother gave her a pointed look, and for the first time, Kat realized her mother saw her as a woman and not a little girl.

"Yes, Mother." She rolled her eyes, her mother so obviously trying to marry her off.

Before Kat could stand, West appeared by her side, holding out his hand to help her. As they walked away, his hand moved to her lower back, touching her possessively. She tried not to shiver, but his touch had such an effect on her. They walked out of the restaurant and out toward the bar.

"That wasn't so bad," he said.

"No, I guess not. What's with our parents? Did you get, like, a flirty vibe from them?"

West snickered. "What? Worried our parents are hooking up?"

"Ew . . ." She pushed away from him. "I cannot in good conscience be screwing you if my mother is with your father."

He pulled her back into his arms. "I know it's weird, but not even that would keep me away from you." He crushed his lips to hers with hungry desperation, like tasting the first rains of spring after an endless drought. Her pulse skyrocketed as he pushed her up against the hallway wall, and she felt his body heat radiating off him. His hands roamed up her skirt, eliciting a gasp that had him gripping her even tighter.

"Let's go to my room. I have an hour before I have to leave for this press event," he said between kisses.

"Do I need to go?" she asked, pulling away slightly. They had to stop before he had her naked in the hotel hallway.

"No, I don't want you to be forced to deal with them. I want to protect you. We'll work up a plan for the press when we get back to the states. This is just the first of many, I'm sure."

"Oh, okay," Kat said, unsure how she felt about being left out of the conversation. She had been stuck on the island too, and something felt wrong about not being there.

"What's wrong?" he asked, always able to read her face no matter how hard she tried to hide it.

"Nothing," Kat said, giving him her biggest smile, and pressed her lips to his to distract him. "Come on, we have an hour." She smiled.

West grabbed her hand, pulling her away from the wall with a grin on his face, kissing and touching her all the way down the hallway to his suite until Kat was panting with need.

He pushed her up against the door with passionate force. His teeth ground against hers and their tongues clashed. She clawed at the lapels of his jacket and pulled him closer still until her knee dug into his rock-hard arousal.

Kat was beyond caring about propriety, consumed by a single desire for all of him—one last time—to give herself to this captivating man who made her feel special and precious and talented like nobody else ever had.

West fumbled with the key to unlock the door, his mouth never leaving hers. Her hands moved to his shirt, tugging at it with heated desperation. She wanted him inside her, the fire of desire he had sparked raging within her. He broke their kiss as she popped each of his buttons free, exploring his toned body with her lips.

"What are you doing to me? I can't get enough of you," he groaned.

Kat vaguely heard the beep on the lock as West captured her mouth again, pushing her across the threshold. Kat was in a reckless frenzy as she undid his belt buckle and felt his hands pull her zipper down her spine. Her breaths were quick and shallow, and all thoughts of romantic seduction were gone as an instinctive need overwhelmed her.

In the distance she heard someone clear their throat, and they both jumped apart faster than she would have thought humanly possible, her dress gaping in the front. They turned to stare at the owner of that offending noise.

Kat's heart plummeted into her stomach, and for a moment she thought her dinner was about to come back up.

West looked at the intruder, his eyes murderous, his hands in fists.

"Christ, Gia, what are you doing here?"

Kat looked between Gia and West and saw what a beautiful couple they made. Gia was so tall and lithe, her blonde hair flowing down her shoulders. Kat's worst fears were already coming true. Without a word, she turned and fled from the room.

Eighteen

West felt helpless as Kat ran from the room. Every inch of him wanted to go after her, but he had to deal with the woman who had managed to break into his room first.

He stalked over to the bar, splashing whiskey into a glass, taking a drink, and glaring at her the entire time. Gia was tall and skinny with glowing skin and long blonde hair, although West knew most of it was made up of extensions. As he looked at her, he thought about how much of her was fake, how she had been pushed to reach certain beauty standards, and now that he looked at her, he didn't find her attractive in the least. Sure, she was still beautiful, but her allure no longer called to him.

Instead he ached for the natural beauty of Kat. Her height fit perfectly in his arms, and her curves hit his hands just right. Her hair, frizzy after days of running around on an island, was just as gorgeous smoothed out, and even more bewitching in braids.

"I ask again, Gia, what are you doing here?"

She walked up to him, her hand slowly moving down his exposed chest. "I was worried about you, of course," she practically purred.

West removed her hand from his body, completely unmoved by her touch. "Well, as you can see, I am fine and you can leave. I don't even know how you got in my room."

She bit her lip coyly. "You'd be amazed what you can get a valet to do for you."

"I'm not surprised," he said dryly. "You were always good at getting what you wanted."

She practically jumped on him, and he took a step back, almost falling onto the bed. "Then why won't you come back to me?" she pouted, her arms circled around his neck.

"Aren't you here with Luke?"

"He's not like you; he doesn't take care of me the way you did. He's not nearly as attentive."

West took her hands from his neck, turning away from the bed, and walked toward the door. "Gia, you're just not what I want. I told you that a month ago and it still stands true."

Her look instantly turned cold, the sexy, coy Gia gone. "Oh, but you want that fat girl?"

She was talking about Kat. He couldn't be bothered to argue that, while Kat wasn't fat, it wouldn't have mattered if she was.

"She won't give you what you want, and you'll get bored eventually. But don't come crawling back to me when you do."

As she neared him, he stepped back. "Get out, Gia, we were done long before Kat, and I want you to stay away from both of us."

She threw her head back and laughed, but not in a way that suggested she found anything funny.

"Kat? God, West, you really will sleep with anything. That was your little backing singer you went missing with? Oh West, that won't last. You'll get bored sweetie; she won't know the first thing about making you happy. She's going to want marriage and kids, and a house in the suburbs. What, are you going to drive your kids to soccer? You don't do those things. You do models and parties. If she really knew who you were she wouldn't want anything to do with you."

Gia patted his cheek as she walked out of his room, and his life, hopefully forever. West thought about what she said. She was wrong. Wasn't she?

He could be all those things Kat wanted; he could be a regular guy and raise a family if that was what they decided to do.

Gia didn't know the first thing about making him happy, but with Kat, he had laughed, felt free, and could tell her about his worries and doubts. She hadn't judged him but had pushed him to think about his future. He had to fix this; she had to believe he hadn't wanted Gia to show up like that.

The thing about clocks is the longer you watch them the slower they move, and tonight Kat felt as if time had stopped entirely. Sick of staring at the clock, she drifted across the carpet to her balcony, like a ghost in the night air. Opening the sliding door, she planted herself on the edge of the patio chair and watched as the city bustled below her, like an endlessly running river, while time stood still.

She kept sneaking glances back at the clock. Thirty minutes had passed since she'd fled from his room. He wasn't coming to get her, that was apparent. He had probably seen his ex and been like, *forget Kat, she's plain, fat, and old. I need to get back with Gia*. A tear slid down her face, and she wiped it away, refusing to let herself be maudlin over something she knew would never happen. Another treacherous tear dripped from her eye, followed by another.

How many times would she cry over this guy? It was ridiculous. She had never cried over a man, and here she was doing it twice in one day. It's not even like she knew how he felt about her. She realized all too late that she loved him, but he had never professed any kind of feeling for her other than lust, and maybe slightly caring if she died on the island.

She turned back to the clock, her only source of time since she didn't have a replacement phone yet.

Forty-five minutes.

He wasn't coming; she was sure of it now. He had to go to the press event.

Kat needed to stop reading romance novels, obviously. She dropped her head in her hands and sang to herself.

Not one of his songs, or even her own, but the tune of "Killing Me Softly" sprang to her mind. That was how she felt, that he was killing her. Music always had a way of distracting her from what bothered her—it was an escape from reality—but more than that it also connected her to her emotions, to her thoughts and needs, and right now it connected with her breaking heart.

She wished she had a new phone and her headphones, because she had the perfect broken-heart playlist to pass the time. She stood up and glanced over the balcony, watching the cars pass below, the lights of the city shining around her. This feeling was exactly why she didn't take risks because every time she put herself out there and was rejected it hurt like hell.

A knock at the door made her turn. Maybe it was him, but he was supposed to be at the press conference. She walked over and peered through the peephole. West stood outside holding a large stack of books in his arms.

She opened the door, saying nothing. His eyes were full of emotion as he wiped away a single tear from her cheek with his free hand. Stepping inside, the door closed behind him with a soft snick as he gently said, "I'm so sorry, sweetheart. It took longer than I thought to get these at this time of night."

He handed her the books, and Kat read through the titles, "*Birds in Song*; *My Hair, My Power*; *Fry Bread with Auntie*

Gwen; *We Are Grateful*." She looked up at him. "West, what is this?"

He stepped back and Kat thought he looked nervous, but that was impossible because West was never nervous.

"You said on the island you had a book that influenced you to play the flute that wasn't even written by someone Native." He nodded toward the stack in her arms. "These are. They're you."

Another tear slid down her cheek, but this time from joy. Her heart had never felt so full in her life. It was the most kind, thoughtful gift anyone had ever given her.

"Do you like them?" His eyes begged her to say yes, and how could she not?

"Of course I do. These are amazing. I don't even know how you found them."

He stepped closer, his hand brushing along her arm, and her body shivered. "I saw a bookstore on the way back from my police interview. I stopped in and asked them to gather what they could find. They weren't thrilled with me when I was back demanding them tonight."

Kat smiled as she flipped through the pages and saw a picture of a little girl having her hair brushed by her mother. The memory of her mother doing the same thing when she was young came back to her. Kat hadn't had a haircut until she was eight, despite nagging her mother. She'd wanted a cute cut with bangs just like all the other girls in her midwestern predominantly White school. But her grandmother had explained that Kat's hair held her memories, dreams, and aspirations. Cutting it could represent the ending of one chapter and the beginning of another. Kat hadn't really cared back then; she'd just wanted to fit in. She chopped it all off and then cried for a week.

West reached for the stack, pulling one out. "This one is my favorite. It reminds me the most of you."

The beautiful images of Native women and girls set against fantastical landscapes held her in awe. West flipped to one of the pages. "All the books reminded me of you in one way or another, but this one especially made me think of your connection with nature on the island. How that connection saved my life. How I will never again take that connection for granted."

Kat read the line from the page West had turned to. "Remember you are one with the earth, one with the animals, and one with the spirit. They connect to you as you to them. Feel their power."

Kat took a deep breath. "It's beautiful. Thank you so much, West. I've never owned books that represent me."

Instantly, he had her wrapped in his strong arms. "I'm so sorry. I was going to wait to give them to you, but now seemed the best time. I didn't know Gia would be there. I sent her away. I promise." He kissed her head and face between apologies.

She reluctantly pulled herself away just enough for their bodies to no longer touch and moved the book to the desk. He searched her face for an answer and continued talking. "Gia means nothing to me. She talked a valet into letting her in. I told her we're through . . ."

Kat could feel his sincerity wash over her; his gaze was so intense it burned through her. She backed away from him. She couldn't think straight so close to him, especially after such a thoughtful gift.

But she found her resolve. "That's just it. If it's not Gia, it's going to be some other woman, and I just can't stack up to them. I know I can't."

He took a step toward her, but she backed away and he stopped his advance. "Kat . . ." Her name on his lips was like a prayer. "Is that what's been bothering you?"

She bit her lip, holding back the tears. He looked so lost, so hurt. How could he not realize that he would eventually break her heart?

"We're off the island now. Penny for your thoughts?" he whispered. His hand flexed at his sides. "Don't hide from me."

Could she open up to him? She owed him at least a piece of herself.

"Just look at you." She waved her hand up and down his body. "You're like a Greek god. You're Weston fucking Monroe, and I'm just . . . me. The girl you left in that hallway." She gave a self-deprecating laugh. "I can't spend the rest of my life comparing myself to every gorgeous woman who comes near you. I'll never measure up."

He took a step closer to her, his hand finding hers. His touch sent shivers through her body. "And why would you? In my eyes, none of them will ever measure up to you."

Her breath hitched as he raised her fingers to his lips and kissed each one. "You don't mean that, West, you'll change your mind." He was standing over her, his fiery gaze burned into her soul, and her skin prickled in anticipation.

"Katrina Nicole Brooks," he whispered, his lips inches from hers. "Tonight I'm going to show you over and over again how much I desire you and only you, because you are the most gorgeous, selfless, resilient woman I have ever known."

Before she could respond, he claimed her mouth with a passionate kiss, making her feel weak in the knees and desperate for more. His hands drifted over her body, exploring every curve and valley as if they had all the time in the world.

Kat couldn't even protest, her arms wrapped around his neck, her fingers digging into his hair. He groaned into her mouth, and she moaned as his hands moved down her back to the zipper. The sound of it slowly being undone left her panting, and she felt the heat of his hand against each inch of skin he revealed. As he removed one shoulder strap, his lips trailed kisses down her neck to her shoulder, where he nibbled at the sensitive area. The other strap soon followed, and her dress slithered down her body until it was a pool at her feet.

West stepped back, his eyes hungrily devouring her exposed body. His voice rumbled, low and controlled. "Are you telling me that all night long you haven't been wearing panties?" Her body shivered in response.

Kat fought the urge to shield her body from his scorching gaze, but before she could act, he seized her wrists, desire pulsing through his eyes.

"I didn't have any that worked with my dress," she said.

A moan of pleasure broke through West's lips as he gripped her ass cheeks firmly. "God . . . if I'd known earlier I would've taken you out in the middle of dinner, bent you over a table, and fucked you right there on the restaurant balcony."

Her whole body sang just thinking about his dirty words. The music, which had been silent for so long, was now a passionate symphony pulsing through her. Instead of letting her step out of her dress, he cradled her frame in his muscular arms and lifted her effortlessly from the ground. His lips caressed hers as he walked them both to the bed. He went to lay her down.

"Wait."

He blinked twice, coming out of a haze.

She stood at the edge of the bed, her eyes burning with passion as she whispered, "I've been wanting to take this off you all night." Her hands moved inside his jacket, her fingertips grazing against the soft fabric of his dress shirt. With one smooth movement, she moved her hands up his chest, under the jacket, and slipped it down his arms letting it tumble to the floor behind him. His shirt still hung untucked from earlier, but it was buttoned again.

He locked eyes with her, and she was overcome with longing. There was an unmistakable look of pure desire on his face, making her feel more beautiful and sensual than ever.

Her hands trembled as she undid each of his buttons, ago-
nizingly slow. Her retribution for all the times he'd played with
her. When the last button released its grip, she moved her hands
up his bare chest, his warmth washing over her and making her
feel intoxicated. With one motion, she pushed his shirt off his
strong shoulders. A gasp of excitement escaped her as she felt
each powerful muscle twitch under her fingertips. He was hers
tonight. There were plenty of women who would love to be in
her position, and yet tonight he chose her.

He grabbed her with an urgency that made her gasp, and she
felt his hardness pressing against her as she allowed him to lift
her in the air. His hands moved from her back, unhooking her
strapless bra and letting it fall to the floor. Her bare breasts fell
into his hands, and he pressed them together, soaking up their
warmth with his hands. He growled. "I'm going to ravage you so
hard tonight, Kat. I'm going to make you scream out my name
until the sun rises, when you'll be begging me to take you even
harder."

Her eyes widened. "What about the press event?"

His eyes flashed as he lifted her off her feet, laying her on the
bed. "I moved it to the morning."

She laughed as he began his descent down her body, worshipping every inch of her skin with his mouth. "Did you really?"

"Of course. I'm Weston Monroe—I do what I want." His
eyes sparkled as he moved to her chest.

His tongue circled each breast before blowing a hot gust of
air across her dusky nipple, driving her wild.

"West," she cried, begging him for more.

He rewarded her with his mouth, devouring the distended peak as she screamed in pleasure and her body jolted with uncontrollable spasms. His other hand coiled tightly around her other breast, squeezing harshly until delicious pleasure shot to her core. His knee wedged forcefully between her legs, and she pressed down onto it desperately searching for an elusive release.

"Uh-uh, not yet," he murmured darkly as he moved his leg away. Kat whimpered in frustration. West seemed to be savoring every moment of torturing her, delighting wickedly in her discomfort.

His hands wandered hungrily over her body, exploring every inch of her with a desperate yearning. His mouth left trails of fire everywhere he kissed and licked and nipped. Slowly, he dragged his tongue down her leg and back up her thigh, pausing just shy of her pussy before starting again on the other leg.

Finally, he pressed one finger inside her, and a gasp of pleasure escaped her. She marveled at how good even one finger could feel after all the tantalizing torture he had subjected her to.

A second finger joined the first, and he switched his attention to one of her breasts while still working both fingers in and out of her slick heat. She felt herself tensing like an instrument that was strung too tightly, ready to break if played. Then his mouth moved to tease at her throbbing clit with hungry laps of his tongue—and the string snapped. Uncontrollable waves of pleasure tore through her as she screamed his name in an ecstatic litany, riding out wave after wave of bliss until there was nothing left but contented exhaustion.

As her soul reentered her body, she felt West kiss his way back up. She grabbed at his belt buckle.

"Why do you still have these on?"

"I was too busy trying to get you naked."

"Off," she commanded.

He slipped off his belt and pants. In the soft light of the room, inch by tantalizing inch of tanned skin was revealed to Kat, a feast for her eyes. Her thirst grew as her heart raced faster and faster.

West grinned, aware of the effect he had on her. "Like what you see?" he teased breathlessly.

"You have no idea," she said in a voice barely above a whisper.

He settled next to her body with ease, their skin slick with sweat and desire. "The feeling's mutual, gorgeous." His eyes burned into hers with need.

And somehow, she believed him. He made her feel gorgeous, and the expression in his eyes said it all.

His fingers plunged deep inside her again, finding places she hadn't known existed and eliciting cries of delight that he lapped up. He brought those same fingers to his lips and let out a low moan as he tasted her. "You're so damn sweet," he murmured against her skin. "I could have lived off of you on that island."

He positioned himself at her entrance, and before she could blink he had thrust himself in all the way. She gasped from both shock and pleasure as he moved in and out of her.

West felt her muscles tighten around his cock in slow, devastating pulls. He threw his head back as he pumped into her, never wanting to leave the pure perfection that was her pussy. "Kat! I . . . Oh god, it's too much!" West had wanted to go slow but while he had been teasing her, he had also been torturing himself. Every inch of glistening golden skin he touched, kissed, and licked sent shockwaves of desire that surged through him until he thought he would burst.

That's what she did to him, she made him desperate to be with her.

She writhed beneath him, desperate for more. He hooked his leg under hers and flipped them over so she was on top. He wanted to see her take her pleasure. "Ride me, Kat. Take what you need."

She gazed down into his eyes, pleasure radiating from her face. He moved powerfully beneath her as she rode him, her passion increasing with each thrust.

She threw her head back, lost in ecstasy as each thrust elicited moans of sheer pleasure from deep within her throat, working the pressure until his name escaped her lips, and sending them both to the brink of surrender.

"Take it, Kat. Take all of me," he commanded while pressing his thumb firmly to her clit. He reveled in the sight of her body as it undulated and twisted in fervid desire, a vision that was only for him to consume and savor. Her curves were luscious and inviting, her ass round and full, her breasts heavy with temptation—all just for him to enjoy and never let go.

As she collapsed onto his chest, their skin met in a symphony of senses as wave after wave of pleasure rolled through her when she came.

"You haven't finished yet, Kat."

She groaned in response, her body unable to deny his power over her.

"Yes, you can," he said more forcefully as he pulled her off the edge of the bed, parted her legs, and positioned himself behind her.

He entered her, pushing himself deep as she writhed in ecstasy calling out his name. Every pump of his hips sent jolts of electricity between them as their bodies slammed together in a passionate harmony that filled the room. He grunted out her name each time his hips sunk deeper and faster.

"Say you're mine," he called out as he pounded into her, never to have once claimed a woman in his life, but this time he meant it. He wouldn't let another man ever touch her again if he could help it.

She moaned and he pushed harder. "Say it."

"I'm yours," she said breathlessly as he seemed to come undone, pumping harder and faster.

His hand found its way between her legs and pushed against the bundle of nerves that held all her pleasure, coaxing out one more orgasm as she shook with the force of it. With one final thrust, he felt his own pleasure erupt within him, the intensity of it beyond anything he had felt before as he spilled into her depths, claiming her for himself.

Kat's body went limp in his arms, and he scooped her up carefully, laying her head on the pillows of the bed. Then he took a towel from the bathroom and gently wiped away the sticky traces of their lovemaking from her thighs.

He climbed into bed beside her, wrapping his entire body around hers as he kissed her tenderly. "Sleep with me tonight?" he whispered against her lips.

She gave a soft laugh in response. "We've slept together every night for days."

"You know what I meant. Now you actually have a choice."

She nodded. "Tonight."

He didn't know what that meant, but they would deal with it in the morning. He let go of her for a second to turn the light off and pulled her back into his arms, letting the feel of her body relax him to sleep.

Nineteen

Kat woke up to strong arms crushing her to an equally strong body. Laying still, she listened to West's even breathing and took it all in. He hadn't admitted that he loved her or anything last night, but he had said a lot. He said she was enough, and for Kat that meant more to her than she could ever express to him. After everything they had been through on the island, Kat really did feel like she was enough for him. That she was stronger than she gave herself credit for.

Deep within her battered, pessimistic soul, she knew he meant it, and she smiled, turning to nuzzle into him. Kat had never thought she could be this happy. She had no clue what their future held when they got back to the States, but something told her West wasn't going to just disappear.

The sheets rustled as West stirred, his eyes slowly opening. Kat smiled and, without thinking, planted a kiss on his lips.

"What was that for?" he said groggily. His voice was always so deep in the morning. It left Kat ready and wanting after just one syllable.

"Just 'cause. You look so cute in your sleep."

West wrinkled his nose. "I'm not sure cute is how I'd like to be described."

"What? You prefer devastatingly handsome?" she joked as his fingers began to massage her scalp.

Sensation sizzled through her nervous system at his touch, and she wished this moment would never end. His mouth covered hers, and she lost herself in the feel of him.

His hands roamed down her body and Kat sighed.

West broke the kiss and sat up, the sheets slipping to around his waist, and Kat shook herself.

She was not dreaming, he was hers, he *wanted* her, and most importantly she believed he was just as lucky to have her. West had done that; he had helped her see that she was strong and worthy of love, even if he hadn't said the words yet. She had survived more than most people would ever experience in a lifetime. She had saved West's life and her own, and deep within she knew even though she may have no direction career-wise, she knew she could do something with her musical ability. The more she thought about it, the more she wasn't even sure she wanted to be a solo musician.

"Where are you going?" she asked, linking her arms around his waist playfully.

He checked the time and groaned. "That stupid press conference. I need to run to my room and shower before I go."

"Want a shower buddy?" she said, laughing.

"Absolutely! But if I let you shower with me I'll be late for sure, and then Stacy will kill me." He stroked her hair, kissing her on the forehead.

"You sure you don't want me to come to that?" she asked, still feeling a little like he wanted to hide her away.

"No, you don't want to deal with them. I wouldn't subject my worst enemy to that."

He was trying to protect her and her identity for as long as he could, she understood that, but still the feeling of being cast into the shadows made her uneasy. It was just one reason she was unhappy with the idea of him acting. He would always be out at red-carpet events and press conferences, and she would be left sitting at home twiddling her thumbs waiting for him to come back to her. No one would know she even existed, or that they were together. She understood privacy for celebrities, but she also didn't want the world thinking he was embarrassed to be with her. And as much as she shouldn't care about what others thought, she had a hard time shaking away those feelings.

"Let's meet for lunch. I want to ask you something." He rose from the bed, pulling his suit on from the night before.

Kat stared in awe, amazed at how he was just as hot putting on clothes as he was taking them off.

She nodded, her voice suddenly missing. She'd spent over a week lost with this man. Shouldn't she be immune to him by now?

"I'll take that as a yes?" He leaned down, giving her one last kiss before leaving.

"Ah . . . yeah . . . I'll be down in the main restaurant with my mom. You'll just have to find a way to get rid of her, seeing as how she's your number one fan now."

West bit back a smile as he opened the door. "I'll see you soon. Wish me luck."

"Like you need it."

"I need everything from you."

And with that, the door closed leaving Kat staring at the empty space, his words circling around in her head.

After her shower, Kat sat on her balcony sipping coffee, reading a book on her Kindle, and watching the traffic drive by. The book didn't keep her attention. Romance had been a terrible choice, but she wanted to get lost in something happy. Instead, she was left thinking about her own love life and all the possibilities ahead of her.

West talked a good game, that was for sure. It was entirely too late for her heart. He owned it, but she didn't know what to do.

What was he going to ask her?

She should have made him tell her before he left, but now she was left sitting on the balcony alone and dying to know what he wanted from her. Sick of reading about someone else's happily ever after, Kat put the book down and finished getting dressed.

West's press conference would start in an hour, and she was going to watch it with her mother. They were going to meet in one of the hotel restaurants, but since she had time to kill, she decided to go for a walk around the grounds of the hotel.

Stepping out of her room, the sunlight filtered through the hallway from the large picture windows. She breathed in the fresh air that flowed through the many openings. Kat loved how much of Indonesia just didn't have walls. Going back to the states was going to be a big shift.

She meandered aimlessly through the various outdoor gardens and hedgerows, taking in the scents and smells of the various plant life, all the while trying not to think about what she'd say to West during their lunch "talk." On one hand, she was glad he wanted to define what it was they were doing, but on the other, she wasn't ready to end it, even though that's what her sense of self-preservation screamed at her to do.

That is, if she had the strength to do it. One look from his gorgeous blue eyes, and she'd cave in an instant. Kat was finding she had no backbone when it came to West, and she hated herself for it. So much for feminism.

Following the path, she almost ran straight into a tall blonde woman. "Oh excuse—" She stopped talking as she looked up into the ice-cold eyes of West's ex, Gia.

Gia looked down her perfect nose as if Kat was nothing more than a speck in her way. "Oh, it's you," she drawled in her Italian accent.

Kat put her head down and stepped to the side, intending to walk around her, but Gia stepped into her path. Kat had never felt so small or insignificant in her life. Gia's skin glowed in the sunlight, and she had a bone structure painters could only dream of. Looking up at her physically hurt Kat's soul. Why West had chosen her over this goddess was still a mystery.

"He'll get bored with you." Gia was obviously just as confused by West's choices.

Kat forced herself to look Gia in the eye, tucking an errant strand of hair behind her ear. "I'm not going to fight you over a man, Gia," Kat started, with much more bravado than she felt.

"That's too bad. You know I would win."

Kat shrugged. "Maybe. And you're probably right, he will get bored with me, but at least I know when to quit the game." She gave Gia a scathing look and turned, walking in a different direction, forcing tears back. She didn't look back to see if her barb had landed or not.

Gia saw the writing on the wall just as clearly as she did. West would eventually realize that Kat didn't fit into his world. She was too plain and too boring for him.

She turned onto one of the outer paths by the nightclub. As she walked closer she saw Luke and Declan talking at one of the tables, both sipping on something. Probably whiskey, even if it was ten in the morning. Kat ducked behind the hedge, hoping they hadn't seen her. It wasn't that she didn't want to talk to them, but . . . no, it was exactly that she didn't want to talk to them. Socializing was not at the top of her list this morning, especially after her encounter with Gia.

As she went to turn around and head back the other way she heard Luke say, "I took care of it. He doesn't have a clue."

That was interesting. Kat's mind began running a mile a minute. Who was he talking about?

"You better have. He knows someone's been skimming funds. It's just a matter of time before he figures out it was us," Declan said.

"I told you, I took care of it." Luke looked around surreptitiously.

Kat held her breath, trying her hardest not to make a sound. Why was she not shocked that Declan had been skimming money from West's royalty checks? But that Luke was involved was surprising. Kat thought he was West's best friend.

Declan's voice rose slightly as he said, "So what did you do? Better not be over-the-top. I told you to keep it low-key."

Luke didn't answer.

"Luke, what did you do?

Luke groaned. "I told you I didn't want to do this. I hired a guy; he said he'd take care of it."

"Shit, you got someone else involved?" Declan cursed again as he kicked the barstool. "What's this asshole going to do?"

Luke looked away from Declan before muttering something under his breath that Kat couldn't hear.

"You're going to fucking blow him up?" Dec yelled. "That's the complete opposite of low-key."

Kat felt shock flow through her body as she put two and two together. Had he been on the deck? Had he been the one to trip West? Had West actually felt someone push him? And holy shit, were they about to blow him up now?

"Don't worry. He planted a device on his car. It will look like an accident."

Kat's stomach churned. She had to warn West.

Without waiting to hear what else they said, Kat took off running down the pathway. She didn't have a phone, and the quickest route to the lobby was through the courtyard Luke and Dec were in. She couldn't go that way. Panic set in as she debated her next move.

She had to get to him and tell him not to get in the town car they had sent for him if it wasn't too late already. The press conference would just be starting. She had to call Stacy. Who even had Stacy's number?

Declan.

Her mind reeled as she rounded the corner to the exit of the resort. Hoping her plan would work, she ran into the middle of the road and attempted to get a taxi.

Out on the road, a car whizzed past, causing her to jump back in alarm. "Wait! Stop!" She waved her arms in the air as she tried to flag down the taxi, but it wasn't like New York or Chicago. There weren't nearly as many taxis wanting to run her over. Kat ran up and down the street, her heart pounding until she finally chased down an empty cab.

"Do you have a phone?" she asked the cab driver as she threw herself in the backseat.

The driver looked at her, confused.

"Ah shit, you don't understand me do you?"

The man's eyes narrowed as he attempted to decipher her words.

Kat held her hand up to her ears like she was holding a phone. "Phone. I need your phone. Call the police."

"Ah!" The man reached into his pocket and held up his phone.

"Yes!" Kat reached for the phone as the man unlocked it and handed it to her.

"How do I call the police here?"

He blinked an inordinate number of times.

"Emergency. Police." Why the hell hadn't she learned basic Indonesian?

"*Ah, ya polisi,*" the driver responded.

"Yes!" Kat sighed, relief swamping her body.

"How do I call them?" she gestured with the phone at her ear.

The driver reached out, taking his phone back, and Kat hoped he knew what she wanted. He dialed 112 and handed the phone back to her.

Lifting the phone to her ear, a voice echoed through the earpiece. ". . .*keadaan darurat Anda?*"

"Oh, for fuck's sake . . . I need to learn more languages." She looked to the driver, staring at her expectantly and waiting for directions.

"Drive to the *Jakarta Globe*, and fast!"

The driver thought for a minute and then nodded. Kat prayed to the spirit he understood her.

She knew there were cops who spoke English. She had spoken with them the day before. Now she just needed to remember their names and convince the phone operator that someone was truly in trouble, and then somehow get a hold of Stacy in time.

Kat squashed the bile that rose in her throat as she thought of West blown to pieces. She couldn't spiral into despair, she had to save him. She only hoped she wasn't too late.

Twenty

W est hated these things, but they went with the territory, and after announcing his retirement, then falling off a yacht and washing up on a deserted island, the press was having a field day.

Stacy, his public relations agent, had flown in the moment he had called her. If anyone could help him spin this situation, it was her.

"You have created quite the frenzy, Monroe," Stacy said as she fiddled with his hair before he went out to talk with the press.

"I know, Stace. If it makes you feel better, it was unintention-al."

Stacy smiled at him in the mirror. "You know I never stay mad at you, but they're vultures out there today. Bobby from TMZ is pissed you canceled last night; he's not going to go easy on you."

West felt his face warm just thinking about the things he and Kat had done the night before. He had done plenty of depraved things in his life, but the feelings of last night had never been there. He cleared his throat, shaking the images of Kat's naked body out of his head. "I had something come up."

Stacy looked down at his lap. "Mmmm, I bet."

West grinned. She knew him all too well. She'd been his PR rep for almost twenty years. Stacy and her wife had always called him out, but he loved her realness; it had made their relationship easy. He really did need to dig into why he couldn't work with single straight women without wanting to fuck them. Maybe it had just been Kat all along he had needed to keep at arm's length.

"Where's the girl?" Stacy asked him.

"Kat? I don't want her involved. I told you that on the phone."

Stacy pursed her lips, holding back what she wanted to say, something she didn't do often.

"What?" he asked her.

"Nothing," Stacy said, going back to fussing with his hair.

West gave her a disbelieving look.

"It's just . . . did you ask her if she wanted to be left out of all this?"

West thought about it for a moment. He hadn't actually asked, but he knew she didn't want to be involved. She had said on multiple occasions that his life of fame would be difficult for her.

"I just know she wants to keep her name out of it as long as possible."

"So, you're just going to tell the press that you fell into the ocean, landed on a deserted island with some girl on your production crew, and nothing happened between you two—even though you've clearly fallen in love with her. Your face says it all."

West scowled at her. "I am not, and no, it doesn't."

"You are so over the moon, baby, and I am so happy for you, but just remember those predators out there are going to read you too. Then they'll eat you alive, so whatever your story, just make sure your face matches."

West wouldn't admit it aloud, but Stacy was right. He was in love with Kat, and he didn't know what to do about it. He wanted to tell her, but he wasn't sure if she was ready to hear it. Women had never rejected him before, other than his mother, who'd had no interest in his life. If Kat rejected him, he wasn't sure he could come back from that.

West nodded, standing to shake out his clothes. "I got this, Stace. You know the press loves me."

"They used to. Now they're pissed you announced your retirement through social media. No one got the exclusive and they've been banging down my and Declan's doors."

West gave her his best smile, but she was still frowning. "I'm sorry. I know you told me not to do it, but Declan said it was a better plan."

"And I told you to stop listening to that dimwit," Stacy snapped back. "Something's off with him, and if I were you I wouldn't trust him."

"You mean the cocaine?" West already knew all about Declan's cocaine addiction. It wasn't news to him, but his behavior had been more erratic lately.

Stacy sighed. "Just make sure all your ducks are in a row, West." She looked out at the press, who seemed to be getting anxious. "Now get out there before they tear this place apart."

———◦○◦———

Kat's knee bounced up and down in the back of the cab as she watched the buildings pass by.

"Could you go faster?" She leaned over between the front seats to get the driver's attention.

He didn't acknowledge her, and Kat sulked in her seat. "Of course you can't go faster. It's just the love of my life that's about to be blown to pieces. Even if I can't be with him, he can't be dead."

Her heart skipped a beat at her confession. Although it had only been to herself and a cabbie who didn't speak English, it was still monumental. She loved West, and she was too chickenshit to tell him.

A voice on the radio piqued her interest, making her sit up straight in her seat. "Can you turn that up?"

The cabbie just shrugged.

"Louder, please." She made the motion of turning a knob and pointed to the radio.

"*Ay*." The cabbie turned the volume knob.

"Yes! Thank you." Kat let out a relieved breath as she heard West's deep voice through the airwaves. They were broadcasting the press conference on the radio. He was still talking, which meant she had time to reach him.

" . . . so you won't tell us who the woman you were on the island with is?" one reporter asked.

"For her privacy, no, I will not be giving her identity at this time. All I'll say is she was just a member of my production team."

Kat ground her teeth. He didn't even say she was one of his musicians. In an instant, he had made her even more anonymous. He had removed himself from her even further.

"How did you get off the island?" another reporter asked.

"A group of fishermen from Sawu Island came by and saw us. They took us back there and helped us find our way to Jakarta," West replied.

They had agreed with the authorities to keep Cocaine Island out of the press for now. They needed time to search, and they wanted to keep it quiet in hopes the traffickers wouldn't leave and find a new island.

The press asked West a few more questions about how they'd survived. He at least gave her props for catching the fish, but not by name. She zoned out for a while, thinking about how she was just the nameless woman by his side, and how if she stayed with him that would always be her lot in life. That loving him wouldn't be enough for her. She couldn't just hang back anymore, riding his coattails.

"What's next for Weston Monroe?" the reporter asked." That got her attention.

"You know, I'm still kind of deciding," West said with what sounded like slight trepidation.

"That's not what your manager said," the same reporter replied.

Kat heard a barely perceptible curse from West under his breath and gave a slight laugh that the radio didn't even bleep it out. Then she went back to worrying about what the hell this reporter was talking about.

West took a breath. "I have accepted a two-picture deal with Onslaught Pictures."

The press room erupted, and Kat's mind swirled with questions as she ignored the rest of the press conference.

When had he done that? He hadn't told her. She believed he'd made the wrong decision, but he was unconcerned with her perception. He was set on acting, and she had no choice but to accept it. Kat realized her issues had nothing to do with the acting but was more about the fact that she worried she would never fit into that lifestyle. At least music she understood.

She was racing—well, racing was too generous a word—through Jakarta to save a man who didn't seem to care one iota about her. Even worse, he had told Declan, who had leaked it to the press. The fact that Declan knew before her just added insult to injury.

"Okay, that's enough questions." A woman's voice cut through the insanity of the pressroom. Kat heard a shuffling sound as they pushed chairs back, the press conference over. "If you have any more questions, you can reach out to me at Stacy Lark PR." The woman's voice came through crisp and clear. Kat knew who Stacy was and had seen her a few times on tour with them. She was authoritative, strong, and never put up with West's crap. Kat liked her a lot, even if she didn't really know her.

The feed cut off, and a disc jockey came on thinking it would be funny to play the latest Weston Monroe single. As the song played, Kat thought about how surreal it was to be hearing her own voice in a cab as she rushed through the streets of Jakarta. She really should never complain again about interesting things not happening to her. She was ready for some peace.

"How much farther?" She gestured, moving her arms in and out, trying to convey distance.

The cabbie held up his thumb and index finger close together, and Kat took that to mean not much farther.

She closed her eyes, focusing on her breath. She had to make it in time.

"That was a clusterfuck, Stace." West walked through the back hallway of the *Jakarta Globe* adjusting his suit coat. "How did Dec even get to them so quickly? I shouldn't have told him about taking the movie deal."

Stacy shook her head as she walked in stride with him.

West stopped, turning toward her. "I know. You said not to trust him, and I think you're right. You know, I've been having money issues."

That piqued Stacy's interest. "Really?"

"Yeah. Money's disappearing, and I know it's not me spending it, or I'm pretty sure it's not completely me. I'm beginning to wonder if Dec has anything to do with it."

Stacy brushed at an invisible piece of lint on her power suit. "I told you that man's a snake. I know he's made you, and me by proxy, a lot of money, but you know better than anyone that you can't have blind loyalty in this business."

West mulled over her words. Declan had always pushed him to give the audience what they wanted. Some people had called West a sellout, and there were plenty of times he'd felt like one. He had made a ton of money, toured the world, and had massive popularity, but had he really done it the way he wanted to? Declan had been the driving force behind everything, like West constantly touring, making albums, and always working. West hadn't minded much. He enjoyed staying busy. But now that he thought about it, Declan was the grand mastermind, so who better to pocket money from the top?

West resumed walking down the hallway, Stacy walking after him.

"Where are you going, West? What did I say?"

"I think you're right. I think Dec's up to something. I want to get back to the hotel and confront him."

"You sure that's a good idea?" Stacy caught up to him, her heels clicking down the hallway. "I'd wait until you're back in the States. Have your accountant find the paper trail."

West halted, and Stacy bumped into him. "Oof . . . are you coming or going, Monroe? Make a decision."

"You're right, I need to wait until I have hard evidence on him."

"You couldn't have figured that out while still walking?" she asked, rubbing her forehead. "Why are you like a solid wall?"

West smiled down at her, remembering another woman who got mad at him for running into her. Everything reminded him of Kat these days.

"Why are you looking at me like that?" Stacy's disgust was evident.

"Sorry, I was thinking of someone."

"Aww, your girl?"

"She's not my—"

Stacy waved him off and resumed walking. "Whatever you say, lover boy. Let's get you back to her."

West tried to hide the smile that crept across his face. He was only too happy to get back to the hotel and talk with Kat. He knew she was going to be mad at him for accepting the acting deal with Onslaught Pictures. Suddenly he felt like he had made a huge mistake. He should have waited until they were back in the States to make that decision. He should have talked with her, but he already knew her opinion on the matter.

It annoyed him that deep down she was right. He was scared to put himself back out there, start his own label, and go back to his stripped-down music. The music that he loved but had never been as popular. He was scared that he was past his prime and would never be as successful as he had been. Acting was a chance at something new, a chance to be on top again, but what if she was right? What if it was the easy way out?

He rounded the corner at the back of the building and saw his black town car waiting for him.

"You coming back to the hotel with me?"

Stacy crossed her arms over her chest. "I'd like nothing more, but your little duplicitous manager has created a mess for me to clean up. I've already received ten texts since walking out here, all wanting your acting exclusive."

West tried to look chagrined. "Sorry, Stace. I shouldn't have told him I'd made any decision."

Stacy leaned against the car as West opened the door. "No, and don't tell that guy shit from here on out."

West gave her a mock salute as he climbed in. "You're the boss."

Stacy laughed. "And don't you forget it!" she said, closing the door, much to the annoyance of the driver who had been standing by.

West leaned his head back on the plush, leather seat and let out a long exhale. How had his day devolved into this? Now he had to talk the woman he was falling in love with into believing that he was indeed falling in love with her, all while acting like his manager wasn't a lying piece of shit.

He needed a stiff drink.

———◆◇◆———

After a lot of hand gestures and pantomime, Kat convinced the cabbie to drive to the back of the building, where she knew they would drop West off and pick him up. There was always a special place for celebrities like him.

The cab rolled into the back with security yelling at him, and he started yelling back at security.

Kat let out a huge sigh of relief when she saw Stacy standing by the curb talking on her phone.

The cab came to a stop as security swarmed the car, yelling at the driver. She had no idea what they were saying, and she didn't care. Kat jumped out of the cab, but a security guard stopped her, pulling her back and yelling at her in Indonesian.

"No! Let me go!" Kat pulled on his arm to get free. She was not going to be this close and fail to save West.

"Stacy!"

Stacy looked up from her call, finally noticing the chaos going on around her.

"Tell them who I am," Kat pleaded as she struggled to get free from the men with very large automatic weapons.

Stacy walked over and flashed her press badge. "Let her go. She's with me."

The guard nodded and let go of Kat's already injured arms, which would have deep bruises on them come tomorrow.

"Thanks, Stacy. Where's West?" she asked breathlessly.

Stacy cocked her head to the side and looked Kat up and down. "He just left."

"No." Kat felt her legs faltering beneath her as she sank to the curb.

"This is a two-thousand-dollar pantsuit, or I'd join you down there, honey. He's headed back to you. What's wrong?"

Kat couldn't breathe. She tried to inhale, but nothing would come in. She felt her lungs shriveling up in her chest. This was what it felt like to die by asphyxiation. She couldn't get the words out. West was going to die. She couldn't say them.

"His car . . ." she spat out. "They . . . messed . . . with . . . his . . . car . . ."

Stacy stepped off the curb and squatted down, lifting Kat's head. "What are you talking about?"

That's when Kat noticed it in Stacy's hand. Her phone! A freaking phone. Kat had been so long without one, she forgot she could call West.

She pointed at Stacy's phone. "Call West!"

Without another word, Stacy dialed West and handed Kat the phone.

It rang two . . . three . . . four times and Kat panicked. He wasn't going to answer.

"What now, Stace?" His deep, calming voice rang through the earpiece, and Kat felt instantly calmer.

"West!"

"Kat? Is that . . . what are you doing with Stacy?"

"Just don't ask questions, okay? You need to get out of your car now."

"Huh? Why?"

"West, I said don't ask questions. Just do it! Get out!"

"I can't. We're just getting on the freeway . . ."

"West, now!"

Kat waited for a reply but didn't hear one. The phone crackled. "West? West? Oh my god, West!"

The phone cut off, and Kat had to stop herself from throwing someone else's phone across the *Jakarta Globe's* parking garage.

Before Kat could think of her next move, a loud boom echoed through the city block.

Twenty One

There was a loud ringing in his ears, then there was nothing but black. As West tried to open his eyes, his entire body protested in pain.

What the hell had happened?

He felt the hard cement beneath his hands as he tried to push himself up, and a firm hand pressed on his back, stopping him from moving.

"Don't move, sir," the voice said.

Every muscle and bone in his body ached, as he tried to clear the fuzziness form his brain. He had been on the phone with Kat; he remembered that. She had told him to get out of the car, which had seemed ridiculous, but something in her voice told him to listen.

He squeezed his eyes shut, willing the splitting pain in his head to go away.

Why won't this fucking ringing stop?

He forced one eye open, and then he saw the car. It was on its side, the front completely blown out. Two other cars had run into it, and their drivers looked to be okay standing next to their vehicles.

Then it all came flooding back to him.

He had yelled at the driver to get out, which had made the driver none too happy. West recalled promising to buy him a new car.

Then they'd both heard a pop from the front, and West knew that sound wasn't good. The driver said the brakes weren't working. West flung his door open, tucking and rolling out of the moving car. Luckily, it wasn't moving too fast in the midday traffic.

West had stood just in time to see the driver maneuver over to the passenger side, flinging himself out. As West had run up to check on him, the car hit a large truck and the entire front had blown up. The explosion had knocked him back, and now here he was lying on the pavement, barely able to string two thoughts together.

He groaned as two men, presumably EMS, rolled him slowly to his back. He heard the two speaking in Indonesian and had no idea what they were talking about. Most likely what to do with him. He would be fine in a minute. He just needed water and some Advil. Now if he could just convey that sentiment to these guys.

"No . . . let . . . me . . . through!" A voice pierced through the din of the ringing, and West felt his entire body come back to life.

She was here.

And then there were hands all over him. Her hands.

Kat was crying and practically lying on him, and he could feel her tears as they slid down his neck. "You're okay," she said between sobs. "Oh my god, I thought you were dead."

"Excuse me . . . miss?" one man said.

"No!" West heard her slap his hand away. "Just give me a minute."

West smiled at his feisty, adorable Kat, and slowly opened his eyes. "What? You worried about me, sweetheart?" His voice was scratchy and barely audible.

Another tear slipped down her cheek as her hand brushed a strand of hair out of his face. He nuzzled his face into her palm. "I'm just glad you listened to me."

West grunted as he tried to sit up. "Help me up."

"Uh, sir . . . that's not . . ." He said in surprisingly clear English.

West gave the EMS guy a look and pushed himself up to sitting with Kat's look of disapproval clear. "You need to be checked out by the doctor."

"I'll go in a minute. I need to know how you knew the car was rigged to blow up."

Kat sat back on her heels and held West's hand, looking down at where their fingers intertwined. "I'd rather not be the one to tell you." She huffed a strand of hair from her face, training her golden eyes on him. "What do you remember about the night you fell off the yacht?"

West's mind was cloudy, much like the night on the boat, and suddenly one piece came together in his mind from the night he went overboard. It had been dark, but he had seen a shadow. Something had moved behind him and he had turned, and that's when he remembered. The shadow, the outline of a face. A face he knew almost as well as his own.

It hadn't been Declan.

"It was Luke! He pushed me off the yacht."

Kat nodded as her hand moved up and down his arms.

"But why?"

"That's a question you'll have to ask him. After I called you, I had Stacy call the cops. She's much better in a crisis with a language barrier than me. They should have arrested him and Dec by now."

"Dec was a part of this too?"

Kat nodded.

West felt a piece of him break off. A piece of his life now gone. He and Luke had been through so much together, and now he realized his best friend had never really been his friend at all. A friend would never stoop so low. Kat had shown him that people could be real and genuine, and as much as it hurt to know that his and Luke's friendship hadn't been real for a very long time, there was still a chance for him to have a real connection with someone.

"I want to talk to him and Declan." West pushed off the ground, but he wobbled.

"West, you were almost blown up. You need to go to the hospital."

"No, not until I talk to them. I must know why. I've been nothing but fucking loyal to them, and they betrayed me." West heard his voice falter and hated himself for having any emotion for either of those pricks.

Something in his expression must have worked because Kat conceded, turning to find Stacy in the crowd.

"Stay here. I'm going to see if the ambulance will take you to the hotel first."

West watched Kat walk to Stacy, and he knew he was the luckiest man in the world. His life had been saved yet again by this perfect woman, and that wasn't even why he loved her. She was strong, sure, but beyond that she was kind, caring, and real. He would always have the true, authentic Kat, and that meant more to him than anything.

One very long ambulance ride later, West was propped up in a chair in the hotel's outdoor café waiting for his moment of reckoning.

Kat was standing behind him fiddling with the zipper on her hoodie. "You sure you want to do this? You could just send them off to prison."

"I need to know why."

"I think the fact that they're assholes would suffice," she mumbled under her breath.

West smirked, knowing Kat had never liked Declan or Luke, and now he would always trust her judgment when it came to who to trust.

Three cops walked in and gave him a quick spiel about not getting out of his chair, not touching them, and some other safety measures. West didn't care. He just wanted answers. And then he saw the bastards. They were both handcuffed, and the cops dragged them into the café.

West's eyes narrowed on the raw marks the cuffs had left on Luke's wrists and almost laughed at how soft Luke was. He wasn't going to survive the Indonesian prison for one second, and as far as West knew, Indonesia didn't have an extradition treaty with the states.

While Declan looked him right in the eye, Luke looked everywhere but at West. He leaned forward in his chair, slightly annoyed that they were standing and he was sitting. The power dynamic felt off.

"Can we get them chairs?"

One cop nodded and two chairs were instantly procured, and they shoved the two men into them.

Much better.

West steepled his hands in front of him. Now what the fuck was he going to say?

Declan made it easy on him, speaking first. "What do you want, Monroe?"

West pushed his hair back. "I just want to know why. After all these years, why the hell would you steal from me?" His eyes shifted to Luke, then back to Declan. "Scratch that. I know why you stole from me. You're a selfish bastard with a cocaine problem, always have been. But why would my best friend try to kill me?"

"I don't know what you're talking about."

"The hell you don't! Kat overheard you guys. Thanks to her I'm still alive, you fucking idiot."

Declan let out a humorless laugh. "No, Luke's an idiot. Once your accountant found that money was missing I knew it was only a matter of time before they traced it back to us. I'm good, but I'm not that good. You know your little buddy here runs through his trust every month faster than his daddy gives it to him? He found out what I was up to and forced me to give him a cut, or he'd tell you. Turns out money is more important to him than loyalty."

West tried not flinch at Declan's words. He wouldn't let them see that their betrayal hurt.

"I told Luke I'd take him down with me if he didn't take care of you."

If Luke could dip his head any farther down, he would have.

West glared at him. "Why the hell would you stab me in the back like that?"

Luke's head snapped up, his eyes a swirling storm of gray. "Because, you just have it all . . . The fame, the fortune, the girls, the looks. Everyone loves you; they want to be you. I just snapped. After thirty fucking years of following you around, I wanted to be the center of attention, you know? Why should you get to have it all? The last thing I was gonna do was fucking beg for money."

Kat snorted behind him, but West said nothing. Luke was a moron, but it wasn't entirely his fault. He was raised by nannies and tutors and needed a lot of therapy he'd never bothered to get.

"I didn't want to kill you. Dec said he'd take me down with him, so I freaked. Then there you were on the deck, drunk as hell, walking right on the edge in the dark. Acting as if nothing could touch you, like you always do. It was so easy. I just pushed the deck chair and as you lost your balance, I gave you a little extra push. But here you are, still alive. Like a damn cat. No wonder you want her so bad."

He nodded toward Kat, and West felt ice go through his body. Luke had caused all of this. He was grateful it had brought him and Kat together, but they also could have died. She could have died. He could never forgive Luke.

Declan laughed as the cops pulled them up. "Must be real good pussy, West. She's got you on your knees. Sorry you had to wait so long. You tell her where you ended up that night at the House of Blues?"

"Shut up, Dec!" West flew out of his chair as panic rose in his chest because he knew what was coming. The cops pulled him back, stopping him from cracking Declan's skull.

Declan looked at Kat. "He didn't come back, did he?"

"Declan, that's enough. Leave her out of it." West's voice was murderously low as he looked at Kat, who was standing stock-still, her eyes moving between him and Declan.

With a smirk, Declan looked directly at West. "How was the lead singer of . . . what was that group called? Body Count? Cute little blonde thing, wasn't she?"

West roared his anger as he ripped free of the cops, getting in one good punch before the cops pulled him back, all while Declan laughed hysterically. He got what he wanted. One backhanded comment and everything was ruined.

He pulled free of the cops.

"I'm fine. I'm fine," he said, straightening his clothes, as Declan and Luke were carted away.

"Fucking hell." West ran his hands through his hair and turned to find Kat, but she was already gone.

He went to run after her, but EMS stopped him.

He was so utterly fucked.

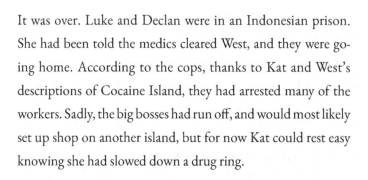

It was over. Luke and Declan were in an Indonesian prison. She had been told the medics cleared West, and they were going home. According to the cops, thanks to Kat and West's descriptions of Cocaine Island, they had arrested many of the workers. Sadly, the big bosses had run off, and would most likely set up shop on another island, but for now Kat could rest easy knowing she had slowed down a drug ring.

The next day went by in a blur of packing and meeting with the authorities and the doctors to make sure she was also clear to fly. Kat's mother fussed over her, still shocked that "that nice boy" Luke could do such a thing as attempt murder. Declan, on the other hand, had always come off as rather sleazy, and no one was very shocked to hear he had been skimming funds off the top for himself.

Kat had been avoiding West all day, refusing to talk to him about where they stood because she couldn't admit out loud that it was over. He had lied to her, and she had never felt so small or insignificant as she had when Declan revealed West hadn't been alone that night all those years ago. Her heart had broken all over again.

Tomorrow they would all board their plane to L.A., and then Kat and her mom would continue to Iowa where she would have to figure some things out.

At lunch together, her mom asked question after question. "Where was West? Why wasn't he eating with them?" Kat brushed off most of them, saying he was with the police or his PR rep, or doing other things important people had to do. Eventually, she would have to tell her mother that her hopes of having a son-in-law were dashed.

Kat stepped into her hotel room, ready to finalize her packing. Maybe afterward, she'd hit the pool, wallow in more self-pity, and continue to avoid West.

"Hi, sweetheart."

Well, scratch the last thing off her list.

Kat jumped at his voice; its deep timbre wrapped around her like smooth velvet. She'd know his voice anywhere. It would forever be imprinted on her soul.

Sighing, she sat in the chair next to him, knowing it was now or never. They had to talk. She was an adult, for fuck's sake. She could do this. She just had to stay strong. Then she looked at his chiseled jawline and the scratch above his eyebrow, which made him look even more dangerous, and she almost lost her nerve.

"What are you doing here?" she asked.

He leaned back, always so relaxed, but Kat knew it was an act. His foot was bouncing up and down with nervous energy. "You know why. After all the shit with Dec and Luke and the cops and doctors, we didn't get to talk, and I know you're mad at me. I just need you to listen."

"So, I misheard the part where you left me in a hallway after making out and then had sex with the tiniest, most petite lead singer on the planet? Oh, and then lied to me about it?"

He bit his bottom lip, and Kat's eyes were immediately drawn to it. "No, that was true."

"And you're not taking the acting gig? I misheard that, right?"

He closed his eyes for a moment. "No . . . that's all true, but listen, Kat—"

She held up a hand to stop him. "Two days . . . we're back in civilization for two days and you've lied to me and cut me out of a major life decision. And I know I'm nothing to you and I'm not your girlfriend, but I'm not going to lie and say it doesn't hurt."

West tried to speak, but Kat stopped him again.

"You don't owe me any explanation right now. We had sex. Mind-altering, life-changing sex, but we never put stipulations on what that meant. We weren't together back then, and we're not together now. I just . . . I guess I'm just disappointed. I thought you would be better."

"I want to be better. I *am* better."

"West, you lied to me. You said you went to the trailer alone that night. I had finally trusted you. I believed that I was enough." Her calm façade began to crack.

West sat up in his chair, his hand reaching out to grab hers and then pulling back. "I know, I'm sorry. I didn't want you to know what an asshole I was. I was embarrassed because I've done some shitty things over the years. But I want to be more. You make me want to show the world there is more to me. And babe, you are not nothing to me, you . . . you are my everything."

She shook her head in disbelief. "If that were true you would have told me the truth."

West's eyes bore into hers, and Kat had to stop herself from looking away. "I'm sorry, I'm still figuring this out. I'm not used to this committed relationship thing, but I know I want it with you because the thought of not waking up to you every morning sounds like my own personal hell."

Kat sat in stunned silence. It was the first time West had wanted to define what they were.

"Last night was our first night apart in weeks, and I didn't sleep at all," he continued. "You're so close. I just want to hold you, and yet you seem so far away from me."

Kat's mind was reeling. What could she say? That she loved him, but she didn't trust him to always love her? That he would one day break her heart and she wasn't sure she could let him do it? That deep down she was still that girl standing in the dark hallway, and she was afraid he was still that guy who'd left her for another?

West grabbed her hand. "Can you say something?"

Kat raised her gaze to look at him. His perfect face looked tired from lack of sleep. "What are you asking me?"

"Move in with me when we get back to L.A."

"And what will I do?"

He shrugged. "Whatever you want. Write music, start your music program for kids."

"So, live off of you?"

"I want to take care of you."

She dropped his hand. "But I don't need to be taken care of."

"Okay, then don't move in with me. We can take it slower, and just try dating like normal people." West sank to his knees in front of her, grabbing both of her hands, and Kat felt a solitary tear slip down her cheek at the gesture. Why had he lied? She thought he'd been open and honest with her, and now she couldn't help but wonder what else he was lying about.

"I write a lot of songs about love and women, but I realize now how hollow they've been because I've never actually experienced the emotion."

Kat looked at their hands intertwined in her lap, willing him not to say it. She would have no defenses if he did.

"That is . . . until you, sweetheart. I love you, and I want to be with you. You showed me that I am more than living in my father's shadow, more than the playboy musician, and that I can still write my own music. You make me want to be more in this world, to fight for those who need it, and to be a voice for those who don't have one. Kat, you own me."

Well, fuck.

What was she supposed to say to that? Her heart swelled with emotion, but she couldn't let it take her over. He lied to her. She had asked him point-blank if he'd been alone that night, and even though he hadn't said no, he had shaken his head in the "no" fashion. He had evaded her.

She felt another tear slide down her cheek, followed by another. How many times would this man make her cry? They weren't even together, and she'd lost count.

His hand wiped the tear off her face. "I wish there was something I could do to make you believe me." His hand came around the back of her neck, and he touched his forehead to hers. Kat inhaled his familiar scent, imprinting the feel of him forever in her mind. Just like this.

She lifted her head, wiping at her nose with her arm.

"I do believe you," she said between whimpers. "But for how long?"

Every ounce of confidence he had given her was laying shattered on the floor at her feet.

West's hand fisted in the hair at her nape, moving her to face him, not rough but just enough to prove a point. Her body went on high alert. "I know you didn't grow up in the most encouraging environment, and I certainly haven't helped things, but what is it going to take for you to believe me?"

"That's just it. I don't know. I've battled this feeling my whole life, and just when I felt that I could be enough for you, a woman you'd be proud to have by your side, I find out you lied to me." He didn't say anything, waiting for her, somehow knowing there was more. Kat took a deep breath, bracing for the truth she would give him; her truth, the raw and unfiltered side.

"I've never been enough, always hovering on being something, but never quite there. Always average, not short or fat, just average. Not sporty enough, not graceful enough, just slightly musical, but not talented enough to make it in this business, not really. Not White enough, but not Native enough, my hair's not straight enough, but it's not gorgeous with thick curls either. I have a good singing voice, but not great, and while my brothers have families and careers and direction, I have nothing. If I stand up for myself, I'm too loud and obnoxious, but if I don't say anything, I'm too quiet and a pushover. I blamed you for ruining my career when, in truth, I ruined it long ago when I became complacent with the way things were and never once tried again. You didn't want me years ago, and now I find out it was easy for you just to replace me with someone else that night. I wasn't enough then. Why would I ever be enough for you now?"

West's eyes softened, his hand coming up to cradle her face. "How do you not see the woman I see? The woman who heals snakebites or catches a fish with a makeshift spear. Who took a bullet that surely would have hit me and then sewed herself up, and then saved me from being blown up? Who wants to bring change to a world that is so resistant to it, and yet fights anyway? The only person who would tell me when a song sounded like crap. Shit, Kat, how could I not want to be with someone like you? To me, you will always be enough. You encompass every piece of me, and I can't get rid of you because it would be like cutting off a piece of myself. There is nothing I want more than to love you. All of you."

She sucked in a breath at his words. It would be so easy for her to forgive him. To trust that he would put her above all others. That she could continue to be this strong, assertive, confident woman who had appeared on the island.

It would have been so easy, but something pulled at Kat, telling her she was still missing something of herself.

At her silence West sighed in resignation. "I will apologize for the rest of my life for nine years ago if that's what you want. I was stupid. I wanted you that night. I couldn't have you. I'm not proud of who I was, but please don't hold that against the man I am now."

She couldn't stop them. The tears spilled out, one after the other, and West held her as they fell. The rush of feeling loved for who she was, along with all they had been through over the past few weeks, culminated in one giant emotional spillover, and Kat needed to think. She couldn't process.

After who knows how long in West's sturdy arms, Kat managed to pull away. "I need time to think," she said between sniffles.

He stroked her hair but said nothing.

"I can't make any decisions right now."

West stood slowly, his powerful body hovering over her. "You're scared, and there is nothing I can say or do that is going to change that. When you're ready to take that leap with me, I'll be there." He bent down, kissing the top of her head before walking toward the door.

He might be right, but she couldn't do anything about it. She had to think, and she had to think away from him. His presence was too overpowering for her to think clearly.

"I'm sorry," she whispered, looking up at him.

West shook his head as he turned to leave. "This isn't over." And then he was gone. The silence engulfed her as she cried the rest of the night until there were no more tears left inside her.

<hr>

The flight from Jakarta to L.A. was interminable. While Tommy Monroe had secured them first-class seats, he had stupidly assumed that West and Kat would want to sit together while he sat next to her mother in the row across the aisle.

She was exhausted and pretended to sleep, but sleep was elusive with West's body radiating all his powerful maleness next to her. She wanted to reach out and apologize to him. Tell him she trusted him, that she loved him more than the air she breathed, and that she wanted him to hold her forever, but she couldn't, her reasons still held true.

What life would she have with him? She'd forever be the woman of Weston Monroe, and while there were plenty of women who would be fine with that, Kat wasn't one of them. She had to have something of her own, something she'd accomplished on her own for herself by her own merits, not her boyfriend's or husband's. She was done spending her life on the sideline.

Not to mention all her other insecurities with all the women that surrounded him daily. She would have to learn to deal with that if she did end up trusting him. Maybe she could, but building that trust back was hard for her.

She watched him through slitted eyes as he read a book. How did he know she found men who read incredibly sexy? It was almost as hot as watching him play his guitar. His sinewy forearms called to her with each turn of the page, and she couldn't stop looking at how his big hands handled the book with as much care as he would a lover. Her body ached for his touch, and she felt warmth pooling in her core. Why oh why was she cursed to be stuck on this plane for eighteen hours with this man?

He was reading the latest spy thriller, probably getting into the mindset of the character he was going back to play. Which reminded her of why she was mad. He'd chosen acting over her. Well, okay maybe not acting, but he knew her thoughts on the matter, and he had decided he didn't care, so what else would he disregard? He'd had a chance to change alternative music, especially for women and people of color, to make it a more inclusive space, but he was throwing it away and Kat couldn't let go of her disappointment.

Eventually, sleep took over, and she awoke to an announcement on the PA asking them to prepare for landing. She felt the weirdest sensation at the thought of returning home. She hadn't been in the United States for over six months.

They had been in Europe touring, and then her trip to Bali, plus her island survival time. It was strange to be back. She figured not much would have changed; no doubt it would be as divisive as ever—a place that needed more love than hate.

She sat up, gathering her things, and noticed West was looking at her.

"Kat." His gorgeous voice rumbled through her. Even in the few hours they hadn't spoken to each other she had missed it. "I meant what I said, this isn't over. I'll give you your space, but then we're going to talk."

She nodded, unsure of what to say. He wouldn't hunt her down in Iowa, would he?

His hand came under her chin, lifting her face to his, and he kissed her lightly, his lips there, then gone. "I mean it, Kat. Don't make me hunt you down."

How did he always read her mind?

His eyes sparkled mischievously, although he was probably serious.

As they walked toward baggage claim, cameras clicked and reporters swarmed them. There were video cameras of all sizes, including reputable news outlets like ABC, NBC, and TMZ, along with amateur bloggers looking to get the inside scoop.

"Weston, can you comment on your manager siphoning funds?"

"Weston, what more can you tell us about the island?"

He was surrounded by a flurry of movement. He answered each question with charm and poise. She was in awe of his ability. Grabbing her and her mother's bags, she slinked away unnoticed.

"That poor man, are you going to help him?" her mom asked.

Kat knit her brow, glaring at her mother. "Why would I help him?"

Her mother gave her a look that spoke volumes.

Kat shook her head, rolling their luggage to the escalator leading to departures. "You don't understand, Mom."

She passed her mom her bag and turned back to get one last look at West, but she didn't see him. Instead, all she saw was Tommy talking to the press.

A firm grasp wrapped around her wrist and pulled her back just as she was about to step on the first stair. "You weren't going to say goodbye?" West asked, his eyes questioning, hurt burning in them.

She sighed. "I thought it would be easier this way."

His eyes narrowed. His hair was pushed away from his face in an unruly mess, making him look even more endearing than usual. She wanted to reach out and push it back, feel the softness of it one last time, but she resisted. "Easier for who?" he asked.

Fair point.

"I told you; I just need time. I need to figure me out, figure us out. There has to be a world where I'm not always your backing singer."

"You're right, you deserve to be front and center."

"I don't want to be front and center, I just need something that fulfills me." West's eyes widened.

Before West had the chance to respond, the media had flocked around him again, questions coming from all directions. One, who seemed to have noticed their heated conversation, asked, "Who's this, Weston?"

Suddenly all eyes were on them, and West grabbed her wrist, not allowing her to leave. "This is Katrina Brooks, my former pianist and backing singer, and the woman I am in love with."

Kat's mouth fell open at his public declaration. Hadn't that been what she was asking for? She didn't actually think he'd do it. He'd just told the whole world he was in love with her, and she didn't know whether to run away or jump into his arms and stay there forever.

"She has a plane to catch, and I have to go; please direct all questions to my PR rep."

The press swarmed in like bees as West pushed her up the escalator. "Go," he whispered in her ear. "Go now before I change my mind. Figure out how to make us work and come back to me."

She looked back as he fielded a question, and for a split second, she almost ran back down the escalator. He loved her, and she loved him. He had just declared it to the entire world, so what was she doing running away?

But something stopped her.

Muscle memory drove her as she and her mom checked in for their flight to Iowa, but inside she wondered if, by walking away, she had just made the worst mistake of her life.

"I'm sorry, dear." Her mother hugged her, fully aware of the emotions roiling within her, and she felt the dam breaking.

No, no, no, no, not in the middle of airport security.

She gulped in large quantities of air, holding back tears as she trudged through security. Why did airports not have a crying room? Considering how many people said goodbye in these places, they really should. Kat put the idea in the back of her mind to patent later as she and her mom walked toward their gate and her future—whatever it held.

Twenty Two

If only someone had invented a whiskey glass that never emptied. West looked over to the bottle that sat on his kitchen counter, cursing himself for not grabbing the bottle outright, but he hadn't quite devolved into that much of a degenerate . . . yet. Over the past month, he had taken his status of functioning alcoholic to a whole new level. His liver was a shriveled mess, screaming at him. He had done such a good job when training, but now what was the point?

After disappointing Kat, he had to find a way to make it up to her and to himself because she was right. He didn't really want to act. After years of being mad at his father for forcing him to do music, when he really thought about it, he hadn't been doing it for his dad. West made music for himself. It took Kat to remind him of why he loved it, before all the fame, production, and world tours. He was ready to get back to basics.

Her words about changing the music industry from the inside, about starting his own label and being a voice for underrepresented artists rang in his mind. But he didn't think he could do it without her. Right now, he was seconds away from hopping on a plane to get her. If he ever stopped seeing double.

He had literally shouted his love for her to the world and, while he had told her to leave, a part of him had hoped she'd turn around and run back to him. She was scared to be with him, scared of getting hurt, and perhaps she had a right to be, but she was also being unfair. He deserved to be trusted; he had done nothing to break her trust. Well, nothing in this decade. He had lied, yes, but his reasoning had been true. He didn't want her to think so badly of him. To think that all he had cared about was whose pants he was getting into that night. Maybe ten, fifteen years ago that had been him, but that wasn't him anymore.

So as hard as it was for him, West had to let her think on her own for now. He had bared everything to her, and she had still left. She'd made her decision, and West was going to have to live with it. For now.

His liver, on the other hand, was not thankful for that decision, and neither was his trainer, who'd come around early that morning, admonishing him for drinking too much.

He'd decided he was going to turn down the movie role but found his mind and body still thrived under a healthier lifestyle, so he kept his trainer around. He needed him, especially now, or he would never get off his couch.

The sound of the front door opening shook him from his ever-revolving thoughts. Since there were only two people who had the code, and his cleaning lady had already been by, he knew it had to be his father.

"Weston." His dad's voice reverberated through his vast house.

West had tucked himself in his back room which looked out at his pool, the large glass doors half open to the warm October air. His father's footsteps grew closer and closer. He had no urge to talk to him. He had been avoiding him for the past month—avoiding everyone, really. His other buddies, who had taken off from Jakarta almost as soon as the yacht had docked, still couldn't believe what Luke had done. While they of course believed West, they struggled to comprehend why he hadn't just gone along with Luke and pinned it all on Declan.

Rich kids always stuck together, for wrong or for right.

His father walked into the room. "I should have known you'd be back here."

"Hello to you too, Father."

His father walked to his kitchen looking through his wine collection, pulling out one of his better reds. West winced at the thought of Kat and her preference for red wine. Everything reminded him of her. His dad poured himself a glass before sitting in one of West's plush gray chairs.

"Are you against answering your phone?" His father gave him a pointed look.

"You clearly know where I live."

"Do you always have to be such a smart-ass with me. It's like you're still fifteen."

West sighed, running his hand through his disheveled hair. He couldn't remember the last time he'd showered. He hadn't shaved in weeks, and a bushy beard was starting to grow. He didn't like to be baby-faced, but he did like to be well-groomed. Kat had tied him up in knots, and now he was unraveling faster than he could put himself back together.

"You're right, I'm sorry. I guess I've never given you enough credit for raising me by yourself."

A gray eyebrow raised in question. "Interesting. And might this be the influence of one Katrina Brooks?

His heart ached just at the mention of her name. "Maybe a little, or a combination of that and surviving my best friend trying to murder me."

"That boy was an idiot thirty years ago; you should have never wasted your time."

"Maybe, but we had some pretty good times." West smiled thinking about all the shenanigans they had gotten into over the years, and he mourned the loss of his friend in more ways than one.

His dad took a sip of wine. "I should never have indulged you two so much. I should have been around more or found you a stepmother."

That got his attention; his father never spoke about his own love life, only complained about West's. "Why didn't you? You only ever said Mom left, but you never seemed to seriously date anyone."

His dad looked away as if caught in a memory. "I loved your mom, loved her so much it hurt my soul."

West could relate.

"But," he continued, "when she got pregnant with you, she didn't want you." West felt the whiskey sloshing around in his stomach threatening to come back up. He had never realized his mother hadn't wanted him. "I talked her into having you, told her I'd take care of her, she'd want for nothing, which was true. The band was at the peak of fame at that point."

"Who was she?" West asked for the thousandth time.

"A singer. I won't tell you who, she's rather famous under a name different to the one on your birth certificate, and she swore me to secrecy. She'll come around if she wants to."

West gaped at him. He had spent his whole life thinking his mom had just disappeared, but in reality his mother had wanted nothing to do with him. In fact, she had chosen her career over him.

"You just let her walk away!" West said, his anger growing.

"No," his father said, calmer than he should've been. "I pushed her. I pushed her harder than I should have. She had you, and I asked her to stay with us, and she did for a while, but she wasn't the mothering type. She couldn't stand it. I drove her away, away from us, away from you, and for that, West, I am forever sorry."

West sat back on the couch, processing his father's words. His father had fought for him while his mother had never wanted him. He had been right that his father had chased his mother away, but not in the way he'd thought. West hadn't been to therapy in a decade, but after this bombshell, he was considering calling up his old doc.

"I don't tell you this to make you question yourself, West," his father said, cutting into his thoughts. "But I want you to think about your Miss Brooks."

West whipped his head up to glare at his father. "She's not mine."

His dad chuckled. "I saw the way you two looked at each other—it was practically incendiary. I've told you about your mother because she's a lot like Miss Brooks, except I think Kat'd make a great mother. But she has to have a purpose beyond that, she has to feel like she makes a difference. You can't solve all her problems, she's too independent. I tried that with your mother and all it did was drive her away. No other woman has ever come close for me."

West saw the weariness in his father's eyes, and for the first time he understood what his dad was feeling. If he felt even a fraction of what West was feeling, he pitied the poor man.

"Have you ever tried to get her back?"

"She's happily married now." He drained his glass and stood up, walking the glass back to his kitchen.

West didn't want to ask, but he did. "Kids?"

"No, I told you, not the motherly type."

No half-siblings running around.

"Listen, son, I know I was tough on you, but music is not just in your blood; it is you. When you play, that is where I see true love. I won't tell you what to do; the decision is up to you, but don't give up on love."

West knew his dad wasn't just talking about music.

"Dad." His father turned and they looked at each other, really looked at each other, and all the years of judgment and anger came to the surface. While they didn't melt away, West felt a shift in their relationship, the start of something new. "What should I do?"

"You can't solve all her problems, but that doesn't mean you can't be there for her. Think about what she needs that she can only get from you. You know that movie we used to watch when you were a kid?"

West leaned back on his sofa. "Which one?"

His dad smiled. "The baseball one. It'll come to you." And with that he walked out the door, leaving West mulling over his words.

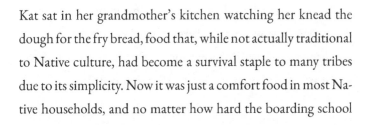

Kat sat in her grandmother's kitchen watching her knead the dough for the fry bread, food that, while not actually traditional to Native culture, had become a survival staple to many tribes due to its simplicity. Now it was just a comfort food in most Native households, and no matter how hard the boarding school had tried to rid her grandma of her memories, she had never forgotten how to make it.

Her grandma worked the dough, turning it into little circles before throwing a couple into the pan of oil. The oil sizzled as the dough hit the pan, a sound Kat had missed throughout her travels. It was absolutely awful food for her to eat health-wise, but if there was ever a time for comfort food this was it. She had gone from eating nothing for days to spending the past few days sitting in this kitchen eating the only food her grandma knew how to cook from scratch. Her heart ached, her head ached, and her entire body ached. She was the definition of a hot mess. How could a woman in her thirties be this broken up over a man?

He's not just a man, he's the man.

She pushed that thought out of her head as her grandma brought over her fry bread, not complete without the butter.

"Not that I'm complaining, dear, but to what do I owe your third visit this week?"

She took a bite and sighed as the fried goodness melted in her mouth. "Can't I just want to see my grandma?" she said, her mouth full of bread.

"Perhaps, if you weren't using me to avoid something."

Damn woman, how'd she know? The older she got, the more she had shed the White assimilation forced upon her and grown into her more authentic Indigenous self. More in tune with the world around her, and apparently that included Kat.

"Katrina, it doesn't take much to tell your heart is troubled. You're unfocused, you barely say more than five words some days, and your mother is worried about you."

"Oh, I thought the spirits told you or something," she laughed.

"No, Katrina, they do not speak to me." Her grandma's face fell, the sadness she never spoke about creeping over her features. "But maybe we can pray to the Great Creator to help you." She walked over to a basket and pulled out a braid of sweetgrass. "Come with me, my dear."

Kat followed her outside to her front porch swing and sat down next to her. It was her grandmother's favorite spot to sit and pray.

While Kat was not one for any kind of religion, she had been to the powwows and various ceremonies where she had seen them light the sweetgrass to signify the beginning of the ceremony, to invite the positive spirits in. A ceremonial act that was sacred for her people. The same ritual was used by families before prayer to invite the good spirits into their homes so that they would hear their prayers. While Kat didn't fully believe in a great creator in the sky, she did believe in energies, and she'd take all the good energy she could get.

Her grandmother lit one end of the sweetgrass braid, and they sat in silence as the smoke swirled around them. Kat inhaled the smoke; the grass let off a sweet vanilla scent that made her instantly calm. She remembered the times, before she had left for UCLA, when her grandmother would take her to the powwows and she would sit and listen to the elders tell the stories of her ancestors, of the battles they fought, of the worlds they discovered, of the spirits they danced with. She would dream of being one of the spirits dancing through the wind, the natural music that nature created.

Music was a part of her, just as it was a part of nature and a part of her people. Music told stories of heartbreak and love, of sorrow and success. Music, at one time, had been Kat's great love, and somewhere along the way she had grown disillusioned by it all, she had lost her passion.

Her mind was transported to West. She saw his face as clearly as if he was standing right next to her. He was reaching out to her, smiling as she grabbed his hand, and she was transported back to dancing with him on the beach on their island. It was just them. No snakebites, no evil drug dealers, just the sunshine, the lapping ocean, and the wind whispering through trees.

He was holding her in his arms while she hummed the tune she'd been thinking about as they slowly danced on the soft sand. Women appeared around them, and though Kat looked at them, West's eyes never left her. He only looked at her, she was the only woman on that beach. The other women disappeared, and Kat leaned up to kiss him but . . .

She blinked and West was gone. She cried out for him, but he had been replaced by a piano. She heard her grandmother in the background. "Oh, Great Spirit, whose voice I hear in the wind, whose breath gives life to all the world, guide our Katrina to see her path."

Kat looked at the keys on the piano in front of her. She played one note, and then the next, and then, as if a great flood had been released, the tune unleashed itself. She felt the music flow from her fingertips as it circled around her in time with the waves and wind. The ceremonial drumbeat of nature played in her head. She didn't know how long she played for, but note after note poured forth from her soul. The sun rose and set as she played, and suddenly the beach was full of others like her. Women and girls, some who looked like her, some who didn't, all singing along to the sounds of her piano and nature.

"Katrina?"

Her grandma called her name, as the scent of the sweetgrass faded away.

"Katrina, what did you see?"

She opened her eyes, looking at the weathered face of her grandmother, her eyes still as sharp and assessing as ever.

"I think I saw what I need to do next." She wiggled off the porch swing. "Thanks, Grandma." Kat bent down to give her a kiss on the cheek before turning to walk down the stairs.

"And what are you going to do?" her grandma called after her.

"I'm going back to Bali!" she called over her shoulder, a smile on her face—the first she'd had in over a month.

Twenty Three

Two Months Later

Nerves rattled around in her stomach as she stood in the car pickup lane of LAX waiting for her ride. After disappearing for almost two months, Kat knew she had some tough conversations ahead of her and no idea how to address them. The first was to the vivacious blonde and spastic redhead who pulled up in the yellow convertible in front of her.

"You rented a convertible? A bit cliché for L.A., don't you think?" Kat said, laughing as she threw her luggage in the tiny trunk.

"Not at all," Lydia said. "It's perfect for our girls' weekend!"

Kat had missed her friends more than she realized, and was happy to see them, smiling brightly as she jumped in the front seat Lydia had just vacated.

Cher hit the gas, and they took off down the turnpike. The air was warm for December, but it was southern California after all.

"So . . ." Cher started. "Tell us all about Bali!"

"I'd rather talk about you two. How's the Beckett Moss show going? I can't believe this is your last weekend of freedom for the next six months!"

Lydia sighed in the backseat. "And you thought West was bad. That man is ridiculously exacting, arrogant, overpowering, and exhausting. We've done twelve-hour practices for weeks."

Kat looked over at Cher. "Is she being dramatic?"

"For once, no. My feet bled so bad after the first week of rehearsals, I'm not sure I'll ever walk the same again."

"God, why are you two still doing it?"

Lydia shrugged, the sound of her gum popping in the backseat. "Money at this point. We're making almost two years salary compared to what we made with West."

Kat let out a long whistle at that.

"But," Cher added, "that makes the whole production team feel like they can treat us all like they own us. They work us like horses. I can't believe they gave us this weekend off."

"I'm so glad they did!" Kat said, smiling as she pulled her wind whipped hair out of her face.

"It's going to be six long months," Cher said as she let out a stream of breath.

"Then what?" Kat asked. "Any plans?"

"I'm going to go back to teaching. The Vegas residency ends just in time for summer. I can start dusting off my resumé. I miss it, and I think I need some stability in my life, and move back to L.A.," Cher said.

Kat saw the peace that washed over her friend's face and thought that might be just what she needed. "Good for you, Cher, they need good teachers. What about you, Lyd?" Kat yelled over the wind.

"Audiobooks!" Lydia yelled proudly.

"What about them?"

"She's been recording them," Cher supplied.

Kat wrinkled her nose in surprise. "You don't even read."

"I do when they're naughty," Lydia said in her deep sultry voice before bursting into laughter. Kat couldn't help it and laughed too.

"Seriously, you're recording smutty audiobooks?"

"I did one for a friend as a favor, and they loved it. Now I've done a few and, apparently, I have the perfect voice for it. After the residency, I'm going to really devote myself to it."

"Wow," Kat said, truly happy for her friends. They seemed to be happy and to have found their footing. Even someone as listless as Lydia had found something she enjoyed and that she was good at.

Cher pulled onto Herondo Street and they crawled their way to their hotel on the beach. It wasn't every day they enjoyed a girls' weekend, so they had gone all-out with a beachside hotel on Redondo Beach.

"What about you, Kat?"

Kat worried her bottom lip. "Can we talk about me later, like after a few margaritas?"

Lydia leaned forward from her seat in the back, her head popping up between Kat and Cher. "No, girl, we're doing this conversation now so we can have fun the rest of the weekend."

Fair point.

"Ugh, fine. There isn't much to say. What do you want to know?"

"You disappeared for three months and said nothing more than not to worry about you and not to give West your new number. So maybe start, I don't know . . . with any of that!" Cher said.

"I had to figure some things out," Kat began.

"And did you?" Lydia asked.

Kat looked down at her hands clasped tightly in her lap, searching her brain for answers that never came.

"Yes and no," she breathed.

"What does that mean?" Cher asked. "You know we're just trying to help you, Kat. We want you to be happy," she added when she saw Kat slump farther down the seat.

Kat tilted her head back, looking out at the ocean ahead of them as it came more into view. "I had this vision when I was with my grandma. I was making music on the beach. I thought that was my calling, so I went to Bali. I thought that was what I was supposed to do."

"That's great, Kat!" Lydia said. "So you wrote a bunch of music?"

Kat gave a humorless laugh. "No, I wrote like a song."

"So, what did you do there for two months?" Cher asked.

Kat shrugged. "I did a lot of meditating, listening to nature, reading. I feel like I've reestablished a connection with nature that I haven't had in a long time."

Both Lydia and Cher gave her a strange look, as if they weren't quite sure what to make of her.

"I promise I'm still a city girl, but there is a place for both in my heart," Kat said. "I just don't know what I'm going to do. I always thought it would be to write my own albums and become a recording artist, but then I met a Balinese girl who was way more talented than me. Her voice and sound were amazing. I think she could really break into the industry. I helped her refine a few of her songs."

"That's fantastic, Kat! And what if you're calling is amplifying voices like yours or others left out of the conversation?" Cher asked.

"That would be great. How do I do that?" Kat asked, sighing as she leaned back against the seat.

"I probably shouldn't say anything. He should be the one to . . ." Cher trailed off.

"Cher!" Lydia said in the backseat.

"Okay, well now I'm intrigued," Kat said, sitting up straight, looking back and forth between her friends. "Spill!"

"West started his own label to produce his music."

Kat sucked in a breath; he had actually done it. She couldn't believe he had listened to her.

"He called me. He needed your number because he wants you to run the label, Kat. You choose the artists, you produce the albums—it's yours. He did it for you, and, girl, it's the most romantic gesture I've ever heard."

Kat felt a tear slip from her eye. Already just the mention of West had her turning into a watering pot. She had left out that part of her trip to Bali. She had connected with nature, and then she had cried. She had read, and then she had cried. She had tried to write a song through her grief and then ended up crying. But she couldn't come back, she had felt like a failure.

She had been convinced her vision was telling her she would write her album on the beach in Bali. But now maybe it had simply meant West was helping put her on her true path. To find exciting new artists who otherwise would have been overlooked by the big labels. Artists like Killo, who she had worked with in Bali.

"But he's just giving it to me. I'll still just be West's arm candy who got his label because he fucks me," Kat protested, knowing she shouldn't care, but still worried what others would say about her only having the label because of West.

"Who fucking cares?" Lydia said, rolling her eyes. "You know how shallow that world is. If it's not one thing, it's another. All that matters is you know you're doing work you care about. And something tells me you'll crush it. You always know the best new artists before the radio ever does, and you fixed half of

West's songs for the better. Especially that first album we were on."

"Thanks, Lyd." Kat wiped at her eyes.

"What are friends for? I still can't believe you and West finally got together." Lydia leaned forward again grinning. "So, what's he like in bed?"

"Lydia!" both Kat and Cher yelled.

They all giggled as Cher pulled the car into the parking lot of their hotel. "He'd move the world for you, Kat. In fact, he's already told the entire world he loves you, and the Weston Monroe I knew before we got on that yacht would never have done that. You did that. Your love did that."

Kat nodded as she got out of the car.

Lydia bounded out of the back. "Okay, enough of this sentimental shit. Let's have some fun this weekend while we're all still wild and free, shall we?"

But Kat wasn't free at all. Her heart belonged to one man for the rest of forever.

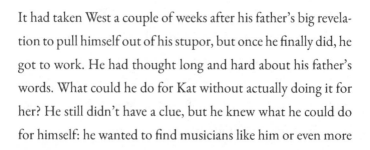

It had taken West a couple of weeks after his father's big revelation to pull himself out of his stupor, but once he finally did, he got to work. He had thought long and hard about his father's words. What could he do for Kat without actually doing it for her? He still didn't have a clue, but he knew what he could do for himself: he wanted to find musicians like him or even more outside the box than him. She had inspired him, had planted a seed on the island, and over time, it had grown into an idea he truly saw as his reality.

Over the past two months, he had called together his sound engineers, producers, and musicians, along with a construction crew. They had turned his pool house into a state of the art recording studio where he would not only record his own music but also take on his own indie artists. Artists of color, women, and various backgrounds who weren't usually seen in their respective genres; he wanted to give them a platform to be seen. Musicians like Kat, with their own unique voices that weren't made for the mainstream but still had music worth sharing with the world, even if they wouldn't make him millions of dollars.

By day he and his crew, whom he had stolen from his former label, worked on building the studio, and by night he started working on his first independent album. Songs that were completely written by him, with no label interference. Songs inspired by his love for Kat, and the absolute heartbreak of losing her.

She had been right: the music was in him. It wasn't his father that had ruined it for him, but the grueling schedules and stipulations the label had put on him. Now he was free to do as he pleased, to make the music he wanted. He felt free. The only thing missing was Kat.

The sound engineers were out in the studio putting the finishing touches on the soundboard when his new administrative assistant came up to the house.

"You have an appointment today, sir. They're waiting in the studio."

"Please, just West," he reminded the kid for the thousandth time. He was the younger brother of Reggie and was just happy to have a job.

The kid opened his mouth to speak and then thought better of it. West waited, but the kid said nothing. "And . . . what do they want?" he prompted.

"Oh, they're here to audition to be one of our first artists. My brother says you'll really like this one." The kid's eyes sparkled with laughter, and West wondered what Reggie was up to.

West strode across his backyard to the recording studio. The reception was empty, which was strange. He'd thought the musician would wait in there. He walked into the master control room to see Reggie and the sound engineers hooking up some speakers.

"Where are they?" West asked.

Reggie angled his head to the live room, and West peered through the glass and saw the figure of a woman. The hairs on the back of his neck stood up. Something about her was familiar.

He saw long, dark hair flowing down her back. She was sitting at the piano, and her fingers graced the keys. The sound was off in the booth and he couldn't hear her, but he hoped to god it was her.

"Leave," he barked, as he left the room and rounded the corner, practically breaking down the door to get to her.

Her head snapped up at the noise, their eyes locking as she saw him burst through the door, and his heart sank. It wasn't Kat, but a different woman whose voice was indeed gorgeous. She stopped playing and stood from the piano.

"Hi, Mr. Monroe. I'm Killo." She offered her hand and West shook it, still in a daze. His heart was breaking again after having his hopes dashed.

"Ah . . . hi, Killo," he forced out. He cleared his throat. "You have a great voice. Where are you from?"

"Bali."

Bali? Something seemed off. His senses told him something was supposed to happen. He just couldn't figure out what.

"Thanks, Killo. You can meet me in the lobby." He heard Reggie's voice through the system, and he watched as Killo gave a nod and walked from the live room.

Such a strange encounter.

She had played beautifully, but he hadn't heard enough to make any kind of decision. Maybe Reggie had listened to more already.

"What did you think?" he heard over the system. West looked through the glass into the control room and almost fell over because there she was. Kat was standing in his recording studio after months of being apart, and she looked prettier than ever. Her hair was down and flowing all around her, while her jeans hugged her perfect curves.

He had waffled between getting on a flight to Iowa and drinking himself into oblivion every single day. He'd even called

Cher to see how Kat was, only to discover she had gone back to Bali. And now the girl playing the piano in his studio made more sense.

He almost ripped off the door as he flew around the corner into the control room, his heart in the pit of his stomach. He stopped dead in his tracks as her nearness assailed him.

"Hi, West," she said, as she dipped her head, not looking him in the eye. He watched her hand stroke the controls on the panel and wished it was him.

He crossed his arms over his chest, standing tall. "Hi? You disappear for months and that's all you got?"

She frowned, her long eyelashes casting a shadow over her downcast eyes. "I deserve that."

He was by her side in two swift steps, the warmth of his breath on her skin. "No, you don't. I'm just surprised to see you."

Her head tilted up at him. "Good surprised?"

"I haven't decided yet."

She backed away, walking around the control room, her arms outstretched. "This is impressive. You did it."

"You know that movie *Field of Dreams* . . .?"

She nodded, a slow smile building on her face. "I am from Iowa."

He gestured to the studio. "I built it for you. You pushed me to see where I fit into this industry. Where I could do something worthwhile. You were right. It's time I made music for myself again, and bring artists along with me who are going to make

authentic music. Artists who are unique and stand for something more."

She gave a slight chuckle. "'If you build it, they will come.' So,
I'm the ghost in this situation then?"

West took a step closer to her but not close enough to scare
her away. "Kat, this is your dream, and my dream is to make
you happy. I realized that. I just want to keep making my music.
Sure, I love being able to give a platform to voices who aren't
always given one, but you are passionate about this work. I think
you should be running things around here, not me. I made this
for both of us, but it's mostly for you.

Kat looked around the space, her eyes wide. "I don't know
the first thing about running a label."

Like a flash, he had her in his arms. He couldn't believe
she was here, the feel of her more intoxicating than any drink.
"Then you'll learn."

West smiled as Kat gave him an annoyed look, apparently not
happy to have her own words thrown back at her.

"How many songs did you finish in Bali?" he asked.

"One," she said, ducking her head. "That's why I brought
Killo. She and I refined many of her songs. West, she's amazing,
and I think you should sign her."

He rubbed her back, pulling her in. "No. You're going to sign
her. I want to do this, but I want to do it with you. This is your
idea, your dream. I'm just here to help you fulfill it. That's why
I asked Cher for your number. I needed to talk to you, to beg

you . . . no, to ask you to do this with me. But she wouldn't give it to me, so I'm glad *Field of Dreams* was right."

Kat laughed out loud at that. "You're so corny."

"Shit, after what you put me through, I get to be," West said with a grin.

"We do this together. As partners?"

West held out his hand and she shook it. "Partners," he agreed.

"The whole acting thing, I don't care anymore if that's what you decide to do."

"I'm not doing it. The IRS is combing through Declan and Luke's funds, and I'll get some money back. I'm not an actor, I'm a musician. You were right. I was scared that I had failed and would fail again, but sometimes you have to get back up and try again. You made me see that because, babe, I love you more than words can even say. These past few months I haven't functioned without you. You own me body and soul, and I can promise you, forever together isn't long enough for me."

A tear slipped out of her eye, and he wiped it away with the tip of his finger. "Don't cry."

Kat let out a little laugh. "I can't help it. You inspired me to embrace who I was. You're giving me a record label to give even more people a voice." She bit her lip, dipping her head.

"West, I . . . I . . . I don't deserve you. You bared yourself to me, and to . . . everyone. And I ran away, I'm so sorry."

West arms grew heavy at his sides as he watched her throat work to swallow. There were still three little words she hadn't said to him, words he needed to hear.

She twisted the turquoise bracelet on her wrist, the one her mother said was for protection. "When I went back to Bali," she started, "there was this day it rained, and I watched as the raindrops hit the ocean. It made me think of you and me, as if we always had just been hanging out on the same cloud, and then we were finally released and landed in the ocean as two infinitesimal little drops separated by the waves. But then we somehow found our way to each other before being torn apart again, and yet we would always float back together, forever destined to come back to one another."

Leave it to Kat to think in terms of the elements. "You're not making much sense."

She smiled. "I love you, West. You're a part of me, and I'm a part of you. It just took us becoming two drops in the ocean for us to figure it out."

She jumped into his arms, wrapping her legs around his waist and her arms around his neck, and kissed him. The heart that West thought had shriveled up and died beat again. She loved him. She was in his arms, and he wasn't dreaming.

"I love you, Kat," he said between kisses as he carried her to the couch in the studio. He laid her down, ripping her shirt over her head. "You are not allowed to leave me again."

She giggled as he kissed her neck. "I'm not going anywhere, Thomas Weston Monroe. I love you more than words."

With that, he had her clothes off quicker than a kid opening presents on Christmas morning. They christened the new control room couch, just the first of many pieces of furniture to be used for their lovemaking over the years.

Epilogue

Kat exhaled in relief as she kicked off her stilettos, feeling the tension leave her body as she sat in the town car. West leaned in to kiss her shoulder.

"You can't wait until we get home?"

She felt his familiar hands at her neck and his husky voice in her ear. "You know I can't resist you."

Even after a year of living together, he still made her feel like it was their first time. He planted featherlight kisses on the soft spot below her ear, sending shivers throughout her body as memories from when they had first been intimate on the island came flooding back. Her skin was still hypersensitive to his touch as his hand brushed across her side and he nipped and kissed down her arm.

"How was your first movie premiere?"

She had been nervous. As she had stepped onto the red carpet, her heart raced and her palms felt clammy. She'd glanced around nervously as flashes of light illuminated her sequined dress from all directions. Although she'd felt small standing next to West in his tuxedo, no one seemed to notice.

"Not so bad. I don't think anyone even noticed me next to you."

West tilted her back against the large leather upholstered seat and kissed her leg. She could feel his warm breath on her skin and every nerve in her body throbbed with desire. "That's really a shame," he murmured as he moved closer to her sex. "You produced the song; I was just your date."

"I . . . guess . . . no one . . . cares . . . about . . . the soundtrack," she said between kisses.

"That's an absolute shame. This was your night. That was your song at the end of that movie."

"It's . . . fine . . ."

"No, it's not, and I intend to make up for their lack of attention." He pushed up her dress. "Why on earth are you wearing this? It makes it rather difficult to get to you." He gestured to her Spanx.

"I had to look good for my first Hollywood premiere; they'd eat me alive if anything was out of place."

"They are all idiots. Your body is perfection just the way it is."

His hands found the top of the shapewear and pulled them down. If it had been anyone else, Kat would have been mortified, but with West she had no shame, no secrets. There was nothing between them. He knew everything about her, and she knew everything about him.

She had never felt so complete, so happy. It had been exhilarating to find out one of the five artists she was producing a record with had a song chosen for the main soundtrack in a movie. And then her happiness had turned to absolute terror when they told her she should join the artist at the premiere.

Kat had felt inferior standing next to the gorgeous Indian woman who sang like a rock goddess. The moment she had heard her demo, she knew that with a little polish and vision she would have a debut album for the ages. While she'd only had one song out for the movie, Kat couldn't wait to release the album. She knew it would easily hit number one on the alternative charts.

West had promised to be there with her every step of the way for their first public outing. The press loved catching them out in public, and Kat was not looking forward to what social media had to say about her. But with West at her side, she realized none of it mattered because he loved her, and he always would, no matter what the rest of his world thought.

They pulled up to their house just as she felt all her undergarments fall from her body. West licked the seam of her core from the bottom to the top, sending shivers down her spine. She moaned in pleasure as his tongue traveled across her, making her body quiver with delight. He lifted his head, and she whimpered at the loss of him. "To be continued inside," he said as he lowered her skirts.

Kat laughed and grabbed her shoes and undergarments as he helped her out of the car. They kissed each other hungrily along the walkway up to the front door. Her body was humming with pleasure, her heart brimming with joy—she would never get used to having someone who desired and loved her so deeply.

West pushed the door open with one hand and pulled her in with the other. He was halfway through pushing up her skirt when a voice broke the silence in the background. "Please stop before I have to gouge my eyes out."

They both froze. Surprise overtook her emotions. There in her living room was her eldest brother, Caleb. Just lounging on her couch as if he owned the place. "Hey, sis. Mind if I crash here for a bit? I'll explain later."

Kat looked at West in question, but he didn't seem to care one way or another about Caleb. West growled in her ear. "Ten minutes, then you better be upstairs or I'll fuck you right here."

Kat's face heated up as the man she loved more than anything walked up the stairs.

Standing, her brother hugged her. He had been much nicer to her since her disappearance. "Love looks good on you."

She smiled, "It does, doesn't it?"

Coming Soon

Kat and West will be back as Cher searches for love.
Uncharted Territory
Coming Fall 2024

Acknowledgements

I am so thankful for everyone who has been a part of this journey. My family who has put up with my imposter syndrome while I learned how to navigate this industry. My fantastic editor Kaitlyn, and my one-of-a-kind artist Krissy, you all made this journey so smooth. Also to my fantastic PR team, I couldn't have managed without your help. And of course, thank you to all the readers for making my debut extra special.

About the author

A consummate daydreamer, Jillian has always been making up stories. Did she do well in high school Algebra? Not so much. But she did write some amazing stories that set her on the path to being an author.

A lifelong lover of romance novels from all genres, there was something she always found missing...

As a member of the Cherokee Nation, Jillian realized a distinct lack of Indigenous representation in romantic fiction, so she writes stories that infuse native identity, love, and joy.

She lives in the Midwest with her husband and kids, who keep her way too busy, but she wouldn't have it any other way. When she's not working or writing you can find her traveling the world, taking in nature, and catching as much live music as she can.

Made in the USA
Monee, IL
01 June 2024

59258193R00204